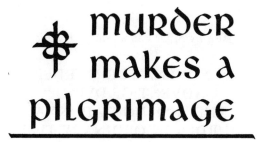

murder
makes a
pilgrimage

Also by Sister Carol Anne O'Marie:

A NOVENA FOR MURDER
ADVENT OF DYING
THE MISSING MADONNA
MURDER IN ORDINARY TIME

murder makes a pilgrimage

Sister Carol Anne O'Marie

Delacorte Press

F c.2

PUBLISHED BY
DELACORTE PRESS
BANTAM DOUBLEDAY DELL PUBLISHING GROUP, INC.
1540 BROADWAY
NEW YORK, NEW YORK 10036

LIBRARY OF CONGRESS CATALOGING IN PUBLICATION DATA

O'MARIE, CAROL ANNE.
    MURDER MAKES A PILGRIMAGE / CAROL ANNE O'MARIE.
       P.   CM.
    ISBN 0-385-31050-1
    I. TITLE.
  PS3565.M347M9   1993
  813'.54—DC20   93-9984 CIP

BOOK DESIGN BY GDS / JEFFREY L. WARD

MANUFACTURED IN THE UNITED STATES OF AMERICA

PUBLISHED SIMULTANEOUSLY IN CANADA

NOVEMBER 1993

10 9 8 7 6 5 4 3 2 1

RRH

To my family,
whose encouragement never waivers;

especially, my sister, Kathleen O'Marie,
Caroline, John, and Noelle Benson,
Hal and Dosie Garden,
Sally and Dave Van Houten,
Joe Crume,
and
Julia and Kate Maree

murder
makes a
pilgrimage

tuesday,
september 21

feast of St. matthew,
apostle and evangelist

✦

"I beg your pardon?" Sister Mary Helen said into the telephone.

The voice on the other end of the line repeated the message slowly and carefully, with the patience of one used to being misunderstood.

"It is my pronunciation, perhaps, Seester," he said in a rich Spanish accent, "that is giving you difficulty?"

In truth his pronunciation was fine. It was his message that puzzled Mary Helen.

"I won a what?" she asked.

Her caller must have decided that she was deaf. He began to shout, "Seester, you have won our contest! You and a companion are to be our guests on a week-long pilgrimage to Santiago de Compostela in España!"

"But, Señor . . . uh . . . " Surprise knocked his name right out of her mind.

"I am Señor Carlos Fraga de la Cueva." He supplied his name again, this time so loudly that she held the receiver away from her ear.

"Señor Fraga, how could I possibly win a contest that I did not enter?"

"Seester, it is I who now must beg your pardon. But your name, it is on one of our winning tickets." Loudly, distinctly, he read her name, her address at Mount St. Francis College, even including San Francisco, California, and the zip code. He concluded with her telephone number at the Alumnae Office.

By now he must be figuring that as well as being a little deaf, I am more than a little dumb, Mary Helen thought, staring out of her small office window at the bright September sky.

"But, Señor," she stalled, racking her brain. When could she possibly have entered a "Trip to Santiago de Compostela" contest? Surely she would remember a thing like that.

"I am the owner of the Patio Español Restaurant." Señor Fraga pronounced each word deliberately. No doubt he was hoping that the old nun would have a flash of recognition. "On Alemany Boulevard, Seester. Do you remember?"

Of course, she remembered the Patio Español. How could she forget it? The place was a block long and looked like a hacienda right out of Helen Hunt Jackson's novel *Ramona*. She and her friend Sister Eileen had gone there recently for a scrumptious dinner with Consuelo Aguilar, a college alumna. As a matter of fact, the dinner and the restaurant had been Connie's idea. "A beginning-of-the-school-year treat" she called it.

With her free hand, Mary Helen flipped back the pages on her desk calendar. "Dinner with Connie A." was scribbled across the bottom of Tuesday, September 7. Just two weeks ago. She remembered being especially pleased to go out to dinner that night—and she certainly remembered why.

Ben, the college chef, always roasted turkeys to celebrate the opening of school. Invariably he roasted too many and used up his leftovers on the nuns.

The morning of the seventh, Ramon, the pastry cook, had told Mary Helen that he was baking patty shells for dinner. It hadn't taken much ingenuity to figure out that they would be dining on turkey à la king that night.

"If I eat another turkey anything, I'm going to start gobbling," she had confided to Eileen, who answered by making several deep, throaty sounds herself.

"You do recall our restaurant, Seester?" Señor Fraga persisted. "We were holding a contest for a trip? *Año santo* in Santiago de Compostela?

"Of course, I remember your restaurant," Mary Helen snapped. The inside of the Patio Español was as impressive as its exterior. The high-ceilinged room was filled with arches and brightly colored ceramic tiles, hand-blown glass, fresh flowers, wrought-iron chandeliers, and a trickling water fountain.

She even remembered what the three of them had ordered: Pacific snapper sautéed in olive oil with garlic and white wine. It came with San Francisco sourdough bread. David, an unlikely name for a Spanish waiter, had asked several times if their spinach *sopa* was hot enough. It was.

"Your restaurant stands out very clearly in my mind, Señor Fraga," Sister Mary Helen said. "What I don't remember is entering your contest."

"You are Seester Mary Helen, are you not?" Señor Fraga repeated, beginning to sound exasperated.

"Of course I am."

"Then you are one of our contest winners," he said with a tone of finality that settled the matter for him, anyway. "You will receive the details of your wonderful trip in Thursday's post. We leave San Francisco for Santiago on October seventh and return on the fifteenth. It is imperative that we know by Wednesday of next week if you accept. *Adios*," Señor Fraga called cheerily, "and congratulations!"

Mary Helen sat at her desk, staring at the dead receiver. How in the world?

"Are you about ready to break for lunch?" She heard Shirley, her secretary, call from the outer office. The two of them had spent the entire morning working on the preliminary plans for the alumnae fashion show.

"I'm starving." Shirley peeked in from the doorjamb.

"Lunch? Is it lunchtime already?" Mary Helen, still dazed, glanced up at her secretary. Shirley's eyes sparkled behind her oversize glasses.

"What is it, Sister? Not bad news, I hope." Pointing at the telephone, Shirley stepped into the small office, where her white hair shone silver under the fluorescent lights.

"No, not bad news. Actually I suppose it's good news. That call was from a Señor Fraga at the Patio Español. It seems that I have won a trip to Spain."

Even the unshockable Shirley took a moment to assimilate the news. "Well, hooray for you!" she said with much more enthusiasm than Mary Helen could muster. "When do you leave?"

"I'm not so sure that I'm going," Mary Helen said. "I'll really have to think about it."

"Everything becomes much clearer on a full stomach." Shirley, gold bracelets jingling, leaned over and patted her hand. "Why don't we eat? I hear the food service is serving tacos today. Maybe that's an omen."

Mary Helen couldn't help laughing. "You go on ahead. I'll catch up and meet you there," she said, pretending to busy herself straightening up the paperwork strewn across her desk.

As soon as her secretary left the office, Mary Helen pushed back in her wide desk chair and closed her eyes. Had she actually forgotten entering a contest? Age could play funny tricks on one's memory, she'd heard. In fact, nowadays old Sister Donata referred to her "forgettory" instead of her memory. But I'm not so very old yet, Mary Helen fussed. Why, I'm only seventy-seven. Or is it seventy-eight? No matter. I am entirely too young to start forgetting something as unforgettable as writing my own name on an entry blank and dropping it into a box.

The word *box* triggered an image in her mind. Come to think of it, she had noticed a brightly colored box at the Patio Español. It was just inside the front door next to a sprawling bouquet of red, orange, and sunshine yellow gladioli. She remembered that much.

After dinner Connie had pushed the heavy wooden door open, holding it for the two nuns. In the warm glow of the restaurant Mary Helen had shivered at the sight of the low fog swirling down Alemany Boulevard. From the corner of her eye she'd spotted the box and a blurred movement. Sure enough!

She bolted up from her chair and switched off the overhead lights. Sister Mary Helen knew exactly who the contest culprit was, and she would confront her immediately.

◆

"I hope you're satisfied," Mary Helen hissed the moment she spotted Sister Eileen in the lunch line.

Eileen's eyebrows arched, and she blinked her large gray eyes. "I beg your pardon?"

"That is exactly what I said when Señor Fraga called."

Frowning, Eileen slid her lunch tray along the counter and picked out a glossy green pear from the fruit bowl. "Fraga? Fraga? That name does not seem to ring any bells," she said.

"Well, it should! Church bells. No, cathedral bells. Does Santiago de Compostela mean anything to you?"

Eileen's cheeks flushed. "For the love of all that's good and holy, keep your voice down, Mary Helen," she said with a touch of the brogue, a sure sign that she was flustered. "Do you want the new faculty members to think that we're fighting?"

One look at her friend's face, and Mary Helen knew that what the new faculty thought was the least of Eileen's concerns. She was playing for time to think up a decent defense. Like any good scrapper, Eileen knew that the best defense is a good offense. Mary Helen knew it, too.

"Don't give me that malarkey." She followed Eileen toward a side table in the spacious dining room which the Sisters shared at lunchtime with the faculty. "Just tell me why you entered *my* name in that contest and not your own."

"I was planning it as a surprise."

"A surprise for what?"

"For Christmas." With a sanctimonious sniff, Eileen cut the juicy pear into quarters and offered Mary Helen one, which she refused.

"Eileen, it is only September. It's not even Advent yet. Furthermore, you have not given me a Christmas present in over fifty years. In fact, you know perfectly well that we never give each other Christmas presents, which, we agreed years ago, simplifies both our lives. What's more, if you intend to start at this late date, what is wrong with a blouse? I can always use another blouse. Or slippers. Or a paperback mystery. I'd love a brand-new mystery."

Sister Eileen began to dust nonexistent crumbs from the edge of the table. The real reason was coming.

"You may find this a little difficult to believe," she began, "but when I spotted the box, I had a very lucky feeling."

"If you were feeling lucky, why in the name of common sense didn't you enter your own name?"

Eileen's bushy eyebrows shot up. "We are talking luck here, Mary Helen, not common sense! I wasn't feeling lucky for me. I was feeling lucky for you."

Without waiting for a comment she went on. "So, following my hunch, I entered your name. I just knew you would win that contest." Her face broke into a wrinkled smile. "And you see? I was right!"

Sister Mary Helen opened her mouth, then closed it again. Although the logic made no sense at all to her, she knew better than to argue. Eileen, the consummate authority on Irish luck, had spoken.

"And so," Mary Helen said, finally accepting a slice of Eileen's pear, "now that I have won this trip, what do you suggest I do with it?"

"Go on it, of course!" Eileen had a determined tilt to her chin and a hint of excitement in her voice. "And I will go with you! Life is too short not to enjoy it," she said with as much infallibility as any Pope could have managed. "Ex cathedra" it was called when the Pope did it: "From the chair of Peter." When Eileen did it, it was called "annoying."

"You and I are going on a pilgrimage to Santiago?" Mary Helen's voice was strained. Several faculty members at other tables were beginning to glance their way. "We don't know a thing about Santiago. Or about making a pilgrimage, for that matter," she said, although that was not completely true.

She remembered reading a recent news story in the *San Francisco Catholic* about Santiago de Compostela, the birthplace of Christianity in Spain, celebrating some sort of Holy Year, although she thought the article had said that the main celebration took place in July. And from her long-ago studies of medieval history, she recalled that Compostela, the oldest shrine in the Western world, had once rivaled Rome and Jerusalem as a center of pilgrimage, although she couldn't remember why.

"Furthermore, this Señor Fraga mentioned something about an *año santo*," she said.

"Holy Year," Eileen translated.

"I know that much!" Mary Helen glared. "What I don't know is why it is a Holy Year in Compostela and not in the entire rest of the universal church? Isn't it the Pope who declares a Holy Year and not the Patio Español? Every twenty-five years in modern times, if my memory serves me correctly. And don't Holy Years generally begin in January, not in October?"

"We'll just have to be finding that out, now, won't we?" Eileen wiped pear juice from her fingers. "And Hanna Memorial Library is full of books that will help us with everything we need to know."

Spoken like a true, if semiretired, librarian, Mary Helen was about to quip, but Eileen rushed on.

"And the sooner the better. What about right after we finish lunch?"

"Right after lunch? I'm working on the alumnae fashion show after lunch."

"Certainly Shirley can do that without you."

"Shirley! I completely forgot about her. I told her that I'd meet her here."

"She doesn't look like she missed you." Eileen nodded toward Shirley, who sat chatting happily with several of the other secretaries. "And I'll wager she will continue to do just as well without you this afternoon."

Eileen was probably right. A fashion show was much more Shirley's cup of tea than hers. As a matter of fact, fashion was Shirley's forte. Mary Helen continually marveled at how everything her secretary wore, including shoes and jewelry, matched. The hues she chose magically picked up and changed the color in her eyes. Today they looked almost emerald, the color of her silk blouse.

Mary Helen pulled at her own pin-striped blouse. The stripe matched her skirt exactly. But then, you can't go too far astray with basic navy blue. As for her eyes, what picks up a muddy hazel?

"Are you nearly finished eating, old dear?" Clearly, Eileen was eager to get their research started.

Feeling a bit like the Devil's Advocate, Mary Helen introduced another problem. "Sister Cecilia. Have you forgotten about Sister President? How are we going to tell her that we are about to take a vacation when we just had one? And don't tell me 'very carefully.' " For a moment Mary Helen thought that she had stumped Eileen. She should have known better.

"What is the sense of being semiretired if we don't skip work once in a while?" Eileen demanded. "And what's more, her world won't end." She winked. "We have an old saying back home."

Sister Mary Helen groaned. Although Eileen had left Ireland more than fifty years ago, she still referred to it as "back home" and could always be counted upon to dredge up an "old saying" to fit the occasion. Quite frankly Mary Helen suspected that she made up half of them. Eileen's next remark confirmed her suspicions.

"Don't worry about the world coming to an end today," she announced. "It is already tomorrow in Australia."

"Since when is Charlie Brown, who, I remember, said that, an Irishman?" Mary Helen asked, but her question fell on deaf ears. Eileen had already deposited her lunch tray on the revolving belt that swallowed up all of the college's dirty dishes. For all her talk about luck, Mary Helen realized as she followed her friend, Eileen seemed as surprised as she that they had won the trip. And, to judge from the speed of her exit, a great deal more thrilled.

◆

After settling things with Shirley, who was happy to carry on alone, at least for one afternoon, Sister Mary Helen went in search of her friend. Outside, the sky was brilliant, and the hedge of cobalt blue hydrangea bushes that ran alongside the main building reflected its color. The building itself glistened in the Indian summer sun. A friendly wind set the leaves of the eucalyptus trees quivering, and the pink-rimmed petals of the lemon-cream Peace Roses still held drops of moisture from the morning's sprinklers.

Mary Helen closed her eyes and took a deep breath. The salty smell of the Pacific was in the air. She heard the college flags snapping atop their pole and from somewhere the *caw-caw* of a sea gull. It must have been a day much like today in Galilee, she thought, when Jesus called Matthew. In the Gospel story for this morning's liturgy Jesus had said, "Follow me." And Matthew, the tax collector, by his own admission had left all, "got up," and followed Him.

God works in mysterious ways, Mary Helen mused, feeling the warmth of the sun on her shoulders and back. For the most part she had stopped years ago trying to figure out the inscrutable whys and hows. Maybe this pilgrimage to Spain was where He was calling her. Who knew? Why, then, was she so hesitant to follow? No reason that made any sense really.

Satisfied that Eileen had headed for the library, Mary Helen ducked back into the building. Eileen was right, of course. Life was too short. The more she thought about it, the more a week in sunny Spain sounded like "just what the doctor ordered," so to speak. Actually she had not been to the doctor since her yearly checkup last January, at which time he had pronounced her "Amazing!"

Her feet clicked along on the red tile hallway toward the Hanna Memorial Library. Just like castanets, she thought, getting more and more into the spirit of the adventure. By the time she pushed open the doors of the hallowed Hanna, she was softly humming the chorus of "Lady of Spain, I Adore You."

Sister Mary Helen found Eileen in the small workroom off the main librarian's office. She was surrounded by black leather-covered tomes.

"We really don't have too much information on Santiago de Compostela," Eileen muttered without even looking up. " 'Galicia is in the extreme northwest corner of Spain. Its climate is generally wet, much like that of Ireland,' " she read aloud.

"Spain is sunny," Mary Helen said stubbornly, unwilling to give up her illusion.

"All I know is that if it's like back home, we had better be prepared and pack our Aran sweaters." She shoved a volume of the 1910 *Catholic Encyclopedia* toward Sister Mary Helen, who skimmed through the statistics of the shrine and the metropolitan see of Compostela, its etymology, and its history.

"Here's something about a Holy Year," she read. " 'Jubilee years (Holy Years) are held when the feast of St. James, July 25, falls on a Sunday. The years come at odd intervals of 6-5-6-11 years apart.' "

Eileen counted on her fingers. "We really are very lucky to be going," she said. "Do you realize what our chances are of being able to celebrate another *año santo?*"

"Very slim-o," Mary Helen grunted, pulling yet another book from the pile. "Listen to this, Eileen. 'Tradition says that the disciples of St. James spirited away his dead body from Spain and set sail for Jaffa. Seven days later the ship, propelled by wind and waves, arrived on the coast of Galicia. A man was riding his horse beside the sea. As the ship neared, the horse bolted and the man was carried out by the waves. Instead of drowning, the rider surfaced covered with cockleshells. Since then the cockleshell has been the symbol of St. James and the badge of a pilgrim to Compostela.' " Mary Helen paused. "Now what do you think of that?"

"It works for me." Eileen looked up from the book that she was perusing.

"How did I know it would?" Mary Helen muttered. "Shall I go on?"

"By all means, old dear. My books just have the facts. You seem to have stumbled on all the good stuff."

" 'The saint's tomb was lost, then rediscovered in 813 by a shepherd who saw little starlike lights over an oak grove. It is sometimes called "St. James of the Field of Stars." ' "

Sister Mary Helen glanced up to see if Eileen was still listening. She was mesmerized. "Do you want to hear the names of some of the famous people who have visited the shrine?"

Eileen nodded.

"St. Francis of Assisi on his way to found his first monastery in Spain; St. Dominic; William of Aquitaine; Louis the Seventh of France; Don Juan of Austria; Marshal Pétain; Angelo Giuseppe Roncalli before he became Pope John the Twenty-third—"

"And us," Eileen added dreamily. "You do have your passport, don't you?"

"You know I do," Mary Helen answered. She renewed her passport and her driver's license religiously, not as religiously as she renewed her three vows, of course, although some convent wag had once remarked that it was close.

"Then what is it that is still bothering you?" Eileen studied Mary Helen's face. "I can tell that something is."

"Several things," Mary Helen admitted. "From all we've read here and what I remember from the article in the *San Francisco Catholic*, the Holy Year starts in January. The Feast of St. James and the culminating celebration are in July. Why, then, are we going in October? And why would the Patio Español sponsor such a trip? To make any sense, it has to be a promotional of some sort. Why would you promote an event when it is almost over?" She paused to let that much sink in. "And then there's still the problem of Cecilia."

Eileen raised her hand. "Whoa! You can ask Señor Fraga about his reasons when you call to accept. I'm sure he has a satisfactory explanation. I have already taken care of Sister Cecilia." She grinned. "I simply left her a note."

The phone in the workroom rang before Mary Helen could squeal at Eileen's news. Even with the receiver pressed against Eileen's ear, she could hear the cold, clear tone in the college president's voice.

"I know how busy you are at this time, Sister dear," Eileen said, her brogue lilting. "I didn't want to take up an appointment space, so I knew you'd appreciate a note instead. Much quicker for you," she rushed on. "Mary Helen is here with me, and we have been reading the most wonderful things about this shrine. It should be a very worthwhile religious experience for the two of us. And it is so steeped in history and tradition. The college, I know, will benefit from our having been. Why, one of us can speak about it to a history class and one to a religion class. It is a small part of the medieval church still left in today's world. Then there is the foreign language department—I beg your pardon?" Eileen paused to listen. "Oh, we will and thank you."

"What did she say?" Mary Helen asked.

"She said, 'Have a good time.'"

"Poor devil, what else could she say?" Mary Helen shrugged, staring with new admiration at her dear old friend, already returning to her stack of books. "What chance did she stand against you?"

Mary Helen checked her wristwatch. "Let's stop for a coffee break," she said. She needed one. The two nuns had been reading silently and to each other for well over an hour.

"Thank goodness you can't find more books on the subject." Mary Helen pushed back a piece of gray hair that persisted in falling over her glasses. "We probably know more about Santiago de Compostela than most of the natives. Let's leave something to the tour guide."

"Right you are." Eileen stretched. "Let's just put these books back on the table to be reshelved, and we'll call it a day."

The two nuns started down the long hallway toward the Sisters' dining room in companionable silence. At this time of day the passageway was deserted. In the name of ecology, someone had flipped off the overhead lights.

"I feel as if we're two moles in a tunnel," Eileen groused, and Mary Helen was about to agree when the rapid clicking of the tiles warned them that someone was approaching in a hurry.

Eileen squinted down the dim corridor. "Whoever that is, the devil himself must be in pursuit," she whispered.

Or the place is on fire, Mary Helen thought, hoping that if that were the case, someone had rescued the coffeepot and a couple of Ramon's fresh glazed doughnuts.

"Is one of you, by any possibility, Seester Mary Helen?" They heard the voice almost before they saw the short, stout man. His dark eyes darted from one to the other.

"I am." Although Mary Helen had never seen the face before, she recognized the voice.

"Seester, I am Señor Fraga from the Patio Español," the man said with a stiff, formal bow. When he straightened up, Mary Helen noticed that his mouth pulled into a thin, tense line.

"We just spoke on the telephone." He was checking, no doubt, to see if she remembered.

"Yes, of course, señor," Mary Helen answered quickly, eager to show him that despite their recent conversation, she did have all of her senses and most of her wits intact.

"Because of our earlier mix-up, Seester, I was anxious to

present this to you in person." Señor Fraga thrust out his hand which held a thick white envelope. "Pulmantur" was typed across its front.

"This contains your information," he said, speaking a bit more quickly than he had on the phone. "There is a pamphlet about the tour, your luggage tags, a list of the documents you will need, and your itinerary. Your tickets, of course, await you at the airport. That is, Seester, if you accept the prize." He paused, studying her face. Obviously he was still not sure whom and what he was dealing with.

"We accept," Eileen announced brightly.

With a look of relief Señor Fraga thrust the envelope toward her.

"Wait just a minute, señor," Mary Helen blurted out.

Señor Fraga looked stricken. "You do not accept?"

"Yes, yes, of course, I do. Thank you. But I do have a few questions."

It took a little convincing, but Mary Helen persuaded Señor Fraga to join them in the Sisters' dining room. After a sprinkling of preliminary chitchat, a cup of coffee, and one of Ramon's fresh doughnuts, Mary Helen could see the man begin to relax.

"As I mentioned in the hall, señor," she began, "I do have a few questions about our trip. I am curious about how many people won your contest. Just I, or are there more?"

"Ten, Seester." He spread both his hands on the table top. "Five winners and five companions."

"The Patio Español is sending ten people to the Holy Year in Santiago?" Mentally she calculated the cost. Roughly it was what Shirley and she had hoped to net on the alumnae fashion show.

Mary Helen noted a melancholy look on Señor Fraga's face when he nodded his head. "Yes, Seester," he said, accepting another doughnut from Eileen.

"The Patio Español is sending ten people to a Holy Year in Santiago in October when, from what I understand, it began in January and its main day of celebration was held on July twenty-fifth. I've given it some thought, señor, and at the risk of sounding crass, I am wondering why."

"Why? Why? Because," he began with a touch of bravado, "Galicia is my province. Santiago is my home."

Their eyes met and held. He took a fierce bite of his doughnut. As he chewed, Mary Helen could almost see his mental cranes turning, appraising her, deciding just how much to tell. When he finally swallowed, Ramon's doughnut seemed to act like truth serum.

"Why? I will tell you why, Seester." His shoulders sagged a little. "To be quite frank, it is because my nephew, my wife's sister's only boy, is a—how you call it?—he is a bum. Thirty years old and no job!" Señor Fraga narrowed his eyes as he picked up momentum. "But always the angle. Sí, always the angle. Now he thinks he will be a travel agent."

The corners of his mouth turned down as if he had just tasted something sour. "A travel agent," he repeated, pausing to let the nuns savor the foolishness of such an ambition. "So what does he do? He sets up an *año santo* trip to Santiago with Pulmantur in Madrid. Promises them ten people. A big man." He stuck his thumbs behind the lapels of his suit jacket. "Not two or even five or six. No. My nephew is a big man. He will find ten. He will run the trip, be the guide. He signs the contract, takes the advance.

"Now, it is getting onto October. The *año santo* is almost over. Pulmantur wants its money." Señor Fraga's face was flushed. Clearly he had worked himself up to a full head of steam. "And the big man? He has no money. He has no pilgrims. His mother, she comes to me."

His voice shifted into a falsetto to imitate his sister-in-law. " 'Carlos, please help my Pepe.' Can you imagine, Seesters, a thirty-year-old still called Pepe? 'I am afraid he will go to jail!' she says. 'Good place for him,' I say. She cries. She goes to my wife, who says that I am a heartless man." Incredulous, Señor Fraga shrugged and stared at the nuns. "Me, a heartless man!

" 'Maybe this is Pepe's big chance,' my wife says. I say, 'Pepe has had enough chances from me.' " He slammed his fist down on the table, rattling the cups. " 'Enough, no more,' I say. But my wife, she begs me, and when I say, 'No,' she cries, and then she stops speaking."

A frustrated and spent Señor Fraga leaned back in his chair and closed his eyes. "It costs me a fortune, but maybe it is worth it after all. At least, my wife is speaking, her sister is out of my hair, and Pepe, he is out of the country for a while. There are nice girls at Pulmantur. Maybe he will meet one, marry her, and stay in Spain.

"But enough of my troubles." He pushed the last bit of glazed doughnut into his mouth and drained his cup. "I must get back to my restaurant." Señor Fraga rose. "*Adios*, for now," he said, bowing formally to each of them. "I will see you on Thursday, October seventh. A driver will pick you up here and bring you to the airport. The time is on your itinerary." He pointed to the envelope that Eileen was still clutching.

"Perhaps you would just as soon we didn't accept the trip," Mary Helen said, feeling a certain sympathy for the man.

Eileen's face fell, but Señor Fraga's fell farther. "No, Seester, we must send ten people to Santiago. I am happy that two of them are religious. I have already given all the information to my accountant."

Accountant? Mary Helen wondered, watching Señor Fraga disappear. With short, quick steps he sailed down the darkened hallway, leaving nothing but the staccato clicking in his wake.

"He surely answered all your questions," Eileen said cheerfully.

And raised a few, too, Mary Helen thought, wondering just how wise it was to go on a tour led by someone who sounded as irresponsible as Pepe.

Eileen suffered from no such qualms. "Our winning was even lucky for Señor Fraga," she noted. "He seems genuinely pleased to have picked out two religious."

Suddenly something that the señor had said and that had puzzled her became crystal clear. "Picked is right!" Mary Helen stared at her friend. Of course, he had "picked" them. He would have picked as many religious as were in the box.

"We are a charitable tax deduction, Eileen," she announced triumphantly. "That's why he is so anxious for us to go, and that is why he said 'accountant.' He may have to pay full fare for eight, but not us. Us he has declared a donation."

At first Eileen stared at her with wide, unbelieving eyes. Finally she dismissed the suggestion with a wave of her pudgy hand. "This fund-raising business is beginning to affect you, Mary Helen. You see tax deductions everywhere." She wagged her head. "Not to press a point, old dear, but I honestly do think it was a stroke of very good luck that I saw that box and that you won this trip. You know, Mary Helen, you really do need a vacation, a chance to get away from everything and just relax."

And what better place to do it, Mary Helen thought, than in sunny Spain?

thursday, october 7

feast of
our Lady of the Rosary

♦

The shrill ring of the convent doorbell cut through the chatter in the Community Room. Much to Mary Helen's surprise, the nuns had gathered there after the last class for an impromptu party to wish the travelers well.

Sister Agnes had prepared her famous spinach dip, Sister Marta had arrived with a steaming platter of buffalo wings, and Anne, with a few of the other young nuns, had seen to the liquid refreshments.

"*Vaya con Dios.* Go with God." Tall, slim Cecilia raised her glass in a toast.

If we're going with Pepe, God had better not be too far away, Mary Helen thought, raising her own glass in return.

"And have a treat on us." Looking over her rimless glasses, Cecilia handed Eileen an envelope with a slight bulge.

Mary Helen was genuinely touched and was about to say so when Sister Therese (who insisted her name be pronounced "trays") burst into the room.

"Your carriage awaits without," she announced to one and all.

"Without a what?" old Sister Donata, her perpetual straight woman, asked.

"Without these two." She pointed to Eileen and Mary Helen.

In the ripple of polite laughter and predictable groans that followed, Mary Helen and Eileen headed toward the front door. Their suitcases were already in the parlor, awaiting the arrival of the driver who would take them to the San Francisco Airport. It turned out to be Señor Fraga himself.

"Good afternoon, Seesters," he greeted them. "You are ready, I see. *Muy bien!*" After snatching up the two suitcases, he carried them to the car, opened the trunk, and put them in. With a flourish he flung open the door to the backseat and held it.

As if it were a chauffeured limo, Mary Helen thought, except, of course, Señor Fraga drove a Toyota, not a limousine.

"You two can't leave without a good-bye hug." Young Sister Anne followed them down the hall.

Inwardly Mary Helen groaned. Why a hug? Why not just a nice, cheerful good-bye with maybe a peck on the cheek? Not that she was against hugs per se, but she'd been noticing of late that it was always the thin young nuns like Anne who were the huggers. When you formed a few rolls in the wrong places, you became a little more circumspect.

None of this seemed to bother Sister Eileen, who was squeezing Anne and looking pleased to do so.

"I brought you each a little gift." Anne reached into her apron pocket.

"You shouldn't have," Eileen protested as Anne handed each a small travel diary. A thin pencil was attached to its back cover.

"Thank you, Anne." Sister Mary Helen was moved by the young nun's thoughtfulness, although she had no intention of using the diary. When she traveled, she was usually too tired at the end of the day to write anything at all. Furthermore, she knew that when she returned home, she'd be entirely too busy to reread it.

"This is such a very special trip"—Anne beamed—"that I thought you might want to capture some of your most exciting moments."

Mary Helen felt a little chagrined. Anne was right. This was a special trip. She should try to jot down something about it, although she rather doubted that a semireligious pilgrimage to a little-known shrine in an out-of-the-way corner of Spain would hold too many exciting moments. She dropped the thin diary into her pocketbook and gave Anne a quick good-bye hug.

"Don't forget these!" Therese's nasal voice echoed down the convent hallway and out onto the porch. In each hand she held a fold-up umbrella. "We wanted to get you a little something you could use on your trip, and I thought of these," she declared proudly, thrusting an umbrella at each of them.

Mary Helen frowned. "Spain is sunny!" she blurted out unthinkingly.

At first Therese looked hurt, and Mary Helen felt like an ingrate. She was just about to apologize when Therese recovered with a sniff. "We'll see!" she said smugly. "We will just see!"

Shoving the second unwanted gift into her carryon bag, Mary Helen stepped into the waiting car.

♦

Wordlessly Señor Fraga zipped along the 280 Freeway toward the San Francisco Airport, just ahead of the evening commuter traffic. Mary Helen's eyes burned, yet she was afraid to close them lest she drop off to sleep. The bump of the tires along the road, the hum of the engine, and the warmth of the October sun filling the car were so soothing that she was sure to fall right off.

And no wonder! Eileen and she had scurried around for the last two weeks, making the necessary arrangements at the college, digging out their passports, purchasing a few traveler's checks, and packing and repacking their suitcases, trying not to forget anything essential yet keep them light enough to carry.

Of course, Mary Helen had checked out a couple of new paperback murder mysteries from the library and stashed them in her pocketbook. She was careful to slip the one she intended to read first into her plastic prayer book cover. After all, there was no sense scandalizing the other "pilgrims" unnecessarily.

There would be plenty of time both to sleep and to read once they boarded the plane. According to the itinerary, Mary Helen figured that the trip to Madrid, their first stop, would take about eleven hours.

A blazing red-orange yolk of sun was sinking quickly and turning the sky into a study of lavender and pink. They passed the National Cemetery; Señor Fraga exited 280 and sped along the Portola Freeway toward San Francisco International.

The airport was a maze of traffic and blinking lights. Hunched over the steering wheel, Señor Fraga maneuvered the lanes for departing and arriving flights, for domestic and international airlines.

With an air of relief, he pulled up in front of their terminal and spoke at last. "Seesters, not to worry. We are here in plenty of time." He glanced at his wristwatch. "In fact, we are early. I will give you to my nephew if I can find him. And then I will see personally to your luggage." He hustled them out of the Toyota and into the terminal.

Mary Helen was curious to meet the much-maligned Pepe.

"Ah, Seesters, here comes the big man now." Señor

Fraga frowned toward a young fellow pushing his way through the crowd.

The two men could not have looked less alike if they'd held a contest. Where the señor was short and stout, his nephew was tall, broad-shouldered, and thin in all the right places.

Nor did he fit Mary Helen's stereotype of a bum. His gray woolen suit was tailored to perfection, his face tanned, and his eyes, like the words of the old Irish ballad, were "dark and . . . roving."

"Ah, Tío Carlos! Early, as always." The young man smiled. Beside her, Mary Helen felt Señor Fraga stiffen.

"Seesters," he said, scarcely hiding his contempt, "this is my wife's sister's boy, my nephew, Señor Jose Nunez de Costa."

With a smile that revealed a mouthful of straight white teeth, Señor Nunez clicked his heels and gave a deferential bow.

"Pepe. Please call me Pepe," he insisted. "It is my supreme pleasure to meet you both." His voice was unctuous. "We are indeed fortunate to have two such religious women upon this pilgrimage." He faced Mary Helen.

If you only knew what we've heard about you and this trip, she wanted to say, but thought better of it. After all, they had eleven hours together on this plane, plus another short hop to Santiago. Not to mention a week in a foreign country. No sense starting off on the wrong foot.

"Except for our friend Consuelo Aguilar we would never have been in your uncle's restaurant." Mercifully Eileen filled the conversation gap. She turned to include the señor, but he had vanished.

Pepe, seemingly unconcerned about his uncle's quick exit, led the two nuns through the milling crowd. "Follow me,

Sisters," he shouted over his shoulder. "We are in the First Class Lounge. I will introduce you to the rest of our pilgrims."

"Thank you, señor," Eileen shouted back, grabbing Sister Mary Helen's hand to make sure that they weren't separated.

"Pepe, Sister." Mary Helen was puffing to keep up. "Please just call him Pepe."

◆

When the three reached the First Class Lounge, Pepe pulled back the heavy smoked-glass door. Chinese stone lions glowered at them from pedestals on either side of the entrance, and the uniformed attendant at the reception desk didn't look much friendlier.

"I moved the rest of your party to the far end of the room." She strained the words through a plastic smile.

With a gracious bow, Pepe motioned the nuns to follow him down the length of the narrow room toward a group of chairs behind a potted palm. Six people sat on the sea green chairs, holding coffee cups and looking uneasy.

"Ah, he's back," a thin-faced man with a graying beard announced. All heads turned toward Pepe.

"*Peregrinos!* Pilgrims," he proclaimed in a loud, cheerful voice, "here are two more for your ranks." Quickly he introduced Mary Helen and Eileen to the man with the gray beard, who turned out to be Professor Roger DeAngelo, and to the professor's wife, Barbara.

"Please call me Bootsie," she said with just a touch of a southern drawl. Next they met Dr. Neil and Mrs. Rita Fong, an Asian couple. Neil quickly made it clear he was a dentist, not a medical doctor. "Before anyone starts telling me about his or her lumbago," he said with an easy smile. Finally, they were introduced to two young women, Heidi Williams, whose hair, eyes, and build reminded Mary Helen of butterscotch drop, and her friend, Lisa Springer.

Settling the nuns in chairs, their host excused himself to hurry back into the terminal in search of his last two missing "pilgrims."

In the awkward silence that followed Pepe's departure, the group made several attempts at conversation. Questions and answers bumped into one another the way questions and answers do when a group tries to establish some common ground.

"How did you happen to be at Patio Español? . . . Do you by any chance know so-and-so? . . . Is this your first trip to Spain? . . . I had an uncle who lived on the Avenues, by Fort Miley."

Eileen fielded the ones that came their way. Mary Helen wondered how long it would take before the chitchat petered out and, for lack of anything better to say, someone would ask, "Whatever happened to the nuns in habits?" That was all right, but its singularly insulting companion, "Don't you think nuns got more respect when they wore religious dress?" raised Mary Helen's hackles.

"I have never been treated with anything but respect, and God help anyone who tries to do otherwise," she was always tempted to answer. So she was relieved when Dr. Fong, peering over his half glasses, noticed that Eileen and she were without coffee and supplied the perfect excuse to leave the group.

"Can I get you some?" Fong asked in a low, soothing voice.

"No, thank you, Doctor." She pushed herself up from the soft chair. "We'll be sitting for a long time. Moving around will do us good."

Sister Eileen joined her at the refreshment table set

against the darkened windows that formed one wall of the lounge.

"Whan that Aprill with his shoures sote,/ The droghte of Marche hath perced to the roote." Out of the corner of her mouth, Eileen whispered the opening phrases of Chaucer's *Canterbury Tales*.

Although Mary Helen hadn't thought of the old classic in years, even a cursory glance brought home Eileen's point. Professor DeAngelo was as hollow-cheeked and melancholy-looking as she remembered Chaucer's scholar to be. His dark eyes, however, which had settled a bit too close to his nose, held a hard brilliance unknown in Chaucer's time: contact lenses.

And the doctor? How had the poet described his doctor? Something about being dressed in "sangwin and in pers . . . lyned with taffeta and with sendal." Actually, that more accurately described the doctor's tiny wife, Rita, in her blood-red blouse and blue-gray pleated skirt. Her coarse black hair was piled high on her head in thick curls that added several inches to her height.

A loud thud drew attention toward the doorway.

"For God's sake, Bud, be careful!" A high-pitched voice filled the First Class Lounge. It belonged to a sixtyish woman with waxy margarine yellow hair.

Rings of underarm perspiration were already formed on Bud's plaid shirt. "What the hell have you got in here anyway, Cora?" he grumbled. "Lead?"

Cora ignored him.

Readjusting a slippery garment bag over his arm, Bud struggled to retrieve a makeup kit.

"Let me help you, Señor Bowman." Like oil poured on seawater, Pepe relieved the man of the carryon luggage and hurried to introduce the newcomers to the group. He began with the two nuns.

Bud shook Sister Mary Helen's hand. "Sorry we're late," he announced to the group at large. "My wife can never get any place on time."

"I could if I had a little cooperation," Cora announced just as loudly.

Treating their sparring as if he hadn't heard it, Pepe moved the couple on to meet the two young women. "This is another of our lucky winners," he said, "Heidi Williams."

Heidi grinned and moved her gum to the side of her mouth. "This is my friend, Lisa," she said, nodding toward her companion.

Bud Bowman's eyes fastened on Lisa, and it was no wonder. Lisa Springer was tall, slender, and as strikingly beautiful as Heidi was plain. Her hair, the color of liquid amber, was pulled back and fastened with a sapphire ribbon that highlighted the blue of her eyes.

Lisa preened a little, almost as if being admired were a new phenomenon or at least one she never tired of. She smiled up at Bud. Only one crooked incisor marred her otherwise perfect face.

"For God's sake, Bud, don't just stand there staring. We've got more people to meet," Cora hissed.

Mercifully a large group of Japanese tourists entered the lounge, and the room took on a pleasant buzz as the Bowmans met the others.

The two nuns made their way back to the urn for a second cup of coffee. "The Wife of Bath," Eileen mouthed to Mary Helen. She rolled her gray eyes toward Cora Bowman.

Mary Helen gave a surreptitious nod. Eileen's right, she thought, remembering the artist's rendition of the famous pilgrims that had hung for years in the hallway of the college's English department. Right down to the woman's florid complexion, gap-toothed smile, and great wide hips. She was even wearing glossy new shoes. It was uncanny!

"Who does that make us?" Mary Helen asked, helping herself to a miniature Danish.

"Why, the Madame Prioress and her nun companion, of course." Eileen winked. "You do have a 'fair forheed.' "

Mary Helen touched her brow. All she felt were wrinkles.

"And I know many a tale about Cecilia."

"Cecilia?" Mary Helen was puzzled.

"Don't you remember, old dear? Chaucer's nun's tale was about Cecilia. The saint, naturally, not ours." Eileen blinked piously. "Although our Cecilia may be a saint for all we know."

"Of course, I don't remember," Mary Helen said, refusing to comment on Eileen's last remark, "and frankly, I'm wondering how you do. I never realized your memory was that good."

Eileen frowned. "What's wrong with my memory?"

"Nothing at all. Actually, it is amazing."

"I have always had a good memory," Eileen groused.

"Yes, I know, but how in the world do you remember all that? It must be years since you read *The Canterbury Tales*."

Sister Eileen's round face flushed.

"How long?"

Airily she refilled her cup. "Not too long," she said.

"How long?" Mary Helen narrowed her eyes.

"Well, if you must know, a week ago." Eileen tilted her head defensively. "I *am* in the library, you know. It is only natural for the girls to ask me for help."

"*Peregrinos!* Pilgrims." Pepe's voice cut off any further conversation. "It is nearly time for us to board our plane. Passports, please." He clapped his hands for attention. "Everyone, please, get out your passports."

Their host's command propelled the tour group into action. Searching through his jacket pockets, the professor looked even more melancholy than before. His wife, who stood nearly as tall as he did, crowded in behind him.

When they were introduced, Mary Helen had judged Bootsie DeAngelo to be much younger than her husband, more the age of one of his students. The black hair pulled back from her face with a colored band and curled softly around her shoulders, plus the youthful figure accented by the short flowered-print shirt flaring over her hips, gave that impression.

Standing nearer her, Mary Helen realized with a start that Bootsie's hair was really too black, almost shoe polish black. The long, thick eyelashes, which she used quite effectively, were much too long and heavy to be her own. She felt a twinge of pity as she noticed the makeup-caked wrinkles etching the corners of the woman's eyes and mouth.

Youth is like spring, Mary Helen wanted to caution her, an overpraised season, but she knew that was something Bootsie DeAngelo must discover for herself.

Her musing was cut short when Pepe again announced, "Passports, please," and the Bowmans began to argue. "I gave mine to you." Cora watched Bud pat the pockets of his slacks.

"Passports, please," Pepe repeated. "It is nearly boarding time."

Dr. Fong's face paled at the prospect of the long flight, and Heidi Williams let out a high-pitched nervous giggle.

Rummaging through her pocketbook, past a paperback mystery and Anne's travel diary, foraging for her own passport, Mary Helen kept hearing snippets of *The Canterbury Tales* in her head. What had Chaucer said about his pilgrims? "Of various sorts"—this group surely was—"gathered together in a flock."

Finally extracting her passport from the bowels of her pocketbook, she wondered if this motley pack would ever

become a flock. She didn't envy Señor Pepe Nunez, who un-doubtedly fancied himself their shepherd. Poor fellow, she thought, watching him shoo the group that moved anything but sheeplike toward the gate, he surely has his work cut out for him.

♦

"Good evening, ladies and gentlemen," the flight attendant began. "Welcome aboard Flight Nine-forty with direct service to Madrid."

Mary Helen hardly heard the rest of the spiel. She was too busy shoving her carryon bag with its bulky umbrella under the seat in front of her and trying to buckle her seat belt. Happily Eileen and she were on the side section of the plane, with two seats together, so they had only each other to bump.

The plane began to roll. "Be sure that your seats are in their upright positions and that your trays are securely fas-tened."

Before the attendant could continue, the flashing of lights and the dinging of bells sent her scurrying and the heavy plane rattled and trembled into a takeoff.

Eyes closed, Sister Mary Helen grabbed the armrest and held her breath. All around her the plane shook and roared. Silently she began a decade of the Rosary and found the familiar, almost unthinking repetition of the Hail Mary com-forting. "Pray for us sinners, now and at the hour of our death."

With the final thud of the wheels against the belly of the aircraft, they were airborne.

"I always forget how much you hate takeoffs," Eileen called above the roar of the plane, which still soared straight up, piercing the cloud cover.

Mary Helen cautiously opened her eyes and peered

around. "I don't seem to be the only one." She pointed to the armrest across the aisle and the set of white knuckles still clutching it. They belonged to Dr. Fong.

Just behind them, Bud Bowman softly comforted his wife. "Relax, babe. It's okay," he said. "Nothing is going to happen now. We're off the ground. Relax."

Cora drew in a hissing breath.

"Relax," Bud repeated, "and leggo of my arm, will ya? You're stopping my circulation."

A sudden ring of bells assured them that they had, at last, reached cruising altitude. Lisa Springer was one of the first out of her seat. Self-consciously she threaded her way down the narrow aisle, surveying each row as she went.

Mary Helen wondered absently if she was looking for anyone in particular. The other tour members were seated in a clump toward the back of the plane. She made a mental check: Bowmans, behind; Fongs, Lisa and Heidi, across the aisle in the wide middle section; DeAngelos, directly in front of the Fongs.

Only Pepe was unaccounted for. Perhaps Lisa had gone in search of him. Before Mary Helen could give it any more thought, the flight attendants began to gallop through the plane with orange juice, pillows, blankets, small utility packs, and, finally, the menu. The next hour was taken up with cocktails and dinner. When the movie came on, both nuns had seen it.

Eileen decided to rest her eyes while Mary Helen delved into her new paperback mystery. With relish, she opened to Chapter One. An eerie quiet settled over the plane. Only the engine hummed. Beside her Eileen began a soft, rhythmic snore. By Chapter Two Mary Helen's own eyes were burning. She closed them. The steady drone of the plane lulled her toward sleep.

"The movie, Bud! Watch the movie, not the redhead."

Cora's words, sounding far away, floated into Mary Helen's sinking consciousness.

✦

Mary Helen awoke with a jerk and cleared her throat. "What happened?" she mumbled. Both aisles were cramped with passengers.

Next to her, Eileen, who was working on the crossword puzzle at the back of the in-flight magazine, pointed to the movie screen. It was back in its tight cylinder.

"The whole bunch is taking an after-the-movie stretch," she said, nodding toward Professor DeAngelo, who, with a wry smile, was stretching his long arms toward the ceiling of the plane.

Mary Helen blinked. In the shadowy light, that twisted grin, his hollow cheeks, and those dark-rimmed eyes gave him the look of a skeleton at a feast.

Too many mysteries, she thought, watching Lisa Springer squeeze past him.

"I am so sorry. Did I bump you?" Lisa asked with exaggerated politeness.

"Not at all." The professor lowered his arms.

"You know, Professor—" she began coyly.

"Roger. Please, call me Roger."

With feline grace Bootsie slithered from her seat and stood behind him.

"You know, Roger"—Lisa ignored the woman completely—"since I first saw you, I have had the funniest feeling we've met before." She put her face closer to his and playfully batted those sapphire blue eyes of hers. "Do I look familiar to you?"

"No. Not really." Nervously he pulled on his beard.

Mary Helen nudged Eileen. "You don't suppose we are going to have a triangle, do you?" she whispered, watching

Bootsie lean her head against her husband's shoulder, whisper something in his ear, then fix Lisa with a "better to eat you with, my dear" smile.

Eileen strained to see whom she was talking about. With a shrug she returned to her crossword puzzle. "What is an eight-letter word for a meddler?" she asked. "It begins with the letter *b*."

Mary Helen thought, but only for a moment. "Busybody," she hissed, "and you are not funny. You know perfectly well that I am simply a student of human nature." She wriggled in her seat to get a better look.

The professor, now stoic-faced, squatted on the arm of his seat as Bootsie's fingers kneaded the muscles in his neck and across his shoulders.

With hardly a backward glance Lisa made her way down the crowded aisle toward the front of the plane.

Rita Fong climbed over her husband, Neil, who was crumpled sideways in his seat. His balding head slumped forward. Deftly she reached down and snatched the half glasses from his nose. He didn't move.

"You can sure tell those two are an old married couple!" Rita nodded toward the DeAngelos.

Mary Helen hoped that Bootsie hadn't overheard. With all the trouble she takes to appear youthful, she surely won't take kindly to being called an "old" anything. "What makes you think that?" she whispered.

"Because if she was the now generation, he'd be doing the rubbing." Rita turned back to reconsider Bootsie DeAngelo. "Maybe I can talk her into enrolling in one of my aerobics classes and learning to relax her own shoulders."

"Where do you teach aerobics?" Mary Helen asked, not that she was really interested. In fact, if the truth were known, she considered aerobics nothing more than finely tuned torture. It just seemed polite to ask.

Half listening to Rita Fong recite her schedule of classes, she noticed that Lisa had found Pepe. It was the first time Mary Helen had laid eyes on him since they boarded the plane, and she wondered vaguely where he was sitting.

The two of them stood by the water fountain in the far front of the plane, laughing and making what old Sister Thomasine, God rest her, used to call "movie star eyes" at each other.

Lisa let her gaze stray for a moment in Roger DeAngelo's direction; then back it went to Pepe and their private joke.

An uneasy silence warned Mary Helen that she had missed Rita's question.

"That would be just grand." Good old Eileen came to the rescue again. "Perhaps in a little while," she said, and Rita, looking very pleased, made her way back to her seat.

"What would be grand?" Mary Helen asked when Rita was out of earshot.

"She wants to show us a few simple exercises that we can do in the aisle, so that we won't develop jet lag." Eileen rolled her gray eyes heavenward.

Mary Helen groaned, visualizing the two of them huffing and puffing in the cramped aisle. "We will be a regular show," she said.

"To hear you, one would think that she was asking us to change into black leotards and do push-ups," Eileen snapped.

The mental picture of the two of them in leotards, no matter the color, struck Mary Helen funny at about the same moment as Eileen began to laugh.

Reluctantly Pepe left Lisa and made his way down the aisle. What a moment for him to begin his official tour guide "how-do," Mary Helen thought, watching him approach.

"You two seem to be enjoying yourselves," Pepe said, smiling benignly at the two nuns. Much the way one would at a couple of lovable old simpletons, Mary Helen thought. And it's no wonder. Here we are thousands of feet in the air, staring at the upholstered backs of seats and laughing.

Pepe pulled in closer, making way for Lisa Springer to pass. The flowery fragrance of cologne wafted after her. With his smile frozen in place, Pepe's dark eyes followed her graceful climb back into her seat.

Forgetting all about them, he moved on to the Bowmans. "Well, señor and señora, how are you two doing? Are you enjoying your trip so far?"

"It's a hell of a long ride," Bud muttered, shifting in his seat.

As if to agree, Bootsie DeAngelo edged around her husband and into the aisle. "I need some exercise," she said, moving toward the front of the plane.

They certainly are a roaming group, Mary Helen thought. She tried to block out all the activity and bury herself in her mystery. She sincerely hoped that Rita Fong would forget her promise of aerobics. No such luck! At that very moment she appeared and clapped eagerly for the nuns to join her for a workout.

Rather than make a scene, Mary Helen and Eileen stood in the aisle, following Rita's lead. At her command they pushed their palms together, rotated their heads, vigorously shook their arms. Hanging on to the sides of seats, they circled one foot, then the other.

Loath to meet the eye of any other passenger, Mary Helen kept her own gaze fixed on the overhead storage bin. Out of the corner of her eye, she did catch a glimpse of Heidi Williams. Actually Heidi was hard to miss. Wide-eyed and snapping her chewing gum, the plump girl was frankly staring. Not that Mary Helen blamed her. The three of them must have been some sight, especially when they attempted the knee bends.

"Now that wasn't so bad, was it?" Eileen said when they were, once again, in their seats.

"For whatever good it did," Mary Helen grumbled, still feeling foolish.

"I am sure that the poor woman was only trying to be helpful." Eileen circled her head once more for good measure. "To save us from jet lag and all of that."

"I'd rather have jet lag," Mary Helen said testily.

Without warning, the overhead lights began to blink and bells sounded.

"Please return to your seats and fasten your seat belts," the captain's voice announced. "Currently we are flying over the Pole and will be experiencing a slight turbulence."

Mary Helen grabbed the armrest and watched Bootsie DeAngelo, holding tightly to seat backs, fight her way down the aisle. The plane lurched, and Heidi squealed as Bootsie fell forward.

Straightening up with a nervous laugh, she leaned against an arm to steady herself. The plane rolled again, pitching Bootsie sideways. Roger grabbed for her and managed to pull her toward her own seat. Together they wrestled with gravity and the seat belt until finally she was settled.

"What's this?" Mary Helen heard Bootsie ask. She glanced over. Bootsie was holding a small, tightly rolled slip of white paper. It must have been on her cushion.

Roger's face was strained and impatient. "Looks like someone dropped a note or something," he said. "How do I know? Just drop it on the floor."

Bootsie unrolled the paper. "Belmont," she read aloud. The plane dropped like an elevator. Her face blanched, and she sucked in her breath.

Books and cups clattered to the ground and bounced around in the aisle. Mary Helen's heart bounced with them.

"Pray for us sinners." The familiar words came to her. Behind her Cora gasped and grabbed the seat back.

Across the aisle Bootsie's face was still pale. It couldn't have been "Belmont," Mary Helen thought crazily, wondering what color her own face was. It must have been the sudden jolt.

"Maybe we can see something." Beside her Eileen's voice was amazingly steady. She pushed up the plastic shade, and the two of them peered out the small window into a sea of absolute darkness.

After what seemed hours, but was probably only minutes, the turbulence quieted and all the signs were turned off.

"How did you like that ride?" the captain's voice asked. Most passengers chuckled appreciatively. One booed. Flight attendants rushed down the aisles, offering after-dinner drinks.

Mary Helen felt exhausted but safe again. The other passengers must have felt the same way because before long a peaceful night silence descended over the plane. One by one, people fished out the blankets and small pillows that they had been given. Covering their eyes with bandit masks, they snuggled down for a few hours' sleep.

Darkness covered them all as the plane, caught in a limbo of time, sped through the night toward the Continent. From here or there came a cough, a soft snore. Mary Helen closed her eyes, trying to relax, regretting her earlier nap.

With the steady pulse of the engines droning through the quiet, she couldn't help contemplating the smallness of the craft and the vastness of the ocean below and the sky in which they hung. The plane, its passengers and crew, together, formed a mere speck suspended in the vast universe. Yet each person contained a whole universe within and each was precious in God's sight and greatly loved.

"If I climb to the heavens, you are there." A line from an

evening psalm wriggled into her mind. "If I take the wings of the dawn, and dwell at the sea's furthest end, even there your hand would lead me, your right hand hold me fast."

Soon they would reach the dawn. The psalmist's words mingled with this morning's Gospel. "Hail, Mary," the Angel Gabriel had said, "the Lord is with thee." Was she, like Mary, able to say at the start of this new day, "Be it done unto me according to thy word"?

The fragrance of spring flowers nearby stirred her from her reverie. Lisa Springer must be moving again. Mary Helen's eyelids were heavy now, but she opened them just long enough to confirm that it was Lisa on her way to the back of the plane. As in a dream, she heard someone else creeping down the aisle, someone with a light step. Was that Lisa again? Poor girl, Mary Helen thought, dropping into a hazy sleep, she must have the fidgets.

friday, october 8

feast of St. Simeon, prophet

◆

The plane touched down at the Santiago airport at about 4:00 P.M., Spanish time. Sister Mary Helen had no idea what time of the night or day it was, San Francisco time, and she absolutely refused to look at her wristwatch. She was tired enough without knowing for certain that she ought to be.

When they had landed in Madrid a few hours earlier, Mary Helen was forced to admit that Rita Fong's aerobics appeared to be working, at least for Rita. The small woman bounced around, taking pictures of anyone who would allow it, meaning anyone too weary to resist.

Unfortunately Rita had a Polaroid camera, so her victims were able to see how awful they looked in exactly sixty seconds.

"Death warmed over," Eileen announced when she saw Rita's candid shot of the two nuns.

"At least you have your eyes open." Mary Helen shoved the picture into the pocket of her Aran sweater, hoping the blasted thing would get lost.

"How did it come out?" Rita called over her shoulder, snapping her husband, who had perked up long enough to answer whatever question Lisa Springer was asking him.

Rita did not listen for their reply. She was too busy corralling Heidi into the group.

"Smile, Heidi," she commanded brightly. "I want to get Neil standing between you two lovely young things."

Neil's face reddened as he complied. Mary Helen found it hard to tell whether the expression on Heidi's face was a grin or a grimace.

Their stopover in Madrid was brief. The bleary-eyed *norteamericanos*, under Pepe's able shepherding, located the plane bound for Santiago de Compostela. Police, looking for all the world like extras from a B movie about a banana republic coup, peppered the *aeropuerto*. Under their watchful eyes, the group boarded quickly.

Now, as the small aircraft taxied into the terminal at Santiago, even Rita appeared to have wilted. No one spoke much beyond the necessary grunts, leaving all the details of disembarking to Pepe, who performed them amazingly well.

Almost before they realized it, the pilgrims, their luggage, and a young woman who had joined them at the airport were aboard a small bus heading for the ancient shrine and their almost-as-ancient lodging, the Hostal de los Reyes Católicos.

Crayon-green fields ran up to the highway. Small carpets of roses spread out in front of slate-roofed cottages, where laundry lay drying on the lawn.

"A *hórreo*." Pepe pointed out the bus window to a small granite storage shed set like an oversize box atop six stone pillars. The roof was peaked with a cross on one end and an obelisk with a ball on its tip on the other. Mary Helen was about to ask about the significance when Pepe took up the microphone.

"I may just as well begin our tour now," he said, balancing himself in the middle aisle. "Right?" He waited expectantly.

The group was apparently too sleepy to respond one way or the other.

Undaunted, Pepe continued. "First let me introduce you to Señorita María José Gómez. She has agreed to come on this tour with us as my special consultant."

Bud Bowman let out a snort, which Pepe ignored. "Now about the *hórreo*. You will see many of them in Galicia. They are peculiar to this area of Spain and are used for the safe storage of grain and corn.

"The Galicians are a superstitious people"—he paused, his showmanship at its best—"so they put both the Christian symbol and the pagan symbol on the roof. They are taking no chances."

There was an appreciative chuckle.

"And Galician women"—he smiled meaningfully at María José—"are said to practice white magic."

Cora, who was directly in front of Mary Helen, turned around in her seat. "That's all I need," she said to no one in particular. "First the redhead, now white magic. My Bud's a goner!"

Sister Mary Helen, wondering what Señor Fraga knew about there being a consultant on the trip, craned to get a better look at María José. The small woman knelt on a front seat of the bus facing them. She wore her coarse dark hair shoulder length, and in a certain light it looked as if it had been rinsed with magenta. A horseshoe headband held it off her face, which was round and clear with a nose a little too flat and too wide to make her beautiful. Her age was hard to pinpoint. Probably mid-twenties, Mary Helen thought.

María José put her hand out for the microphone. Her dark eyes darted playfully from Pepe to the tour members. "White magic is good magic," she said in a low, gravelly voice. Again, everyone chuckled.

Eileen nudged Mary Helen and pointed to a woman walking along the roadside with a large wicker basket of wet laundry on her head. "Talk about carrying a heavy work load," she said.

Out of habit Mary Helen groaned at the pun.

In the distance, above the softly rolling hills, the sky was a study in white and brilliant blue. As the bus wound its way toward town, Sister Mary Helen watched the mobile clouds gathering, dispersing, suddenly piling into great darkening mountains. There was an energy in the sky that gave the rugged landscape a special beauty and made her wonder, uneasily, if Sister Therese had been right about the umbrellas.

"Do you think it's going to rain?" She nodded toward the clouds.

"It always rains in Galicia." Eileen looked puzzled. "You know that."

"How would I know that?"

"I read it to you in the library. Don't you remember?"

"I remember no such thing," Mary Helen said with more conviction than she felt.

Eileen yawned. "That's why we wore these heavy sweaters"—she tugged at her Aran knit—"and why the pilgrims to Santiago dressed in broad-brimmed felt hats, heavy capes, and the thickest of sandals. You do remember that?"

Before Mary Helen was forced to any admission, Heidi Williams shot out of her seat.

"There it is!" she shouted, pointing out the window. They all strained to see where she was pointing and were rewarded with the sight of the magnificent cathedral spires looming in the distance.

"*Mon joie,* Heidi." María José stood in the middle aisle. "It is an ancient custom," she said, "that the first one in a group of pilgrims who spies the towers shouts, '*Mon joie,* I am the king.' That person becomes the king of the group, or, in your case, the queen."

"Attagirl!" Bud called out. Pepe clapped, and Heidi let

out an embarrassed giggle. María José went on to explain the legend of St. James, the symbolism of the cockleshells, and several other things that Mary Helen did remember reading in the old *Catholic Encyclopedia*.

Feeling a bit smug, she scanned the buildings on either side of the narrow streets, searching for the cockleshells over the doorways. To her amazement, the streets and doorways were crowded with hundreds of young people walking, bicycling, talking in groups.

"You will feel right at home here, Professor," Pepe said when the bus stopped to let a group of hooting young men cross. "This is a university town. There are one hundred thousand people; fifty thousand are students."

Mary Helen wondered if Pepe made up those statistics, although from where she sat, they seemed correct.

Within minutes the bus turned into Santiago's central plaza. Sister Mary Helen sucked in her breath. It was as if she had been catapulted back several centuries. The glorious baroque cathedral, the ornate buildings surrounding the plaza had the undiluted ambience of a medieval town. It would not have surprised her in the least to see Chaucer's long line of mounted pilgrims riding up to the *hostal* and dismounting for a night's lodging.

What she saw instead were several bellboys clad in gray and Kelly green uniforms hurrying out of the hotel with carts to collect their luggage. Before they all left the bus, Pepe gave them detailed instructions on how to register at the hotel, where to exchange their money, and the time and place of dinner. He suggested that until then they take a nap or explore the town.

"Whichever suits your fancy," he said with a flourish. After leaving the bus, he disappeared into the hotel with María José, undoubtedly to "consult," Mary Helen thought wryly.

Like two zombies, Eileen and she followed the bellboy, who could more accurately have been called a "bell grandfather," through a courtyard and down a hallway lined with copies of the works of Goya and El Greco toward their assigned room.

"This place is absolutely gorgeous," Eileen whispered, but Mary Helen was too tired to appreciate their palatial surroundings. Once they had tipped the man, both nuns shed their shoes, removed their glasses, slid into their canopied beds, and fell into a deep sleep.

A gentle yet persistent tapping woke Sister Mary Helen. At first she feared it might be rain. When she was a little more awake, she realized that someone was knocking on the heavy wooden door of their bedroom. She glanced at her watch. Without her glasses she could not make out the time. No matter; it was still set on San Francisco time, and at the moment she was too groggy to calculate the difference.

"Yes," she said, opening the door a crack. Her eyes met the eyes of Dr. Neil Fong.

For a moment he looked confused. "I'm so sorry, Sister," he said, blinking and fussing with his half glasses. "I hope I didn't disturb you. I thought this was Lisa's room." His face paled. "I just wanted to show her the Polaroid my wife took in Madrid." He fumbled in his jacket pocket, pulled out the photo, and held it up for Mary Helen to see.

Without her glasses, the figures were simply a blur, yet she smiled and muttered, "That came out very nicely."

"I am sorry if I disturbed you."

"It is high time we were up anyway." Eileen stood behind her. "What time do you have, Doctor?"

"Six. Just six o'clock," the dentist answered, and, apologizing again, hurried down the thickly carpeted hall. Mary Helen watched until he turned the corner.

"Only six o'clock." Eileen yawned and sat back down on

the high bed. "And dinner is not until nine. I will never make it. My stomach is still on San Francisco time."

"That's odd," Mary Helen mused.

"I think it's quite normal. And you don't mean to tell me that you're not a wee bit hungry, too."

"Not your stomach, Eileen! Dr. Fong. Don't you think it is a bit odd that he'd drop by the room to show Lisa Springer a Polaroid picture when he is going to see her at dinner in a very few hours? You don't suppose he is smitten with her, do you? She is a beautiful girl, you know, and really quite a flirt."

"How do you know that?"

"Didn't you watch her on the plane last night?"

Eileen let out an exaggerated sigh. "Now don't be making up situations where none exists." She slipped on her shoes. "His wife may be asleep, and he's wanting some company. Or he's restless after the long flight and just wanted a reason to roam around."

"Why roam in a hotel when there's a whole lovely, quaint little town at your doorstep?" Mary Helen put on her glasses and pulled back the heavy drapes. In the twilight she spotted a gray-headed man crossing the patio. "There goes Professor DeAngelo. See?" She hung out the open, screenless window. "He's going for a walk. Why didn't Dr. Fong go with him?"

"Perhaps they didn't run into each other." Eileen pushed herself off the high bed. "Now, I'm starving! For all your noticing of things, did you happen to notice a place in this hotel where we could get a cup of tea? Maybe hunger is what's making your imagination work overtime."

Sister Mary Helen let the drapes fall. Eileen was probably right. She was imagining things. No wonder! During her years at Mount St. Francis College, she had been involved with several murders. She shivered. Was she beginning to view all events with a jaundiced eye? This trip was to be a pilgrimage, a holy journey, a time to relax and be rejuvenated.

Mary Helen straightened her skirt and ran a comb through her hair. "Not only did I spot a little room with wooden tables," she said, "but before we left home, I stuck a couple of packages of shortbread cookies in my pocketbook."

Without further delay the two nuns went in search of a cup of tea. The little room with wooden tables turned out to be the hotel bar. Save for the bartender, who was busy lighting candles in the center of each table, the place was deserted. The pair moved quickly to an unobtrusive table, sat on the red cushioned chairs, ordered their tea, and broke open a package of cookies.

They had just asked for refills when Heidi Williams appeared in the doorway. "Thank goodness there's someone I recognize here," she said, joining them. "I can't find anyone."

The flicker of light from the candle on the table caught a strand of gold in her butterscotch hair. Mary Helen noticed that her eyes were red and puffy. She had either suffered a severe attack of hay fever or been crying.

"Is everything all right, Heidi?" Mary Helen asked softly.

Heidi reached in her pocket for a tissue. "Yeah," she said, swiping at her eyes. "I'm okay. I was just feeling a little lonely, I guess. I couldn't find anyone around, and this whole place is so—so spooky."

With a wave of her chubby hand, she dismissed centuries of Spanish Romanesque architecture and a vast collection of priceless works of art.

"We're glad you found us." Eileen offered her a cookie. "But where is your friend Lisa?"

"I never should have asked Lisa," Heidi mumbled through a mouthful of shortbread. "It was my trip, you know. I won it."

"Isn't Lisa your friend?" Sister Mary Helen had wondered about the pair since she'd met them. Even on first appearance, they presented a very odd couple.

"We used to be real close," Heidi said, swallowing, then clearing her throat. "We're next-door neighbors, and we've known each other since we were babies. Lisa and I were like this in grammar school and high school." She crossed her index and middle fingers.

"But then in our senior year she got a scholarship and went away to college. In college she changed. A lot!" Heidi bit emphatically into her cookie, leaving Mary Helen to guess what she meant by change.

"When I won the trip, I was going to ask my cousin Doreen, but my mom said, 'Why not ask Lisa next door? You two used to be such good friends.' "

Heidi's puffy eyes narrowed. "So I asked her, and sure enough she said yes. My mom and her mom were glad, but I should have known better. 'You'll have fun,' my mom said. My dad'd kill me if I had fun the way Lisa does."

"Where is Lisa now?" Mary Helen asked. What she really wanted to ask was "How did college change Lisa, and what in the world does she do for fun that is worthy of murder?" Certainly it couldn't be that rather amateurish flirting she had noticed on the plane.

Heidi shrugged. "I really don't know where Lisa is now. I was getting out of the shower when I heard someone knocking on our bedroom door. Lisa must have answered because I heard muffled voices. Then she hollered, 'I'll see you at dinner,' and I heard the door slam." Heidi's eyes began to fill again.

"We are just about to take a little look-see around the hotel ourselves. Get our bearings, so to speak, before dinner," Eileen said brightly, "weren't we, Sister Mary Helen?"

It was news to Mary Helen, but she nodded in agreement.

"Why don't you come with us?" Eileen patted the girl's plump hand.

"If you won't mind." Heidi's chin quivered.

"Mind? Don't be silly. We would love having you. . . ." Eileen let her voice trail off.

Slowly the threesome made their way through the sumptuous hotel. They wandered into the Gothic chapel with its filigreed columns and its magnificent iron screen, which Ferdinand and Isabella had built for the medieval pilgrims. Mary Helen wondered what the royal couple would think of its modern-day use as a concert hall and gallery.

They strolled through the four patios built by the monarchs as refuges for the exhausted pilgrims. In its heyday the Hostal de los Reyes Católicos had been the foremost hostel in the world. So many came that the enormous *hostal* could not accommodate them.

The trio stopped to admire the magnificent paintings on the walls and to peek into spacious lounges with overstuffed furniture, ornate fireplaces, and exquisite flower arrangements.

For all their meandering through the hotel, they did not come across one other member of their tour group. In fact, except for two or three uniformed maids, they did not run into another living being. Spooky, Mary Helen thought, using Heidi's word to describe her own feeling.

They paused momentarily and waited in the hallway while Heidi went in to use the rest room.

"Where do you think everyone else is?" Mary Helen asked, glad that they were alone for a minute.

"If they have any sense at all, they are resting in their rooms." Eileen sagged down into an antique velvet-covered chair in the hallway.

"Here you are!" Pepe's voice roared down the empty hallway. "I am glad I found you," he said, waving a list of names and room numbers. A tousled-looking María José followed in his wake. "I was just making sure that all my *peregrinos* remember that dinner will be served at nine o'clock in the Salón Real."

"There's even a seashell for a basin in there." Heidi burst out the door of the rest room.

"Ah, another of my lovely ladies." Pepe bowed, and Mary Helen watched the color rise from Heidi's jaw right to her hairline. "I was telling the Sisters that dinner will be served in the Salón Real."

"Where is that?" Heidi asked, wide-eyed.

"Just off the courtyard to your—" Seeing the puzzled look on her face, he stopped. "But never mind your pretty head. I will call for you in your room myself, Señorita Heidi.

"Sisters"—he turned toward them—"María José, my wonderful assistant, has arranged for a group of bagpipers to entertain us during our aperitif." Pepe winked. "You need only follow your ears to find the dining room."

Eileen's eyes glowed. "Bagpipers, is it?"

"Yes, indeed, Sister. And since you seem to have a touch of the Celt in you, would you honor us by pronouncing the benediction before our meal?"

"Assistant?" Mary Helen watched Pepe disappear down the hallway. "I ask you, Eileen, how in the world did María José go from consultant to assistant in a few short hours?"

Eileen didn't seem to be listening.

♦

Back in their bedroom, as they tidied up for dinner, it was obvious that Eileen was stewing. "Benediction! No one ever asks me to give the benediction, Mary Helen. You are the one who usually says grace on these kinds of occasions. What in the name of all that's good and holy shall I say?"

Mary Helen turned from the mirror, where she was

straightening the bow tie on her blouse. "In over fifty years of friendship I have never known you to be at a loss for words. I seriously doubt if tonight will be the first time."

"Let me think." Eileen brushed imaginary lint from her suit jacket. "Something Celtic. Perhaps from one of the saints." A mischievous glint shone in her gray eyes.

Mary Helen groaned. "Not that prayer of St. Bridget."

"Why not? Now, how does it go?" She paused, although she didn't fool Mary Helen for a second. Eileen had proved time and again that she had a wonderful memory. Mary Helen knew it was especially keen on nonsense.

"I'd like to give a lake of beer to God." Her brogue thickened, and she sounded as pious as St. Bridget herself. "Because the happy heart is true. . . . /I'd sit with the men, the women and God,/There by the lake of beer. We'd be drinking good health forever,/And every drop would be a prayer."

Mercifully the bagpipers will be on hand, Mary Helen thought, closing the heavy bedroom door behind them. If she does really start that thing, with any luck at all I can signal them to drown her out.

◆

By the time the two nuns arrived for dinner at the Salón Real, most of the tour members were assembled. The promised bagpipers played loudly and, if Mary Helen could judge by the smile on Eileen's face, extremely well.

From just inside the door she surveyed the long room. As its name promised, the *salón* was indeed *real*. Chandeliers with tassels and tiers of electric candles hung from the carved wooden ceiling. Tall-back chairs surrounded lavishly set tables. With regal detachment, the monarchs in dark, stiff portraits presided over the gathering from their places of honor on the side wall.

Formally dressed waiters milled around with trays, offering flutes of the local white wine. At least Mary Helen assumed it was local because Professor DeAngelo kept sniffing his glass and commenting for all to hear on the "hardy Galician bouquet."

Next to him, Bud Bowman rolled his eyes and muttered something about nothing hitting the spot like a cold beer.

Cora glared.

"You look lovely this evening, Cora," Eileen said, hoping no doubt to avert another Bowman spat. To Mary Helen's surprise Cora's face became even rosier. She was blushing!

Nervously Cora touched her waxy yellow hair, which was tightly curled. "I was afraid I had left the hot rollers in too long," she whispered to Sister Eileen.

"Not at all! Your hair is lovely. And your dress is stunning. It is a perfect color for you."

Self-consciously Cora swished the emerald green silk skirt that was draped softly over her broad hips. "Thank you," she said.

In Mary Helen's opinion, the thing that was really stunning was the diamond and emerald necklace hanging in Cora's open neckline, not to mention the enormous diamond ring on her finger.

"I thought that I'd dress up a little for the occasion," Cora said, accepting a second flute of wine. "How often do you win a trip to Spain?"

Straightening the bow tie of her own new pink blouse, Mary Helen surveyed the room. Actually every one of the women had dressed up quite a bit for the occasion. Rita Fong, who stood next to her husband, if you considered a yard apart "next to," wore a voile outfit of the softest periwinkle blue. It gathered dramatically at her waist, proving for all who had eyes to see, the value of regular aerobics.

Bootsie DeAngelo was sheathed in a burgundy crepe

dress that draped her tall, slim body in all the places that crepe should drape. Wine in hand, Bootsie wandered away from her husband toward the Fongs, who seemed happy for a distraction.

As soon as he could do it politely, Dr. Fong left the ladies and sidled up to Sister Mary Helen. "Let me apologize again for disturbing you this afternoon," he said, his words barely audible.

Why is he whispering? Mary Helen wondered as she assured him that he had caused no disturbance at all. Was there someone he didn't want to overhear him? Who? Quickly she dismissed the idea, chiding herself for being suspicious. The man is simply reserved. They smiled at each other in awkward silence. Mary Helen was relieved when Bud joined them.

"Did you two happen to get a gander at the cathedral yet?" Bud asked. "While Cora was fussing with her hair, I went over and took a peek. Now, that is really some church," he said, in what Mary Helen considered would be undoubtedly the understatement of the trip.

"Did you get a chance to see it yet, Doc?"

Neil Fong blinked as if he were trying to remember, then flashed a look toward his wife, who was totally ignoring him.

You either saw it or you didn't, Mary Helen thought impatiently. So what is all that blinking about? She adjusted her glasses and focused on Dr. Fong's face, which to her surprise had drained of color. Neil was spared by Bud Bowman's low whistle.

"Speaking of ganders, get a gander at what's coming," he said.

Mary Helen turned to watch Pepe glide into the *salón*. Lisa Springer clung to his right arm. She was ablaze in a raspberry lamé chemise which did outstanding things to her flaming hair. On his left arm was Heidi, again looking, Mary Helen thought sadly, very much like a butterscotch drop.

Smoothly detaching himself from both women, Pepe moved about the room, slapping backs and kissing hands. Mary Helen was thankful that she held her wine in one hand and her pocketbook in the other. Furthermore, she had no intention of doing any juggling.

Pepe took in the room. "Aha! I see we are all here. *Bueno! Bueno!*"

All but María José. Mary Helen wondered where she was. Before she could ask, the tiny woman, strikingly glamorous in a strapless gown of black velvet and silver lace, slid in through a side door. Her dark hair was pulled back from her face and held in place by an ornate comb. Even from across the room, Mary Helen saw that her eyes were blazing. She could almost feel the heat emanating from the small, angry body.

Like a polished host, Pepe ushered each guest to a seat at the round banquet table. Cleverly he placed himself between Lisa and Heidi with María José directly across from him, as far away as one could get at a round table.

Tapping a crystal goblet, he called upon Sister Eileen to pronounce a blessing. Mary Helen held her breath. She need not have worried. Eileen's prayer was short, sweet, and, much to Mary Helen's relief, considerably duller than the one that she had threatened.

Once they were seated, the waiters immediately began to serve oysters on large half shells. Conversation bubbled like the white wine that the steward poured into the glasses.

Pepe, avoiding María José's eyes, raised his glass and toasted the health of the group. Not to be outdone, Bud Bowman toasted Pepe. Cora looked so pleased that her husband toasted María José as well.

Directly across the table from Mary Helen the De-Angelos sat tight-lipped, the way people do when they've had words. Creases like small spokes formed around Bootsie's set mouth.

Perhaps they're tired. Mary Helen gave them the benefit of the doubt and speared an oyster. She might have believed it, too, if Bootsie, with a swish of her long dark hair, hadn't deliberately turned her back on her husband and focused her frosty blue eyes on Cora, who sat to her left. "You look lovely in green," Bootsie said loudly.

Startled by the unexpected attention, Cora sputtered but not for long. Within seconds the two women had lowered their voices and were carrying on an animated conversation. They were so absorbed, in fact, that they hardly seemed to notice that the waiter served a delicious plate of what looked to Mary Helen like potatoes and peppers mixed with giant sardines. Nor did they pay much attention to the wine steward refilling their glasses.

Sister Mary Helen wished that she could hear what they were saying. To be honest, she wished that she could hear what anyone was saying. As is sometimes the way with round tables, everyone was talking to someone, but no one was talking to her.

To her right, Sister Eileen and Dr. Fong were engrossed. Whatever the topic, Eileen carried most of the conversation. To the right of her husband, Rita Fong was giving María José and Bud Bowman a lesson in reducing muscle stress. Or at least it appeared that way from the places she was pointing out on her neck and shoulders. From the look on María José's face she wasn't profiting much from the lesson.

Heidi listened intently to whatever Pepe whispered to her, giggling softly, now and again, before taking a sip of wine. Directly across the table Roger DeAngleo was pontificating.

It is just as well his wife's back was to him, Mary Helen thought, watching Lisa Springer, her full mouth set in a little pout, pretending to vacuum in every syllable. Wordlessly she stoked his male ego—and from the look of it, that wasn't all she was stoking—into a roaring flame.

The professor, seemingly enamored by her flattering attention, hardly stopped for breath. Watching them, Mary Helen recalled a stanza from an old poem of Swift's:

> 'Tis an old maxim in the schools,
> That flattery's the food of fools;
> Yet now and then your men of wit
> Will condescend to take a bit.

From where she sat, Roger DeAngleo seemed to be sucking in considerably more than a bit.

Sipping her wine, Sister Mary Helen settled back, resigned to observing her fellow pilgrims. Actually she rather enjoyed it. She was constantly amazed at how much one can learn about people by merely watching them.

For example, although the friction between María José and Pepe was overt, there was also something definitely amiss with the DeAngelos. And she suspected as much about the Fongs. They, however, were the hardest to read. On the other hand, the bickering Bowmans were having a wonderful time, and Lisa and Heidi seemed to have made up whatever differences they had had.

And differences do occur when you're traveling with someone, married or no. It is not easy. Even Eileen and she had their moments. Glory be to God! she thought facetiously. We've been on this jaunt for only two days. We'll be killing each other before the week is out!

Heidi giggled, and from across the table Lisa and Roger DeAngelo mouthed in *simpatía*, to put it "Spanishly." Another fascinating phenomenon, Mary Helen mused, is how quickly relationships develop on tours. Perchance it was the being thrown together in a kind of time warp. The unfamiliar places, the strange customs, and the foreign language set a stage for instant intimacy.

Whatever the cause, one minute we're perfect strangers; the next we're regaling each other with the most personal details of our lives, much as Heidi had done this afternoon.

Heidi wriggled in her seat. Although her afternoon had gone poorly, her evening was more than making up for it. In fact, as the center of Señor Nunez's attention, Heidi was positively glowing and paying no heed to Lisa Springer, who, with sparkling eyes, kept looking at Roger DeAngelo.

Watching them, Sister Mary Helen suspected that these two girls could go on indefinitely. She, on the other hand, hoped to call it a night soon. The combination of rich food and mellow wine made her eyelids heavy. She glanced hopefully toward her host.

Checking his watch, Pepe pulled himself away from Heidi's adoring gaze long enough to signal the maître. Within moments, the bevy of waiters appeared to remove the entrée and to replace it with small dishes of carmelized custard.

"Our dessert, *leche frita*," Pepe announced. "Fried milk."

Thanks be to God, Mary Helen thought, placing her hand over her wineglass. She didn't know how much longer she could remain upright at the table.

"How are you doing, Sister?" Heidi, momentarily alone while their host again conferred with the headwaiter, turned toward her.

"Fine, dear. But more to the point, how are you feeling?" Mary Helen asked as if she didn't know.

Heidi beamed. "Fine, now." She giggled. "I guess I was just being silly this afternoon. I hope I wasn't a pain."

"Never," Mary Helen said, and, with her final spoon, attacked the thick dessert, a first cousin to flan.

"You'll never guess who Lisa was with . . ." Heidi began. Much to Mary Helen's chagrin, Pepe tapped his goblet for attention.

"My dear pilgrims." He rose, waiting for everyone to abandon all conversation before he continued.

"Who was she with?" Mary Helen whispered, but butter-scotch Heidi was once again enthralled.

"Did you enjoy your first banquet in España?" Pepe asked.

The group clapped appreciatively. Bud Bowman put his baby fingers in his mouth and gave a loud whistle.

"Hear! Hear!" Lisa Springer raised her glass and winked at Bud.

Cora scowled at her husband, who whistled a second time. Mary Helen wasn't sure if the glare was for the whistle or the wink.

With a bow Pepe went on to outline their schedule for the following morning: breakfast at eight; a tour of the cathe-dral at ten; dinner at two-fifteen. Mary Helen hoped that Eileen was jotting it all down.

"Tonight," he said, "you are free. Some of you may be tired and wish to retire early. But for those of you who wish to prolong the evening"—he glanced meaningfully across the table at María José—"the hotel has several public rooms that are open with music for dancing. . . ."

Pepe's words continued on, but Sister Mary Helen's mind was already climbing the stairs to her room.

"What do you say, old dear?" Eileen, her gray eyes twin-kling, leaned toward her. "Is it to bed or to boogie?"

Mary Helen moaned. "I am exhausted. How about you?"

Eileen nodded in agreement.

"I can't quite figure out why." Mary Helen squirmed out of her chair. "Is it jet lag or the heavy food?" She gathered up her pocketbook. "Maybe it's the wine."

"Perhaps, just perhaps, mind you"—Eileen followed her as she threaded her way through the crowd—"it's our age."

Mary Helen stopped short. Pushing her bifocals up the bridge of her nose, she glared at her friend. "I prefer to think it is the wine," she said, "don't you?"

♦

Five minutes after they turned out the lights, Mary Helen was wide-awake. Maddening, she thought, struggling to find a comfortable position. Not a half hour ago I thought I'd fall asleep in my dessert. Now I'm in bed, and I can't even doze.

"Are you awake?" she whispered, hoping Eileen had the same trouble. Her only answer was a soft, rhythmic snore.

Irked, Mary Helen rolled onto her side, punched up her pillows, and tried to think sleepy thoughts. The sound of laughter floated up through the floorboards, and a familiar tune, although for the life of her she couldn't remember the words.

Footsteps came down the corridor, one set, two sets; then a loud burst of conversation. Mary Helen strained to hear. Although the words were muffled, the tone was abundantly clear—red-hot anger!

A door slammed, and Mary Helen pulled the covers up over her ears. The band switched to a raucous number, and the floor seemed to vibrate with the beat.

"Eileen," she whispered, hoping for company. No response. How can anyone sleep through that? Mary Helen wondered, pushing back the covers. She lay in the darkness with her eyes shut. Was it jet lag? If she had it, why didn't Eileen?

Suddenly the room seemed very stuffy with the musty odor of old furniture and the heavy red velvet drapes taking over. Air! That was what she needed: some cool night air to help her sleep.

She tiptoed across the room, fighting down the urge to jiggle Eileen's bed. Although from the sound of things I could jiggle to my heart's content and she'd never notice, Mary Helen thought with a twinge of envy.

Mary Helen pulled back the heavy drapes and flung open the window. To her surprise the Plaza del Obradoiro was filled with people, all kinds of people. It was as if darkness had brought the city roaring to life. She remembered reading in one of the books in the Hanna Memorial Library that at night Santiago de Compostela changes into a colorful, fascinating maelstrom. It was colorful and fascinating, all right, but from where she stood hardly dangerous. If anything, at least this part of Santiago seemed bright and cheerful and contented.

Large groups of students laughed and cavorted with one another. Children ran and played tag while their mothers gossiped. Older couples peacefully circled the plaza, passing bustling tourists laden with shopping bags. A policeman, his nightstick protruding from his yellow rain slicker, stopped to chat with a couple of men in berets. Amid them all a lone flutist stood beside his open case. A few sprightly notes floated up on the night air. Listening, Mary Helen felt a pang of sympathy for the boy's mother, who had probably hoped for a Spanish James Galway.

She leaned farther out the window. The ledge was wide enough to sit on, and she was tempted to try it, maybe even dangle her feet. Only the thought of slipping and landing in the plaza in her nightdress stopped her. Not that she would have any particular worry if that did happen. It was Eileen who would be left with some fancy explaining to do to Sister Cecilia and the other nuns, especially Therese. Mary Helen amused herself thinking about what decorous Therese would say about such a fall from propriety. She chuckled at her own pun and wished Eileen were awake.

Outside, marbled clouds gathered around the apricot

moon, and Mary Helen smelled rain in the air. Poor Therese! Although she could drive you to drink without a cent in your pocket, she did try to be kind. Much as Mary Helen hated to admit it, they probably would need her umbrellas.

A sudden volley of sharp, angry Spanish took her by surprise. Whoever it was had just stepped out the front door of the *hostal* and was directly below.

She leaned out as far as she dared and caught a glimpse of a head and an ornate comb. As the figure stalked across the plaza, Mary Helen recognized María José. She squinted. Was that Pepe trailing her?

As impervious to those around her as they were to her, María José gesticulated furiously, stopping now and again to turn on Pepe and stab at him with her finger. Pepe, gesturing every bit as wildly, continued to dog her until the two of them disappeared behind one corner of the cathedral.

"What's the matter?" Eileen's groggy voice startled her.

"Nothing. I just can't sleep."

"Get into your bed, old dear. That might help."

"I was in bed," Mary Helen began, exasperated, but it was too late. Eileen had drifted off again.

Mary Helen sighed. Maybe that was good advice. Besides, if she stayed there in front of the open window, her feet were bound to get cold. Once that happened, she would never get to sleep.

Back in the soft, roomy bed she pulled the covers up over her shoulders and tucked her toes into the end of her nightdress. Dance music seeped up through the floor. The band was playing a medley of "oldies but goodies." Maybe the guests were winding down. From the sound the band certainly was.

Resolutely she closed her eyes. But her mind refused to shut off and wandered downstairs. Were the other tour members still there or had some gone off to bed? By dessert Cora had looked exhausted. Were the Fongs enjoying themselves? Odd little man, Dr. Fong. Did he dance? She'd bet Rita did.

And the DeAngelos. Was Bootsie still sitting, tight-lipped, ignoring her husband, or had they made up? She hoped so. Obviously María José and Pepe had not. Too bad!

With Pepe gone from the *hostal,* who was with poor Heidi? I hope she's still having fun. In fact, I hope they're all having fun. Mary Helen shifted into a more comfortable position, her thoughts growing fuzzy.

Oddly the only one she wasn't concerned about was lovely Lisa Springer. Do or die, Lisa would have a good time. Mary Helen would bet money on it. More power to her, she thought dreamily, more power to her.

An angry small girl, whose face was vaguely familiar, but whose name Mary Helen could not quite remember, grabbed both her ankles. Shocked, Mary Helen struggled with this strange girl who carried a load of wet wash in the wicker basket on top of her head.

"Stop it this instant!" she shouted.

The girl simply smiled as if she hadn't heard and, holding tight, forced Mary Helen's toes into a large shell-shaped basin filled with ice cubes.

"Now, the soles." The girl bared her teeth. The left incisor was crooked. The ice clinked as Mary Helen pushed hard against the bottom of the basin and wiggled wildly to wrench herself free from the girl's icy grip.

"Stop it!" she shouted even louder, and this last shout was probably what woke her. She lay there, heart pounding, relieved that it was a dream. A least part of it was. Her toes were icy cold. The window! She had left the window open.

Shivering, she crossed the room. To her surprise the Plaza del Obradoiro was completely deserted. Except for the patter of soft rain upon stone, all was stillness. The plaza, delineated as it was by four large and beautiful buildings, picked up the sound. And the low, steady trickle of water filled the quiet night.

Leaning out to pull shut the window, Mary Helen thought she saw someone standing on the steps of the cathedral. She squinted into the shadowy darkness. Probably just a reflection of some sort. In the dim light it looked like a person. But nobody stands that still, especially in the pouring rain.

A cough floated up from the floor below. Someone else must be standing by an open window, she thought, creeping back to her bed. Somebody else can't sleep. She fluffed up her pillow and closed her eyes, feeling suddenly very tired. Exhausted, actually, and old, like St. Simeon, whose feast had been today. Poor old fellow had wished to live long enough to see Jesus, and as soon as he saw the Child, his first words were "Nunc dimittis. . . . Now you can dismiss your servant in peace. . . ."

She wondered, sleepily, if, when his bones began to ache and his eyes began to fail, Simeon regretted his wish. There was a Chinese proverb about being careful what you wish for because you may get it. Odd—isn't it?—that you must be careful what you wish for, even if it's seeing the Christ Child or wishing that everyone downstairs has fun.

◆

Carpeted footsteps padded past the bedroom door. Two sets? Three sets? It was difficult to tell. Someone stifled a giggle. The party's over, Mary Helen thought, wondering what time it was. By now, however, she was too sleepy to care. "Nunc dimittis. . . ."

saturday, october 9

feast of St. John leonardi, priest

♦

Sister Mary Helen awoke with a fierce craving for a cup of good, strong, hot coffee. Blinking, she rescued her glasses and wristwatch from the nightstand. No wonder! It was already seven-thirty.

Except for a gentle sough from Eileen in the next bed, the room was deadly quiet. No footsteps in the hall. No rumble of a chambermaid's cart. The soft gurgle that water makes after a rain and the bark of a faraway dog were the only sounds she heard. It was as if the whole of Santiago were still in bed.

Orange spears of sun shot through the open drapes, and particles of dust twirled and climbed up the beam. "As thikke as motes in the sonne-beem." The line from *The Canterbury Tales* popped into her mind, and with it her fellow pilgrims. How were they doing this morning? Surely some must be up by now.

Kicking her feet out of the covers, Mary Helen rustled around, hoping to rouse Eileen. Eileen didn't budge. "Hopeless," she muttered, dressing quickly.

With a click the bedroom door closed behind her, and Mary Helen stood in the ornate but empty hallway, wishing she had paid more attention to Pepe's instructions about time and places for things.

A well-dressed man, looking all business, emerged from several doors down. On a hunch she followed him and with no trouble at all reached the *hostal's* dining room at about the same time as Cora Bowman.

"Good morning, Sister." Cora, her cheeks still creased with sleep, seemed genuinely glad to see a familiar face. "I'm dying for a cup of java. How about you?"

Before Mary Helen could answer, an ancient waiter in a stiff white jacket bustled them to a vacant table. Actually most of the tables in the spacious room were vacant. In the center of each a haystack of French rolls, buns, and croissants waited with butter curls and small jelly packets for the hungry to arrive.

"*Café con leche, señoras?*" the waiter asked, a silver pot poised in each hand.

Mary Helen hesitated, but not Cora. "Without milk this stuff will put hair on your chest," she snapped, pushing forward both their cups.

"Buffet." The waiter nodded toward a long table down one side of the room. It was laden with platters of meat and cheeses, pitchers of juice—orange, pineapple, tomato, grapefruit—mounds of fresh fruit, and boiled eggs in large cockleshell bowls.

"Buffet," he said in well-practiced English. "When you ready, please help."

"Did you sleep well?" Cora asked, breaking off the corner of a croissant. Inwardly Mary Helen groaned. She hated to talk before her first cup of coffee, but how was Cora to know that?

Fortunately all Cora needed was an audience. "If you did sleep, it was a miracle," she said. "What with that big row in the hallway. Enough to wake the dead, if you ask me. Except Bud, who sleeps like a dead man anyway. It would take Gabriel's horn to wake him up." Cora stopped, undoubtedly searching for her original point.

Mary Helen raised her eyebrows to indicate that she was listening and took another sip of the thick, sweet coffee.

"All that racket!" Cora was back on track. "Bud and I had a nightcap downstairs with the others. Then we went up to bed. When we left, they all seemed to be having a ball." She shrugged. "Pepe was dancing with the single girls. He must be worn out this morning. I was just falling off to sleep when I heard shouting and banging doors. I couldn't make out the words, but whoever it was was hopping mad."

Cora broke off another corner from the croissant, popped it into her mouth, and chewed it as if it were hard work.

"I'm dying to find out what it was all about. It was our group. I'm sure of that," she said, and waited for Mary Helen to ask the obvious question.

Mary Helen bit. "How do you know it was someone in our group?"

"Because they were speaking American!" Cora was definite.

Mary Helen chose to explain that any number of people in the *hostal* might speak American English, not that Cora cared. Nor did she want to admit that she had heard the same angry conversation. It was far too early and far too lovely a morning to worry about anyone else's quarrels.

Furthermore, she had not yet even glimpsed the cathedral. Although they were touring it officially later in the morning, Mary Helen decided she'd like to slip in now for a quiet look, say her morning prayers, perhaps attend an early-morning Mass.

She was about to excuse herself when Cora waved toward the entrance. "Another early riser," she whispered as though they had formed a secret club. "Bootsie. Over here," she called, pulling back a chair.

Bootsie DeAngelo hesitated in the doorway. Her eyes darted around the room until she spotted the two of them.

"You didn't sleep either, I see," Cora said when Bootsie was seated.

At least, she has the good grace not to mention how she knows, Mary Helen thought. Bootsie's face was as white and taut as rice paper. Overnight the lines around her mouth and eyes had sprung into deep wrinkles. Her hair, blue-black and limp, was pulled back with a youthful padded cloth head-band that only made her look older.

"*Café con leche, señora?*" The waiter was at her elbow.

Bootsie put her hand over her cup. "Tea, if you please," she said in a slow, hoarse drawl.

Cora and Sister Mary Helen both had refills. "Are you feeling all right?" Cora frowned. "I hope you're not getting a cold."

Bootsie shook her head. "Strange food, strange bed, a little jet lag," she said, staring into her teacup. "And the rain! Did you-all hear it pouring? Then, early this morning, that giggling in the hallway." She gave an involuntary shudder. "But nothing bothers my Roger. He's upstairs, dead to the world."

"Bud, too!" Cora, rejoicing with a fellow sufferer, bent forward and began to berate her husband's sleeping habits. Bootsie, too exhausted to do anything but listen, agreed; that suited Cora fine.

With no experience to add to the conversation, Mary Helen drained her cup. Wondering how to escape politely, she fumbled in her pocketbook. There was Anne's travel diary. If she didn't write something now, she'd probably take it home empty.

Since neither Cora nor Bootsie needed her attention, she opened it. "October 9," she wrote on the top of the first page. "Saturday. Going to see St. James." Enough! She'd fill in the details later.

Mumbling excuses about prayers and Mass, which her companions neither seemed to hear nor to care about, Mary Helen made a hasty exit.

Once outside the *hostal,* she paused, still unable to believe that she was actually in Santiago de Compostela. Overhead the bowl of sky was an after-the-rain blue, and the air was fresh and crisp. The Plaza del Obradoiro itself was nearly deserted. The few people who were in the flagstone square seemed in a hurry to be on their way. Pigeons, their necks ringed in rainbows, bobbed along, picking at crumbs and drinking from puddles.

One enterprising young man, probably a student, was already setting out his wares. From where Mary Helen stood they looked like windup plastic birds. She wondered idly how the pigeons would take to their intrusion.

Midway across the huge plaza she stopped to drink in the magnificent cathedral. Moss and lichen streaked the granite facade, giving it a greenish tinge. Two towers soared into the sky, framing a shorter central one with St. James the Apostle atop it. Mary Helen craned her neck. James, dressed in flowing cape and wide-brimmed, cockleshelled hat, with a pilgrim staff in his hand, looked ready to step right out of his niche and into the plaza below.

She started up the long flight of stairs, the stone worn with the feet of centuries. Kings and saints, rogues and beggars and poets all used these same steps, she reflected, planting her foot firmly on each one.

Maybe even St. John Leonardi, she thought, remembering the medieval pharmacist whose feast the Church celebrated today. Maybe he walked this way, and in time unknown saints, saints yet to be born, will use the same stairs that I now touch.

Mary Helen paused just inside the main entrance of the cathedral under the Pórtico de la Gloria—the Door of Glory —to let her eyes adjust to the sudden dimness. She drew in her breath. The triple-arched masterpiece was magnificent, rampant with hundreds of figures. Fascinated, Mary Helen found prophets and saints, angels and children, all carved by Maestro Mateo in the twelfth century, still relaxing against the pillars and along the arches. Smiling and winking, lounging or chatting, they awaited the Last Judgment.

Their joy was contagious. Mary Helen smiled. In fact, she might have laughed aloud if the cathedral hadn't been so silent. This was her idea of the dreaded Last Judgment, too, an upbeat affair where God, in His unconditional love, invites each one of us to enjoy a paradise of music and laughter and winking saints.

The cathedral, like most cathedrals, was built in the form of a Latin cross with long, narrow aisles and soaring arches. The hushed interior was nearly empty. A woman in a blue smock was dusting, and here and there a lone worshiper hunched over a pew, obviously deep in prayer. Mary Helen tiptoed, hoping not to disturb anyone.

Before her, the sanctuary was dominated by the ornate silver repoussé on the wall and on the altar. Above it all sat St. James himself, glittering in silver and gold, surrounded by angels. Eight enormous cherubim held a massive carved and gilded canopy. As startling as the baroque sanctuary was, especially in contrast with the quiet elegance of the arches, the two were somehow harmonious.

The high altar was empty, but a faint aroma of incense hung on the air. Obviously Mary Helen had missed the early Mass.

Before I settle down to morning prayer, I'll just pop in for a quick visit to the shrine of St. James, she thought, tiptoeing around the side of the sanctuary. It seems only polite.

According to the guidebooks, the apostle's remains were kept in a crypt below the main altar. A narrow door to the left of the sanctuary led the pilgrims down to it.

Carefully she squeezed through the door marked *"Entrada"* and followed the narrow, worn steps down to a stone chamber hardly large enough to hold four or five people. It was as quiet as a tomb! No wonder, Mary Helen thought, suppressing a nervous urge to laugh, it is a tomb!

A bronze plaque on one wall proclaimed Pope John Paul II's visit to the shrine, where the pontiff had celebrated Mass. Across from it a heavy, wrought-iron gate closed off the tunnellike hallway leading to the silver coffin which was adorned with figures of Christ and the twelve apostles. The now-familiar cockleshell pattern decorated its lid. A single light shone down, and hammered silver absorbed the glow.

A tattered purple velvet prie-dieu stood in front of the gate like a double guard to protect the saint from his visitors. Slipping behind the kneeler, Mary Helen moved up to the gate. It was locked. She peered at the crypt from every angle and caught a glimpse of the edge of an altar and a bouquet of flowers.

That altar was probably where the Pope said Mass, she thought, and the flowers looked perky and fresh. People must go into the enclosure. She shook the gate, but it was so securely fastened that it didn't even rattle.

There has to be another entrance, she thought, feeling a sudden inexplicable urge to touch the casket, which tradition held contained the remains of St. James and two of his disciples. Perhaps the gate–prie-dieu barrier fanned her desire. Perhaps it was the realization that both the Pope and the florist had been inside. What's good for the goose is good for the gander! Whatever spurred her on, she was determined to have some physical contact, however slight, with a man who had known and loved and touched Christ Himself.

Glad that the cathedral was nearly deserted, Mary Helen hastily climbed up the steps. In the shadows behind the main altar, she opened a carved wooden gate and crept into the chancel. Groping in the semidarkness, she felt her shin hit a kneeler. The harsh scrape of wood against granite reverberated up through the stone arches.

Mary Helen froze, waiting for the sacristan or a guard or even the woman in the blue smock to investigate. When no one appeared, she edged her way toward another small door with a set of steps.

Blindly she touched the stone wall and, testing each step with her toe, felt her way down. As she descended, the strange musty odor became stronger.

Once she reached the bottom, the small light drew her toward the casket. Mary Helen squeezed around the altar, careful not to upset the vase. Her foot caught on something. The edge of the linen altar cloth, no doubt. She looked down, hoping that she hadn't pulled the whole thing awry.

But it wasn't the altar linen at all. It wasn't even white. Whatever had tripped her was shiny and red. Raspberry red. Even in the dim light, it shimmered. Wondering what it could be, Mary Helen freed her toe and squeezed around the marble pillar.

She must be quick. Someone else was sure to come down into the crypt soon, someone who was bound to realize that she was neither the Pope nor the florist. Not even the cleaning lady. She didn't want to be caught on the wrong side of the gate. Too hard to explain. Somehow she knew that her "goose and gander" theory wouldn't cut it.

Eyes closed, Sister Mary Helen whispered a prayer, stretched out her hand, and touched the silver lid. She expected it to feel cold, not wet and sticky. Distracted, she opened her eyes and fished in her pocket for a tissue. What in heaven's name could be leaking down here? Mary Helen glanced up at the ceiling, then down.

Her heart gave a sickening jolt. She stared disbelieving at her open palm where the flickering light played on a clot of bright red, sticky blood.

Steadying herself, she stretched forward to examine the side of the casket. A streak of red was smeared from the corner of the lid down one side—as though a bloody rag had been dragged over it. Then she saw it . . . on the marble floor below, awkwardly stuffed behind the ornate casket. It was not a rag at all. It was a body. Rivulets of blood snaked down from a gaping head wound onto the shimmering evening dress. They ran like scratches across the raspberry lamé.

Mary Helen crouched beside the casket and peered at the face, half covered with strands of auburn hair. Vacant blue eyes stared back at her. The tip of a tongue protruded from swollen purple lips. Across the throat was a thick, cruel welt. Someone had strangled her. Someone had strangled Lisa Springer.

The room moved around her. Mary Helen grabbed a cold pillar to keep from moving with it. A scream—her own? —ricocheted off the stone walls, echoing and reechoing until it faded into a whisper.

She leaned heavily against the marble altar. The musty smell mingled with the sickening odor of blood. She fought back the nausea rising in her throat. What now?

A creak overhead startled her. Was someone coming? An unsuspecting worshiper? Another tourist? The murderer?

Sister Mary Helen stumbled up the narrow stairs. She must tell someone, anyone, quickly. She ran past startled worshipers and frowning cleaning ladies in blue smocks, past a priest on his way into the confessional.

Still shaking, she exploded into the blinding light of the Plaza del Obradoiro. Temples pounding, she hurried across the huge flagstone square, unaware of the straggle of tourists and unsuspecting townsfolk preparing for the start of a brand-new day.

◆

Breathlessly Sister Mary Helen flung open the bedroom door and burst in on a startled Eileen.

"Where in heaven's name have you been?" Eileen's face was still pink and wrinkled from sleep. "I woke up, and you were—" She stopped in mid-sentence. "What is it, Mary Helen? Your cheeks are flaming. And the rest of your face is as pale as if you just shook hands with the devil or stumbled upon the dead." Staring, she sat down heavily on the edge of her bed. "Oh, no! It can't be. Tell me you didn't."

Mary Helen made straight for the room phone. While she waited for an operator to answer, she took deep breaths, hoping to quell the sick throb pulsating through her whole body.

"Drink this." Eileen offered her a chunky glass filled with water.

Mary Helen pushed it away and listened intently. "Señor Nunez, *por favor*," she ventured, hoping that was what the operator had asked. Apparently it was.

"Good morning. This is Pepe," he announced cheerfully.

"Pepe, this is Sister Mary Helen," she said, wondering crazily why his cheerfulness irked her so.

"Ah, Sister, may I be of some assistance?"

You'd better believe it, Mary Helen wanted to snap. Instead she cleared her throat, steadied her voice, and, without preamble, told him of her discovery.

By the time Mary Helen replaced the receiver, Eileen's face had gone gray. She drained the glass of water herself. "What did he say?" she asked hoarsely.

"I'm not sure. I know it started with *Dios mío!*"

"What do you mean, you are not sure? You were just on the horn with him."

"After his first horrified gasp, he rattled away in Spanish. I haven't the foggiest notion what he was saying. The only words that I could make out clearly were God's name, Lisa's, and *policía*."

Mary Helen sank down on the edge of the bed next to her friend. They sat in uneasy silence, each one lost in the whirling of her own imaginings.

"What do you suppose we should do now?" Eileen asked.

Without warning, Mary Helen launched herself off the bed and went for the phone. "I have no idea, but I know who will." She gave the operator an overseas number.

"You *cannot* call Kate Murphy now. Do you know what time it is in San Francisco?" Eileen counted backward on her fingers just to make sure. "Mary Helen, it is nearly one o'clock in the morning. Hang up!"

Even if Mary Helen had wanted to, it was too late. The phone was already ringing. The only thing worse than a late-night call is one whose caller hangs up.

♦

Kate Murphy was dead tired, yet she could not seem to fall asleep. "Twelve-thirty," the luminous dial on the alarm clock read. She snuggled near her husband and flung her arm around his waist. Maybe Jack's steady, deep breathing would calm her down, put her to sleep, too. She tried to imitate his rhythm but couldn't.

Frustrated, she rolled away. She felt hot, almost feverish. What was the matter with her?

The day had started out all right. Little John had his regular appointment with Dr. Trotter. Kate spent all morning in the pediatrician's crowded waiting room. At least it felt as if she had been sitting for an entire morning in that hard plastic chair.

Baby John, eager to explore, squirmed in her lap and banged his set of bright plastic keys against her knees. Kate, wishing that she'd brought his blanket, finally let him creep around on the dirty carpet.

Delighted with his freedom, John babbled, "Dah-dah-dah," and banged the keys on the floor. Smiling up at Kate, he threw them across the waiting room. Apologizing to the woman they hit, Kate retrieved the toy and pulled a soft rabbit from her carryall for him to play with. John gurgled happily and threw it across the room.

"They do that," a haggard-looking woman next to her said, wiping her toddler's runny nose. "They think it's a game. Don't make the mistake of looking like you are enjoying it," she warned. "He'll keep it up."

Smiling, Kate picked up the baby and rocked him in her lap. How could she look as if she weren't enjoying it when she was frankly delighted by everything that the baby did? His slightest new discovery, his attempts at sounds, his unexpected smiles all gave her joy.

The only thing that she did not enjoy about him was the prospect of leaving him to go back to work. And that was coming all too soon. She banished the thought from her mind, but not before she'd experienced the heavy, empty lump that began in the bottom of her stomach and grew until it filled her whole body.

"This is my fourth daughter, Stephanie," the woman next to her confided. "She is two. All my girls are two years apart," she whispered as if the baby might overhear. "The three older ones have the measles. My husband's home with them. Steffie has been real cranky lately, and I'm afraid that she's coming down with them, too." Automatically she felt the child's forehead and raised her little blouse top to peek at the rash on her stomach.

As if to prove her mother's point, Steffie dropped the cloth book that she was playing with and let out an earsplitting wail.

As the little girl moved from a wail to a screech, John's lips curved down, his chin quivered, and despite Kate's bouncing, he joined in. Soon, as if in solidarity, every baby in the waiting room was howling.

"Good night, what happened?" Dr. Trotter's nurse swung open the inner office door and stood there in her stiff white uniform, frowning at the mothers as though somehow they were responsible.

Without another word, she flipped the light switch, once, twice, three times. Magically the crying stopped and the babies blinked up, fascinated by the long tubes of light.

"The doctor will see John now," the nurse announced, much to Kate's relief. There was no telling just how long the light trick would last.

Dr. Trotter had pronounced John in A-one condition. "You, on the other hand, Kate, are looking a bit peaked," he said. "Are you getting enough rest?"

Kate was taken aback. Actually, until he mentioned it, she hadn't thought about it. When she did, she realized that for the past few days she had been feeling unusually tired.

"When John goes down for his nap this afternoon, you take one, too," he suggested, and Kate had followed the doctor's orders.

Maybe that's why I can't sleep now, she thought, listening to the rustle of the bedroom curtains in front of the open window. Although San Francisco had been unseasonably warm today, almost hot, now a cool night breeze blew in from the Pacific. A full moon shone into the room, silhouetting the bedpost and the chest of drawers. Next to her Jack's breathing was deep and steady. Across the hall she heard the baby whimper. Baby dreams, she thought, wondering, for maybe the millionth time, what babies dream about.

Twelve forty-five and she was still wide-awake! Kate closed her eyes and tried to wipe everything out of her mind. What was the matter with her?

As if to answer, the dry, empty lump returned larger than ever. It filled her whole body and made it ache. She counted the months. Nine. John was nine months old. She had stretched and juggled her maternity leave as far as was possible. Within days she must make her decision about whether or not to return to the San Francisco Police Department. Tears stung her eyes. Kate forced them back. She loved her work. She enjoyed being a homicide detective. She missed the guys, but not as much as she was going to miss little John.

Sniffling, Kate wondered where that police chief was now. The pregnant one in Texas that she had read about who could hold down her job and be a mother as well. She'd like to call her and ask what she did about that horrible empty feeling.

Kate rolled back toward her husband. Should she go back to work or take an extended leave? Jack had left it up to her. He would be happy with whatever she decided, she knew that. It was she who had to make up her mind, and soon.

The shrill ring of the telephone cracked through the silent room. Kate tensed, the way she instinctively did when the phone rang in the middle of the night. Jack and John were safe. Could it be Jack's mother? No one ever calls at this hour with good news.

Quickly she reached over her husband and picked up the receiver. "Hello," she whispered, but Jack was already awake. He perched himself up on his elbows to listen.

"Kate, I'm so sorry to wake you up this way. In the confusion I had forgotten about the time difference."

It took Kate a few seconds to recognize the voice. "Sister Mary Helen." She sank back to her side of the bed. "Confusion? What confusion? Where are you? Didn't you tell me just last week that you and Sister Eileen were going to Spain?"

"Yes, dear. I did, and we are. In Spain, that is. But something unfortunate has happened."

"Something unfortunate? In Spain?" Kate Murphy was incredulous. Sister Mary Helen had a knack for being in the right place at the wrong time. Or was it the wrong place at the right time? From the San Francisco Police Department's point of view, in the wrong place most of the time. Over the years this phenomenon had led to Kate Murphy and Sister Mary Helen collaborating on four different homicide cases, with Sister Eileen never far away. In the process they had become fast friends.

In Kate's opinion, this trip to Spain was a much-needed vacation for the two nuns, and she had sincerely hoped that they would come home well rested, particularly if she decided to get a nanny for John. She intended to pick their brains for the proper person. For this important task she wanted both of them at their best.

"Yes, dear. Are you there? I am still in Spain, Santiago de Compostela, to be exact. The most dreadful thing just happened."

"What's that, Sister?" Kate sighed, hoping against hope that she didn't know the answer.

"Well, Kate, I decided to visit the tomb of St. James the Apostle on my own. And when I did, there in the crypt was Lisa Springer. There was an enormous gash on her head and across her throat. . . . Well, Kate, it looks as if she has been . . . as if she was . . ." Apparently Sister Mary Helen was having a difficult time getting her mouth around the words.

"Murdered?" Kate said.

"I'm afraid so."

"And who is Lisa Springer, Sister? One of the members of your tour?"

"Yes." Suddenly the voice sounded so faint and far away that Kate wondered if something had happened to the connection.

"Can you hear me, Sister?"

"Yes, dear."

Still weak. Shock, Kate thought. "Have you notified anyone?" she asked gently.

"Of course I have." From the tone Kate knew that some of the old starch was coming back. Good.

"Just before I called you, I called Señor Nunez, our tour guide, and he in turn will notify the police, I'm sure."

Then why in the hell did you call me? Kate wanted to blurt out, but there was no need.

"What I want to ask you, Kate, is what should we do next?"

"Nothing, Sister. Do nothing! As I've tried to tell you so often, murder is police business. Furthermore, you are in a foreign country. You don't even speak the language. The best thing that you can do is stay out of it."

When Mary Helen did not respond, Kate realized that she had been shouting. Perhaps she was coming on a little too strongly. She softened her tone.

"It really is better, Sister. You should cooperate with the local police, of course, but really it is wiser to let them handle it."

Still, Sister Mary Helen said nothing. The phone lines crackled. Kate wanted to bite her tongue. "Not that I mean you aren't wise," she added lamely. Then after a pause, "Of course, you can always call me if you need me, Sister," she said. The instant she heard Mary Helen's "Thank you, dear," she wished that she had bitten her tongue.

Replacing the receiver, Kate snuggled down under the

covers and moved closer to Jack. He put his arm around her, and, with a shiver, Kate nestled comfortably into his familiar hollows. She closed her eyes, ready, at last, for sleep.

Jack began to laugh.

"What's so funny?"

"I was just thinking about Sister Mary Helen."

"What about her?"

"She gets herself into such messes in English. Can you imagine what she is capable of in Spanish?"

"I don't want to imagine it," she said, "especially since I told her to call me if she needs me. What in the world got into me?"

"You can't help yourself, hon." Jack pulled her closer. She felt his warm breath in her hair. His lips touched her cheek, her throat. "What you've got is a bad case of the motherly instinct." His whisper tickled her ear.

Even as his lips moved down her neck, she felt that dull pain start all over again. It began in the pit of her stomach.

♦

The two nuns did not have to wait long to find out what action the local police would take. As Mary Helen replaced the telephone receiver, a sharp rap sounded on their bedroom door.

Eileen jumped. "Who is it?" she called out.

"*Policía. Por favor*, to come," a deep voice answered.

Cautiously Mary Helen, her knees still wobbly, cracked open the door and peeked out. A tall, muscular fellow with a small, neatly trimmed mustache stood in the hallway. His navy blue uniform, leather holster, and gun looked official enough, but Mary Helen was taking no chances. "Please may I see your credentials, señor?" she asked.

The man stared blankly at her. "*Por favor*, to come," he said louder.

"Your credentials, señor?" Mary Helen tried a pleasant smile.

Obviously bewildered, the man frowned. "To come," he said, omitting the *por favor*.

Mary Helen felt Eileen at her side. She held a pocket-size Spanish/English traveler's dictionary. *"Habla usted inglés, señor?"* Eileen asked with a touch of the brogue.

The dark eyes brightened. "No, no, no!" He shook his head emphatically, then began a volley of Spanish aimed directly at Eileen, who stood there looking blank.

"Now see what you've done," Mary Helen hissed. "Put that thing away. It's better to say nothing than to say the wrong thing."

"Señor, please." Undeterred, Eileen put up her pudgy hands, trying to stop him while she searched for the appropriate phrase, but it was too late.

"Señor Esteban Zaldo y Arana," the policeman, or at least Mary Helen supposed that was who he was, announced finally. Rolling his eyes, he gestured toward the hallway and pointed to his holster.

"That's credentials enough for me, old dear," Eileen said. Mary Helen agreed.

Silently the pair followed the man through the magnificent vaulted hallways hung with tapestries and works of art. They followed his clicking heels down a flight of marble stairs.

"Do you feel like a heretic on your way to the Inquisitor?" Eileen whispered as they turned a corner.

Mary Helen nodded. "I should of stood in bed," she said, and Eileen giggled with nervousness.

Abruptly Señor Zaldo stopped before a closed door, knocked, and, without waiting for a reply, flung it open. "To come," he said. With a nod of his head, he left his two captives standing in the doorway of a small, dim room, where the rest of the tour members, all talking at once, were corralled. Their voices rose, each one outblustering the last, with Cora shrilling above the rest.

"That's everyone," Cora announced, but no one seemed to notice.

In the confusion Mary Helen glanced around. Heavy draperies covered the windows, and the room had the musty smell of little use. Along one wall bookshelves stretched to the ceiling. An ornate desk dominated the far corner, and bulky velvet-covered chairs bordered the worn carpet.

The room once might have been a library. Right now it looked to Mary Helen more like a catchall room, one that was used to store extra furniture or to fill whatever need arose. Every large institution had one, she knew, like the old priests' dining room at Mount St. Francis. At the very thought of the college her stomach somersaulted. Please God, no word of what had happened would reach there, at least until she did.

Pepe and his "assistant," María José, stood in the center of the fray. María José, black eyes flashing, was attempting with little apparent success to calm the group.

Only Heidi, red-eyed and pale, sat on one of the heavy chairs. Dr. Fong stood over her, an empty glass in his hand and a worried expression on his round face.

"*Silencio, por favor!*" the deep voice boomed from the doorway. Señor Zaldo had returned.

Eyes shifted uncertainly toward him as a tense silence settled over the group.

"*Gracias.*" He smiled, justifiably proud of what he'd accomplished. Another volley of Spanish preceded a name. "Comisario Ángel Serrano y Cobas," he announced with great respect. Obviously they were about to meet the top dog. Stepping aside, Zaldo made room for the gentleman in question.

Sister Mary Helen didn't really know what she'd expected, but it certainly was not what she saw. At first glance Comisario Serrano looked like a statue that she had spied in one of the gift shops at the Madrid airport, a statue of Sancho Panza. Like Don Quixote's legendary squire, he was short and squat with a round little belly. In Comisario Serrano's case his paunch pulled against the buttons on his shirt and caused his belt buckle to dip slightly south. The legs of his gray suit sagged and formed pleats over the tops of his shoes.

A tonsure of gray hair in need of a trim circled his head and seemed to fit the cherubic face. Not that Ángel Serrano reminded Mary Helen so much of an angel as he did of an aging and harmless gnome.

That is, until their eyes met, and Mary Helen knew that this was a man to be reckoned with. She watched him take in the group with eyes "as bold as lions, roving, running, leaping here and there." The long-forgotten simile jumped into her mind, although the name of its author did not. How did the rest of that passage go? Eyes that "speak all languages."

His eyes were quite articulate. Mary Helen wondered if his speech would be as clear. Fortunately for all concerned, Comisario Serrano spoke perfect English with a hint of a British accent that he might very well have acquired at Oxford.

"Good morning, ladies and gentlemen," he began, taking time to smile and nod his head toward each member of the tourist party.

Putting the names with the faces, of course! Mary Helen nodded back and noticed the man register momentary shock when he saw María José.

"My deputy, Señor Zaldo, tells me that he managed to round you all up despite the early hour, and if Señor Nunez will kindly confirm the fact . . ." He glanced toward the extremely pale Pepe standing between the DeAngelos. When

Pepe returned a weak nod, the *comisario* continued. "Good! Good! Now we can get on with it."

"Get on with what?" Bud Bowman exploded.

"If you will allow me, señor." Ángel Serrano's voice was most congenial. "Señor Nunez, I am told, informed you that one of your group, Miss Lisa Springer, met with a most unfortunate accident." He paused.

For effect, Mary Helen thought.

"On further investigation, we fear that it was not an accident after all but that Miss Springer was murdered."

"You don't think that one of us did it, do you?" This time it was Cora.

A loud groan from Heidi cut off anything else Cora was going to say. "How could this happen?" Heidi wailed miserably. "My mother'll kill me!" As soon as the words left her mouth, Heidi broke into fresh sobbing.

Dr. Fong, looking more helpless than a doctor should, even if he was a dentist, put his hand on her shoulder.

"Cora—Mrs. Bowman, that is—has a point, Comisario." Roger DeAngelo stepped to the center of the carpet, rather like the group spokesperson. "Wouldn't you be better off going after the scoundrel who did this?"

Ever supportive, Bootsie DeAngelo moved beside her husband. "Maybe it was one of those awful muggers, Inspector." Bootsie's voice was uncharacteristically shrill. "Did you think of that? Did that poor woman have her purse with her when you found her?" Her face was still as white and taut as it had been at breakfast.

"Thank you, madame, for your suggestion." Comisario Ángel Serrano bowed courteously. "We will, of course, give this possibility some thought, but at present I will have to ask each of you where you were last night and whether or not you noticed anything unusual."

An uncomfortable silence followed his announcement.

Mary Helen noticed Roger DeAngelo stiffen. An electric glance shot between the Fongs. María José's flashing eyes turned on Pepe. Cora seemed to gloat as if somehow she'd finally discovered what last night's commotion was all about.

Mary Helen herself squirmed, wondering how much of what she had seen and heard during the night was relevant to the case.

Comisario Serrano wasn't missing any of it. "So, if you will kindly make yourselves comfortable, I have arranged for the hotel to provide some breakfast. Señor Zaldo will escort you, one at a time, to a temporary office I have set up.

"María José Gómez, you may come with me now, please," he said in a voice that gave nothing away.

Within minutes a small army of waiters in stiff white jackets marched into the room, carrying silver coffeepots, cockleshell bowls filled with fruit and eggs, heaping baskets of rolls, butter, and jam. The feast, which they set on the enormous desk, was very like the one Mary Helen had seen in the *hostal* dining room barely an hour before.

Without warning she felt dizzy. So much had happened in such a short span. Life is so fragile, she mused, sinking into the nearest chair. A cloud of dust rose around her. A waiter handed her a cup of coffee.

Before long the pungent aroma of strong coffee, mingled with the smell of dust, became cloying. She wondered why María José hadn't returned. She wished someone would open a window and was very glad to hear Officer Zaldo call her name. The sooner she got out of this room, regardless of the reason, the better.

With almost medieval courtesy, Ángel Serrano ushered her into what looked like a manager's office and made sure that she was seated comfortably.

"The manager has been so kind as to lend me his accommodations," he said, as if to answer her question. His bright eyes sparkled. "Now, Sister." He pulled an overstuffed chair from behind the desk and settled himself.

Mary Helen noticed that only his toes touched the floor. Not that that had anything to do with anything, she thought. Quickly, and as unemotionally as possible, she related the story where the story began, with Señor Fraga and his Patio Español.

In spite of her best efforts, her voice quivered when she described her discovery of Lisa's body, the smeared casket, the curls clotted with blood, the swollen, discolored face, and the thick welt across her throat.

All at once her hands felt cold. Despite the warmth of the room, her teeth began to chatter. "I'm sorry, Comisario." Mary Helen clenched her teeth in an effort to control them.

Comisario Serrano pushed up from his chair and walked to the door. Almost miraculously he produced a snifter of brandy. "Sip this, Sister," he said. "You are in shock, of course, and with good reason. You are undoubtedly not used to this kind of thing."

With a nod of thanks, Mary Helen took a swallow. It burned all the way down. If you only knew, she thought, feeling unexpected tears sting her eyes. Not that one ever gets used to "this kind of thing," as he put it. She rummaged in her sweater pocket for a tissue.

"Shock," Comisario Serrano repeated. "You have had quite a shock!"

When Mary Helen pulled her hand from her sweater pocket holding a bloodstained tissue, the *comisario* looked a little shocked, too.

"We can expect to find your fingerprints in the crypt?" he asked matter-of-factly.

Nodding sheepishly, Mary Helen handed the tissue to him and dug in her pocket for another. Wiping her eyes, she watched him turn the soiled tissue over in his hand.

"And last night, Sister," he said, studying her face, "what did you do last night?"

Mary Helen recounted her evening, including being unable to sleep, hearing people arguing in the hallway, watching Pepe and María José quarrel in the plaza, and finally hearing the early-morning revelers in the hallway.

She was glad that was all she'd heard since she was afraid that she was beginning to sound like an inveterate eavesdropper. Comisario Serrano didn't seem to care about her manners. "Anything else?" he pressed.

Feeling foolish, she told him about looking out onto the deserted Plaza del Obradoiro and thinking that she saw a figure standing on the cathedral steps.

The *comisario* fell silent.

"Surely, it was just a shadow," Mary Helen ventured. "You know how night shadows can be, and it was pouring rain," she added, hoping that he wouldn't think that she was an old lady given to flights of fancy. "Nobody stands that still in the pouring rain."

"Unless the person does not want to be noticed, dear Sister."

"Who in the world would care about being seen on the cathedral steps?"

Even before his dark eyes pinned her like sharp needles, she knew the answer. "Our killer, Sister, that is who."

Although the office now seemed stifling, a shiver ran down Mary Helen's spine. Had she actually seen Lisa's murderer?

"Whom have you told about this?" The sharpness in the *comisario*'s voice startled her.

She ransacked her memory. "No one really."

"Not Pepe Nunez?"

Mary Helen shook her head.

"Not even your traveling companion?"

Again Mary Helen shook her head. She really had not had the time or the opportunity to talk to Eileen, not that Eileen would repeat it.

"Do not tell anyone, Sister, not even Sister Eileen."

Mary Helen was aware that the *comisario* had not consulted a list but knew Eileen's name right off. This fellow is going to be interesting to watch, she thought, wondering absently how long it would take him to discover her call to Kate Murphy and whether or not she ought to tell him first.

Before she could decide, he rose from his seat, bowed, and ushered her toward the door. "Tell no one, Sister. Do you understand?" He peered at her.

Of course, she understood! Mary Helen tried to hide her annoyance. His words were abundantly clear. Perhaps he did think that age made her a bit senile in the memory department.

"I won't tell anyone, Comisario," she said, "not even Sister Eileen." Her cheeks flushed as the reason for his concern erupted in her mind and sent a wave of panic through her body. If I saw the killer, perhaps the killer saw me. If he knows that I saw him and that I told someone else about him, then we are both . . . She dreaded drawing the logical conclusion.

"Good show!" the *comisario* said, saving her from it. With a deep and final bow, he escorted her from the room.

♦

Back in the small, musty catchall room, the morning dragged on. Breakfast lay virtually untouched. As each tour member left, then returned, the mood in the room seemed to darken. Not even opening the thick drapes to let in the crisp October sunshine helped.

Mary Helen drank an ocean of coffee. She looked around in vain for a magazine, even a Spanish one, to take her mind off the experience of finding Lisa. She wished crazily that she had brought along her paperback. In it, the murders were all make-believe and the villain caught in 270 pages. She attempted to write something, anything, in her travel diary, but the only word that came to her mind was *horrible*.

The catchall room was unnaturally quiet. With each passing hour suspicion and distrust grew and spread. When the group realized that María José had failed to return, tendrils of fear coiled around them.

In the prevailing tension Bootsie DeAngelo paced nervously while her husband made quite a show of reading and rereading the Spanish titles on the row upon row of bookshelves. The Fongs made every effort to avoid each other, not easy in a room this small. When their eyes did meet, Neil Fong looked away quickly. And no wonder, Mary Helen thought, watching Rita. The anger in her cold, dark, almond-shaped eyes would freeze a pillar.

Finally the *comisario* called for Sister Eileen. Heidi curled up in one of the heavy velvet chairs. Before long she was asleep. Now that Fong's vigil over the girl seemed unnecessary, he joined his wife. Despite the obvious coolness between them, they sat close together like a small, safe unit in a hostile camp.

Mary Helen wished that she could get Heidi alone, but there didn't seem to be much of a chance. Not now anyway. She wanted to ask her about her unfinished remark during last night's dinner. "You'll never guess who Lisa was with . . ." Heidi had said, and she was probably right. Mary Helen would never guess, although from the strain in the room, she put her money on Dr. Neil Fong.

Mary Helen checked her wristwatch. Eileen had been with Comisario Serrano for nearly twenty minutes. She wondered what was taking so long. After all, Eileen had been fast asleep the entire night. Mary Helen could vouch for that. She hoped that her friend wasn't filling him full of her "old sayings from back home," as she was wont to do when she was in a pinch.

With a swish the door swung open, and Eileen, her face flushed, entered. Before she was settled in her seat, the *comisario* called for Pepe. He was the last. Their ordeal was nearly over.

"How did it go?" Mary Helen asked in a low whisper.

"Fine, old dear, just fine." Eileen's brogue was unusually thick. Something had excited her. "That Ángel is quite the character." She rolled her eyes heavenward.

"Ángel, is it?" Mary Helen asked. "And what took you so long?"

"Nothing really. We were just talking about Ireland. He spent several summers there when he was a lad going to Oxford. He knew many of the haunts I knew, and lo and behold, he even knew my third cousin on my mother's side, Mary Agnes Glynn, from Ballygloonen. They went to a dance or two together." Eileen blushed. "He said he remembers that Mary Agnes—Aggie, we called her—was quite a looker."

"I am waiting out here, sweating through your interrogation, and you are in there talking about your mother's third cousin?" Mary Helen felt her blood pressure rising.

"Who, by the way, married quite well, did our Aggie. I told the *comisario* that we have an old saying back home: 'Many an Irish property was increased by the lace of a daughter's petticoat.' "

Mary Helen groaned, but Eileen went on as though she hadn't noticed. "It is, no doubt, his technique. Making you feel at ease like that. There's another old saying back home—"

Mary Helen glared. Unabashed, Eileen smiled. "Yes, indeed. 'You must crack the nuts before you can eat the kernels.' "

"You are no nut at all." Mary Helen lowered her voice and resisted the temptation to rephrase her last remark. "You were asleep."

"How did the *comisario* know?"

"He could have asked you or me."

"Entirely too simple," Eileen said, and smiled over at Bud Bowman.

"Anyone want to play cards?" Bud asked in an attempt, no doubt, to get something going, even a conversation. "Pinochle, maybe?" His eyes roamed the room like a friendly Great Dane looking for a playmate.

Mary Helen was considering taking up his offer, more as an act of charity than anything else, when Bootsie DeAngelo exploded.

"How could you, you cretin? How could you suggest cards at a time like this?" she shouted. Then, her nerves obviously reaching their limit, she burst into high hiccuping sobs. Almost a keening, Mary Helen thought.

Bud's face fell.

"Who are you calling a cretin?" It was Cora. Any veneer of the friendship they had enjoyed at breakfast vanished. She rose like a mother bear to protect her own. Florid-faced, she stumbled for an epithet to return to Bootsie. "You—you—you fish-eyed old bag!" she spit out in frustration.

Bootsie stopped in mid-hiccup. An uncomfortable silence filled the room. Cora was right. Bootsie's blue eyes did have a fishy coldness to them, and although she was not strictly elderly, she was much older than she tried to appear.

Seemingly satisfied that she'd hit pay dirt, Cora put her hands on her hips and waited for round two.

"Now see here, Cora." Roger DeAngelo pulled himself up to his full height and stepped in front of his wife. His dark eyes blazed. "You are definitely out of order."

"Who are you calling 'out of order'?" Bud Bowman found

his voice. "If I remember right, it was your missus that started the name-calling."

Dr. Fong peered over the top of his glasses and put his arm protectively around his wife's shoulders. Stiffening, she shook it off.

Heidi stirred in the chair but did not wake. She must have been up all night, Mary Helen thought absently, to be so tired.

"This will get us nowhere," Dr. Fong said, his face draining of color. "Let's at least act civilized."

"Why don't you stay out of it, fella?" Bud doubled up his fist and glowered first at Fong, then at DeAngelo.

"Someone better stop this or it's sure to turn into a donnybrook," Eileen whispered to Mary Helen.

Before either of the nuns could act, tiny Rita Fong stepped to the middle of the room. "Ladies and gentlemen," she said in a no-nonsense voice, "we are all obviously tired and upset. Fighting among ourselves will do us no good. We have had a long trip, a short night, and a very stressful morning. What we all need to do is relax. We need some deep breathing. Everyone stand."

Like obedient robots, they stood.

"Tall, stand tall! Ready, ready, ready." Her voice boomed off the bookshelves. "Up tall, tall, tall. Taller. Shoulders back. Feet apart. Arms over your heads. Stretch those lazy spines. Stretch. Stretch taller."

Mary Helen watched in amazement as tiny Rita stretched her arms and her back until she loomed almost tall. She held the pose as still as a statue. Mary Helen felt suddenly light-headed.

"Breathe," Rita commanded. "Breathe deep. Deep. Deep. Deeper!"

Standing tall and breathing deep was how an astonished Pepe found his group of *peregrinos*.

◆

As soon as Pepe left the office, Comisario Ángel Serrano pushed himself back in the swivel chair, propped his feet on top of the manager's desk, and closed his eyes. Peace, at last! He needed it to think.

After a morning filled with chatter the small office was richly quiet. "Quiet as a nun," the English poet had written. The chap must never have run into the two I just met, Ángel thought, rubbing his burning eyes.

In the stillness he heard the rhythmic drip-drip-drip of a rain gutter in the patio below. From somewhere tires swished on the still-wet street. Silverware rattled in one of the hotel's dining rooms.

What a mess this tour of Nunez's had become! There was something about the young man that Ángel didn't like, didn't trust really. He was too suave, too well dressed. What did the Americans call it? Too "yuppie"—strange word. Ángel pulled at his tie to loosen it. His shirt collar chafed at his neck. Was he really gaining kilos as his wife, Julietta, claimed or was she using too much starch in the laundry?

Julietta would probably like him to be more like Pepe Nunez. At the thought of her, his stomach rumbled. It was almost time for his dinner.

The whole of Santiago would soon stop for dinner. María José must be home by now. Thank goodness that he was able to send his only niece home. His sister, Pilar, would have had his head if he had detained her. Although it would serve her right. Maybe scare her a little. Quickly he dismissed the notion. María José, he knew from years of experience, did not scare easily. He wondered crossly how she had managed to get involved with this Pepe and what the duties of an assistant to a fellow who did nothing but show people the sights actually were.

When he asked her, she had shrugged impatiently. "Tío, I have told you and Papa both that I intend to be a business-woman, support myself, see the world, break out of Galicia. I want to be a liberated woman. I will take whatever opportunities arise to do this." Her jaw was set. "This is not just an adventure. I view Pepe Nunez and his tour as a business opportunity."

For the life of him, Ángel Serrano could not see why, but it was fruitless to say so. All this liberation business happened when María José went to the university: liberation and her magenta-colored hair. He and his brother-in-law had figured both would pass, but neither had, and Pilar seemed to be encouraging her.

"And now, what of your opportunity, Ho-Ho?" He used her childhood pet name, hoping to soften her up for reason. "It seems to have propelled you right into the middle of a murder."

Undaunted and clearly unsoftened, María José's dark eyes met his. "Tío," she said in that irritatingly positive tone of hers, "it has produced another opportunity. Don't you see? I can continue on this tour with Pepe and work as a sort of assistant to you."

Ángel sent her home. Maybe having only sons is a blessing, he thought, determined to talk to his brother-in-law. Ho-Ho had always been a handful. Someone had better tighten the rein on that girl before it was too late.

Wasn't this just his luck? Bad enough to have his own niece involved in a murder, let alone in the murder of an American tourist. It would mean notifying the embassy in Madrid—clearly the mayor's responsibility—but notifying the mayor fell to his lot. Better to leave it until after the noonday meal. The mayor always reacted better when he was full. Surely Canon Fernández had already reached the mayor.

Thank goodness he had made it clear that he was not to be disturbed for any reason.

And, of all places to find the victim, in the cathedral! *Murder in the Cathedral.* His mind jumped back to Oxford, where he had first read that play, then back again to Santiago and to the canon, whom he had been avoiding all morning.

What would the canon say when they finally met? Plenty, Ángel knew, visualizing the bantamlike priest, ranting and strutting, lamenting the sacrilege, somehow blaming the police in general, and Ángel in particular, for what had happened. Idly Ángel wondered what kinds of rites would be required to exorcise a cathedral. But that was the canon's problem. His was to discover the murderer. And what a muddle it was.

"Maybe it was a mugger," the professor's wife had suggested in her slow drawl. When he had seen her alone, Barbara DeAngelo, for some reason called Bootsie, with the blue-black hair and those cold blue eyes, stated very clearly and concisely that on the previous night she was in the lounge with her husband, the Fongs, and the Bowmans. Lisa Springer, Heidi Williams, María José, and Pepe Nunez joined them a little later. The Bowmans left early. Dr. and Mrs. Fong were the next to go. Not too much later she and her husband left. About ten-thirty, she thought.

"We were just exhausted," she said, "and we both went to bed. My husband fell asleep immediately. I read for a while and then turned off the lights. Although I didn't sleep very well, I don't remember hearing anything unusual until Pepe roused us this morning.

"Surely it was a mugger who did this," Bootsie repeated, and Ángel did not argue. He knew, however, what she did not. Santiago had its share of thieves, drunks, and even wife beaters. But it had very few murderers, and none so heinous as to commit murder in the crypt of its beloved St. James.

A staccato rap on the door propelled Ángel upright in his chair. *"Pase!"* he barked, clearing his throat and bending over a sheet of paper on the desk.

"Comisario!" Officer Esteban Zaldo, eager and efficient, clicked his heels and stood at attention. Ángel motioned for him to sit down. Zaldo even sat at attention, back straight, heels together. His mustache was straight and rigid. Only the half-moons of perspiration forming under his arms indicated that he was human.

For some reason his formality irritated Ángel, although he knew it shouldn't. Esteban was a dedicated and effective police officer. Being successfully able to contain that bunch of American *peregrinos* in one room ought to be proof enough.

Ángel pulled in his chair and doodled down one side of the paper on his desk. "I'm glad to see you, Esteban," he said.

Zaldo allowed a small, pleased grin to play at the corners of his mouth.

"We have a problem." Ángel turned the paper around and started down the other side. "There is absolutely no question in my mind that one of these Americans is the murderer." Ángel glanced up. "But which one?"

Esteban frowned, undoubtedly indicating that he, too, understood the seriousness of their predicament.

Ángel read aloud from his notes. "Barbara, called Bootsie, DeAngelo claims to have been in bed all night with her husband. Her husband, Professor Roger DeAngelo, verifies it. Henry Bowman, called Bud, slept all night. Snoring, according to his wife, Cora. She was just dropping off to sleep when someone, she claims, was quarreling in the hallway outside her room." He consulted his paper. " 'Fighting tooth and nail,' to quote her exactly."

"Do we know who that was, Comisario?" Esteban's dark eyes were sharp.

"The Fongs, I suspect."

"Did they admit it?"

"Not at all!" The *comisario* grinned at Zaldo, who was still a bachelor. "Married people don't admit that they fight, Esteban. We discuss things. And they did admit that they had a discussion, which, according to Dr. Neil Fong, may have become a bit noisy. 'Loud enough to wake the dead,' to quote Cora Bowman."

"Do we know what they were fighting about, Comisario?"

"Only what they tell us." Ángel chuckled. "The dentist claims that his wife was upset that they had stayed downstairs so long. She was tired and had kicked him several times under the table."

"Kicked him?" Esteban's mustache twitched. "That little thing kicked him?"

Although Rita Fong was tiny, to Ángel's way of thinking her small person emitted a giant's strength. Was it the command in her voice? The brightness of her dress? Or was it those eyes, which peered at him like two hard lumps of polished jet?

"That is his version," Ángel said. "She claims that she was concerned because he was drinking too much wine and wine is not good for him. She says that was what they were discussing in the hallway and that he became angry, shouted, and stalked away."

"That was the commotion Señora Bowman heard." Zaldo's eyes brightened. "Perhaps the doctor went outside for a breath of air, met Señorita Springer, tried to make drunken advances. When she refused, he struck her."

"That is an interesting theory, Esteban, except that both the Fongs agree—and it is one of the few things that they do agree upon—that Dr. Fong returned a few minutes later, sick and penitent, and that they spent the rest of the night in bed together."

As far as possible from each other, Ángel supposed, feeling a twinge of pity for the doctor. He himself hated going to bed angry. After a row with Julietta, rather than sleep in a tense bed, he always apologized and Julietta was quick to forgive. For some reason Ángel could not imagine Rita Fong forgiving at all.

"What about the murdered girl's friend, Heidi?" Esteban interrupted the *comisario's* reverie.

"Aha! Heidi." Ángel turned over his paper. Gum-chewing Heidi had provided him with a wealth of information. "She told me that she and Lisa went to bed about three this morning. Pepe had left the hotel briefly with María José, who, at least in Heidi's view, was furious with him."

At the mention of Ho-Ho's name, Esteban squirmed uncomfortably. "I am sorry, Comisario, that your sister's only daughter is involved."

"It is not your fault, Esteban." Nor mine either, he thought, regardless of what his sister, Pilar, would say. Maybe he should have put Ho-Ho in jail for a few hours. Teach them both a lesson!

"María José told me," he continued, "that she was angry because Pepe had not bothered to escort her to the banquet. Then afterward he had danced with the other single women while he left her sitting."

Ángel's stomach growled so loudly that he cut short his niece's rendition of the evening. "She went home early," he said, dreading the thought of checking out her alibi with his sister. "Pepe returned to the hotel, where they danced until closing time, and he escorted the girls on a moonlit walk around the university."

Zaldo's eyes narrowed.

"All very aboveboard," Ángel added quickly. "When they finally went to their room, they found a note had been shoved under the door. For Lisa."

"A note! From the murderer?"

"From an admirer, according to Heidi, although they might be one and the same."

"Where is this note?"

"Heidi tells me that the murdered girl tore it into little pieces and flushed it." Bad on the evidence and bad on the plumbing, Ángel thought, pushing himself up from his chair. Zaldo shot to attention. "At ease, Esteban. At ease. We'll talk more after dinner." He put his hand on the officer's rigid shoulder. "Why don't you go home and have your dinner, too?"

"But what about the nuns, Comisario?"

"The nuns?" Reluctantly Ángel sat back down and motioned for Officer Zaldo to do the same. "You don't think that one of them is the murderer, do you?" He ran his fingers around his tonsure. "One was asleep all night. And the other one? She did have something interesting to add. She happened to look out the window sometime during the early-morning hours and spotted what she thought might be a person on the cathedral steps.

"On the other hand, she claimed that whoever it was stood so still that perhaps it was only shadows. Not a word about this to anyone, Esteban, until we can check it out further." The clock in the tower struck two.

"But after dinner. Facts are better on a full stomach, don't you agree? The nuns, however, I think we can safely rule out."

The young officer's boots scraped nervously against the carpet.

"What is it, Esteban? Is there something about the nuns that you have not told me?"

"While you were interrogating the Americans, Comisario, I took the liberty of checking with the hotel's manager to see if any telephone calls were placed."

"And?"

"One, Comisario. To San Francisco. From the nuns' room." With a flourish, Esteban Zaldo produced a slip of paper with the number.

Ángel accepted the paper and stuffed it into his coat pocket. "Good work, Zaldo," he said, watching his subordinate try to conceal a satisfied smile. "We'll look into this as soon as possible." He checked his wristwatch. It was two here in Santiago. That made it six in the morning in San Francisco. If he expected cooperation from whoever was on the other end of the line, he had better wait an hour or two.

"But for now, I insist," he said, "that we stop for dinner."

With a click of his heels, Esteban Zaldo turned sharply and, shoulders squared, strode from the manager's office.

As the stiff back passed through the door, Ángel Serrano couldn't help wondering about Officer Zaldo. Perhaps the poor chap has been watching too much American television, he thought. Those black-and-white reruns of, what was that program called? "The Streets of San Francisco"?

♦

"Peregrinos!" Pepe wrung his hands nervously. "Your attention, please!" He raised his voice, although it was hardly necessary. Except for Rita Fong's steady aerobic commands and assorted grunts and wheezes from the participants, the small room was quiet.

When Pepe entered, it went deadly still. All of them stood immobile. If Mary Helen hadn't known better, she would have sworn that she heard nine hearts thudding like pistons waiting for their guide to continue.

And was it any wonder? Although hope ran high that Lisa's murderer was a random mugger, in their inmost beings, Mary Helen suspected, they all knew it was one of them. Had Comisario Serrano discovered which one? For the moment she couldn't decide which was worse: to know that you were doing aerobics with a murderer or just to wonder if you were.

A glance at the frozen faces of her companions assured Mary Helen that they all were having the same misgivings. All except one, that is. But which one? She realized she was shaking.

Pepe cleared his throat. "The *comisario* has said that we may go on with our scheduled events until further notice."

The group gave a collective sigh of relief, as if the short reprieve indicated that the murderer might be an outsider after all.

Pepe fumbled with the itinerary. "We missed the cathedral tour, of course." His face changed to an unbecoming turkey red. "Dinner is in the cafeteria downstairs."

"It's about time." Bill Bowman broke the silence and smiled broadly. "I'm so hungry I could eat a horse. How about you?" He grinned at Bootsie DeAngelo.

Will he never learn? Mary Helen wondered, watching Bootsie recoil in disgust. "How can you eat at a time like this? How can any of you eat?" Her cold blue eyes narrowed and roamed the room, challenging them. "For God's sake! One of us has just been murdered!"

"Jeez, lady"—Bud shrugged—"I was only making conversation."

"And just who asked you to?" Bootsie spit out, her nerves apparently still at the breaking point.

An uneasy silence filled the room. Bootsie DeAngelo's husband stepped up behind her and touched her shoulders. "Calm down, sweetheart," he whispered.

"Don't you patronize me, Roger." She framed each syllable through clenched teeth and shrugged off his hands.

"Understandably we are all upset." It was Dr. Fong's soft voice. As he spoke, his glasses slipped down his nose. "But there is really no sense in taking our feelings out on one another."

"Just what we all need! First a health nut, now an amateur psychologist," Bootsie snapped.

"You need more than an amateur shrink." Unfortunately Cora Bowman felt called into the battle. "You need a full-blown—"

"Speaking of being full-blown," Bootsie interrupted with a nasty sneer.

Cora's face flamed. Her jowls shook with rage.

"Now, now, please," Pepe began, but no one except Sister Mary Helen seemed to notice.

Rita Fong stepped to Cora's side and pulled herself up to her full height. "Only a very insecure person needs to be so insulting." Her almond eyes were sharp. "Or a person who has something to cover up with a smoke screen, I believe they call it."

"Rita!" Dr. Fong choked.

The silence in the room was electric. Bootsie DeAngelo's taut face was an unhealthy white. Mary Helen herself felt a little light-headed.

"As long as we are talking about a smoke screen." Professor DeAngelo spoke deliberately, his dark eyes made even harder by his contact lenses. "Perchance, you, Mrs. Fong, are the one who followed that poor girl."

Cora sprang to Rita's defense and glared at DeAngelo. "Just what makes you think it was a woman, Mr. Romeo—Professor?"

"Jeez, all I was trying to do was make with a little light talk," Bud Bowman grumbled to Eileen, who nodded sympathetically.

"How dare you?" DeAngelo's lean face tightened with anger. Mary Helen watched him clench and unclench his fists. "How dare you speak to me like that? You gap-toothed busybody!" he shouted.

Cora's hand flew to her mouth as if she had been slapped.

"Hey, guy, watch your mouth with my wife. Nobody insults my Cora." Bud pointed a thick finger at DeAngelo. "One more word out of that yap of yours, and I'll knock you into the middle of next week."

DeAngelo stuck out his chin in defiance, as though begging Bowman to throw the first punch. Mary Helen feared that he would have, too, except for a long, loud, piercing shriek from Heidi.

Everyone spun toward the girl in surprise. With all the ruckus, Mary Helen had almost forgotten about poor Heidi.

"Stop it! Stop it, all of you!" she screamed. "Lisa's dead, and no one cares. Everyone's saying hateful things. Stop it!" Exploding into sobs, Heidi collapsed into the nearest chair, covered her face with her hands, and wept.

♦

"This is turning into some vacation," Sister Eileen grumbled as she and Mary Helen entered the high-ceilinged dining room on the ground floor of the *hostal*. It had taken several minutes for Pepe to quiet Heidi, make peace among the Bowmans, Fongs, and DeAngelos, and herd his pilgrims into the ornate cafeteria. But he had done it with aplomb and without, Mary Helen noticed, the assistance of María José. Where *had* the girl gone?

Dinner was a silent, strained affair that seemed to drag on much longer than the wall clock indicated. If there ever had been a chance that the group might gel and begin to enjoy one another, the scene in the catchall room had taken care of that.

When they sat down, Pepe babbled a little, probably

from habit. It was obvious that neither Heidi, on his left, nor Bootsie, on his right, was listening. Maybe he wasn't even listening to himself. Bud Bowman, eyes down, dived into his pumpkin-colored soup while Cora stared vacantly out a dining-room window onto a rose-splashed patio. Rita Fong pushed her salad around her plate, occasionally slipping a lettuce leaf onto the plate in front of her husband, who didn't seem to notice. Next to her, Mary Helen felt Professor De-Angelo's long, narrow left foot jiggle nervously as he chewed.

There were several attempts at civilized conversation, one or two promising volleys with Eileen tossing the ball. But these too hit the ground, even before the entrée was served.

"Give it a rest," Mary Helen muttered when Eileen introduced the topic of the weather. The food, the decor of the room, and the ancient traditions surrounding the Cathedral of Santiago de Compostela had already fallen flat.

With a resigned shrug, Eileen returned to her plate of steamed scallops. The general consensus seemed to be: eyes down, shovel it in as quickly as possible, and grunt politely now and again.

One by one the other pilgrims and even Pepe excused themselves until only the two nuns and red-eyed Heidi were left at the long table. Mary Helen stared absently at the clutter of half-filled plates and half-empty crystal glasses and popped the last piece of a tart into her mouth.

"I could do with a bit of fresh air and exercise," Eileen said, replacing the delicate china teacup on its saucer. "How about you, Mary Helen?"

Mary Helen nodded. Actually she would have preferred a quick siesta, but she suspected that it was useless to try to sleep. All morning she had kept herself distracted, but she knew that just below her consciousness lurked the image of Lisa. The moment she closed her eyes, the girl was sure to appear, twisted behind the silver casket, her lips swollen and purple with the tip of her tongue protruding, the blood-matted curls, the staring eyes like two round vacant holes. And with it all, the surrealistic shimmering of the raspberry lamé. Yes, indeed, fresh air and a bit of exercise were just what the doctor ordered.

"We do have time for a stroll before our next event?" Eileen asked in that Irish half question, half statement way of hers. She rummaged through her pocket and pulled out a sheet of paper. "Let's see," she scanned it. " 'October 9. Saturday afternoon: Free time to explore the city.' We are not expected to meet again until supper at nine. Perfect!"

Eagerly Eileen pushed back her chair. "How about a quick walk down one of those quaint streets surrounding the cathedral?"

It's a quick *talk,* you want, old girl, Mary Helen thought, pushing back her own chair. And so do I. So much had gone on this morning, and they hadn't had a minute alone. She was quite surprised, therefore, when Eileen turned toward Heidi and asked, "Would you care to join us, dear?"

Heidi's hazel eyes filled with tears. Mary Helen held her breath. She didn't know if her nerves were up to another deluge. Not that Heidi could help it. She was in shock, the same shock that had all their nerves on edge. A change of scene, fresh air, and a little exercise would do them all good.

"We would be very happy for your company," Eileen coaxed.

To Mary Helen's amazement, Heidi gave in immediately and ran off to change from her high heels to her tennis shoes.

"Before the girl gets back down, Mary Helen, tell me what you thought of those flare-ups before lunch," Eileen spoke quickly. "I'm dead to know."

"If you are so dead to know, why did you ask Heidi to come along with us? You know she'll be right back. And if we don't want her hysterics again, I think we'd be wise to change the subject."

"Not at all." Eileen pursed her lips. "Getting it out of her system might be the best thing for her."

"Spare us, O Lord." Mary Helen rolled her eyes toward the ornate ceiling.

Ignoring her, Eileen continued. "That is why I made the decision to ask Heidi to join us."

"So that she could get it out of her system?" Mary Helen narrowed her eyes. "Who do you think you are kidding?"

Eileen shot Mary Helen her "I will not deign to dignify that with an answer" look and hurried on. "I realize that if we were alone, we could pool information, talk freely. And since Heidi is with us, that will have to wait. But it did occur to me that if we asked Heidi to join us, we might be able to find out something about whom Lisa was with yesterday afternoon. Also, where the girls went last night and with whom, when Lisa left the room . . . You know, old dear, 'pump her,' as they say."

"Who says that?"

Eileen's bushy eyebrows shot up. "All those detectives in the books say that. If anyone should know, you should."

"Eileen, you never cease to amaze me." Mary Helen feigned more amazement than she actually felt. "You, of all people, should know enough to keep out of police business. Kate Murphy is always telling me that. And if my memory serves me correctly, you are always agreeing with her."

"And neither of us is fool enough to think for a pig's wink that you are going to do it. So we might just as well get started while the trail is fresh."

Mary Helen studied her friend fondly and realized, once again, what it was that had kept them pals for over fifty years.

◆

Ángel Serrano dawdled over his last swallow of wine. Across the dinner table his wife, Julietta, eyes closed, leaned back in her chair. With her plump hands folded on her stomach and her eyes shut like that, it was difficult for him to tell whether or not she was asleep.

Soon he must go back to work. Before he did, he wanted to tell her about the murder. At least about María José's involvement in it before someone else did. Or before Pilar arrived at their front door with a full head of steam.

Long ago, when their sons were babies, they had made it a rule never to talk about his work at the dinner table. Even now with the boys grown and gone, Julietta kept the rule. Actually, if Ángel remembered correctly, it was she who had made the rule in the first place.

Surely by now she must have heard about the dead body in the cathedral. Everyone in town must be buzzing about it. He wondered if Julietta was awake. He knew exactly what she'd say if he asked her. "Don't be silly, Ángel. I never take a siesta. I am just resting my eyes."

He studied the familiar face. Where once it had been sharp and firm, it was now soft and full with tiny laugh lines like cobwebs around her eyes and at the corners of her mouth.

Her hair was still black, thanks to Ricardo, the hairdresser, but mid-life had filled out all those delectable curves that had haunted him in his youth and sent him running back home from Oxford to win her. Gad, how he desired her still!

"What is it, Ángel?" She must have felt him staring.

"You don't want to know." He rose from the table.

Her smile brought all her soft wrinkles to play. "I'll bring our coffee into the parlor," she said, standing up, too, "so we can talk."

In the front parlor they sat side by side on the worn brocade sofa, sipping *café con leche* while Ángel told her about

Pepe Nunez's tour, the discovery of a dead American tourist, and María José's involvement.

Julietta clucked sympathetically.

"So be prepared for Pilar," he said, setting his empty cup on the coffee table.

"Too late." Julietta shrugged. "She already called on the telephone."

Ángel groaned. "What did she say?"

"Nothing much. She is very distressed about Ho-Ho's being in danger. She wants you to forbid the girl to continue on the tour. She called Pepe Nunez a scoundrel and poor Señor Zaldo, who summoned María José, a fascist."

"What did you say?"

Julietta shook her head. "Nothing."

"Nothing? How did you manage to get away with saying nothing to Pilar?"

"I simply pretended, God forgive me, that we had a very bad connection."

Ángel Serrano glanced up at the clock on the mantel. Three-thirty. That would make it seven-thirty in the morning, San Francisco time. A little early, but he'd take a chance.

"Before I go back to work, I want to place one phone call," he told Julietta, then riffled through his jacket pocket, searching for the scrap of paper Zaldo had given him with the number the nuns had called.

"Why don't you get yourself a notebook to jot down these things?" she asked him for the millionth time. Without waiting for his answer, Julietta gathered up the cups, blew him a kiss, and left him alone.

Ángel placed the number with the long-distance operator. While he waited for his connection, he heard the faint rattle of china. Julietta was clearing the dining-room table.

He wondered whom he would reach. Because nuns had made the call, Ángel expected that the number would be a convent. Possibly they called the mother superior to see what they should do. Perhaps nuns had rules to govern such things.

Therefore, Ángel was taken aback when the groggy voice of a man barked, "Hello?"

◆

The harsh rasp of the telephone jolted Kate Murphy awake. Jack groped for it, then flipped on the bedside lamp. After a moment's listening he held out the receiver. "For you, again," he said, closing his eyes.

"Who is it?" Kate struggled up on her elbows.

Jack shrugged. "Comisario somebody or other."

Across the hall Baby John began to whimper. The phone had awakened them all. Yawning, Jack threw back the covers and reached for his robe. "I'll change the baby and give him some juice," he said. "Maybe he can go back to sleep for a while. Maybe we all can." He frowned at the phone.

"I know you received a midnight call, so I am most apologetic for calling you again so early and disturbing your rest," a male voice began. Kate tried to place the accent. Hispanic, surely, yet there was a touch of British.

"I am Comisario Ángel Serrano of the Santiago Brigada Judicial. As I explained to the gentleman who answered your telephone, I am calling about Sister Mary Helen. Somehow I imagined that I would reach a convent."

"With that one you never know what you'll reach," she said.

"And why is that?" the *comisario* asked.

Kate toyed with the idea of telling him that Sister Mary Helen was an internationally wanted criminal and that he should lock her up along with her equally wanted sidekick, Sister Eileen, but thought better of it. Although the *comisario* sounded pleasant enough, she knew from past experience that to deal with the two nuns, he'd need all the good humor he could muster. Better not waste any on her jokes.

"Just kidding," she said. The long-distance wires clicked rhythmically while she explained as succinctly as possible that she was a member of the San Francisco Police Department's Homicide Detail on pregnancy leave and about her past dealings with Sisters Mary Helen and Eileen.

"Ah, I see" was Ángel's only comment when she finished.

Kate sympathized with the poor man. It was a great deal to absorb.

"When Sister called me, I advised her to cooperate with the local police, of course, but to stay out of it." Whether he knew it or not, she figured the *comisario* would end up appreciating that bit of counsel.

"We have quite a puzzle here," he said quietly.

Kate felt an unexpected rush of adrenaline. "After I talked with Sister, one thing did bother me."

"Oh?"

"The motive. Why would anyone kill that young girl? These people, the tour group, I mean, were together only a few days. Surely no one develops a murderous urge that quickly. Do you suppose it was a random killing, Comisario? By a mugger or some such person?"

The *comisario*'s "no" echoed across the wire.

"Then there must be some previous connection between the young girl . . ."

"Lisa Springer." Ángel supplied the name.

"Between Lisa Springer and someone who is on that tour." Kate twisted a piece of her hair around her finger and pushed it into a curl. "What we need to do is to begin with a background check. Don't you think?" she added, astonished at how easily she had fallen into the familiar role.

Ángel readily agreed.

Kate swung her feet out of bed and fumbled for the note-pad on the bedstand. Carefully she copied down the names and addresses that Ángel dictated.

"What about your leave of absence?" he asked when they finished. "Will this be too difficult to do?"

"No problem at all," Kate said with assurance. "Just as soon as it seems civilized, I'll put a call in to my partner. I know that he'll be happy to help, although, you understand, not officially."

With perverse pleasure she visualized Inspector Dennis Gallagher fuming, swearing, berating her, and invoking saints to preserve him from nuns in general and Mary Helen in particular. She knew that finally, after thanking the Almighty for his coming retirement, Gallagher would get down to business and help her.

Contrary as it seemed, Kate missed the old bear and his ranting. Although Denny was the baby's godfather and they saw him often, it was somehow not the same as when they worked together.

"I'll get back to you as soon as possible," Kate said.

After a grateful Comisario Ángel Serrano had given her both his office and home phone numbers, the line went dead.

"You miss it, don't you?" Kate had not heard Jack reenter their bedroom. Tousled and tired-looking, he nearly filled the doorway. The baby slept peacefully in the crook of his tanned arm.

With a pang Kate watched her husband crawl back into his side of the bed and gently settle Baby John between them.

"Let's start this parenting business right, hon," Jack whispered. "Rule number one: Everybody sleeps late on Daddy's day off."

Kate felt warmth from the baby's small body. With one finger, she touched his blond curls, moist and tangled with sleep, then studied his chubby, outstretched hand. His thin eyelids were almost blue.

"I guess I do miss the detail," she said softly across their sleeping child, "but not as much as I'm going to miss him." She felt inexplicably teary. "I wish I could have both."

"I know, hon." Jack punched his pillow until he made it into a comfortable ball.

"What are we going to do?" Kate asked, annoyed that clearly he was going back to sleep.

"Maybe I can invent a bulletproof knapsack and you can take him to work with you like a papoose."

"I'm serious."

"Me, too, hon. We can call you Mama Sleuth and Not-a-Clue. SFPD's wonder team."

"Very funny. But really, pal, I am dreading the day we have to leave him. And it's coming soon, too soon. Who will we find? Your mother says that she'd love it"—she tried to keep her tone objective—"but that's not fair to anyone, do you think, Jack?"

His muffled snore told her that their conversation had just become a soliloquy. From the small crack between the edge of the shade and the window frame, faint streaks of sun stole into the dim bedroom. Kate closed her eyes, listening to the soft sounds of breathing, savoring its peace, wanting the night to last.

Yet strangely she also wanted it to be midmorning. She yearned to be up and moving and full of purpose. With the baby balanced on her hip, she'd put in a call to Inspector Dennis Gallagher, and the two of them would have the pleasure of hearing the godfather roar.

◆

"Let's wait for Heidi outside," Mary Helen suggested, eager to examine the Plaza del Obradoiro in broad daylight. The figure, or whatever she thought she'd seen last night on the cathedral steps, was preying on her mind. Surely it was only a shadow formed by a gargoyle or the stone edge of a building jagged in the moonlight. The plaza had been too silent, the form too motionless to be anything else.

As the doorman pushed open the heavy glass doors of the *hostal*, a strong wind caught it and nearly tore it from his hand. Small eddies skimmed along the flagstone entrance, throwing up dust and tiny stones. Squinting, Mary Helen looked up at the cathedral towers, which rose like flames into the darkened sky, where black, ragged clouds were being hurled about.

This is not the time to look for a single shadow, Mary Helen thought, watching shadows of all sizes and shapes roll across the huge plaza. To her amazement, it was nearly deserted.

"Where is everybody?" she asked before thinking.

"Siesta time, señora," the doorman answered, still holding tightly to the glass door.

"Do we need Therese's umbrellas?" Eileen asked, pointing up at the sky.

"In Galicia rain is an art," the doorman said, not answering her question at all. "In Galicia the rain caresses you." With a courteous nod he pulled the door shut.

"Caresses you?" Eileen wondered aloud. "What in heaven's name does that mean?"

"It's probably a polite way of telling you that you're going to get soaked to the skin," Mary Helen said, and left Eileen to fetch the umbrellas.

Padding down the hallway, she passed Heidi's bedroom. The door was ajar. "Are you nearly ready?" Mary Helen called in. No answer.

"Heidi?" Feeling uneasy, she pushed open the door a crack more. "I've come back for our umbrellas. I think you'll

need something, too, for the rain. . . ." Mary Helen let her
voice trail off.

Red-eyed and immobile, Heidi stood in the middle of
the bedroom. Belongings were strewn everywhere almost as if
Heidi had attempted to collect and pack them yet had not
had the heart for it.

"What is it, dear?" Mary Helen put her arm around
Heidi's shoulder. The girl was trembling.

"What am I going to do with all her stuff?" Heidi asked
in a thick voice. "I can't just leave it here. Somebody has to
take it home." She shut her eyes. "I can't touch it. Every time
I touch it, I think of her dead and everything, and I . . ."
She bolted for the bathroom, leaving no doubt in Mary
Helen's mind about what the girl did whenever she touched
Lisa's things.

Sister Mary Helen sympathized. She wouldn't relish
packing Lisa's belongings herself, yet someone had to do it.
Maybe she'd talk to the *comisario* about moving Heidi to another room and sending in a policewoman to pack.

She heard the toilet flush, the tap running, and water
splashing. Heidi must be pulling herself together. The wisest
course was to get her out of here. Mary Helen snatched up a
half-slip from the floor, rescued a pair of panty hose from the
end of one bed, then grabbed a brush full of amber hair from
the dressing table, and pulled open the drawer in the armoire.

Shove everything in, she thought, sweeping a green
headband from the chair. The more out of sight, the better.
The drawer was empty save for a tattered snapshot.

Odd, Mary Helen thought picking it up. There were two
girls in the picture posing in front of an ice-cream store. One
was obviously Heidi, a much younger Heidi, probably about
fourteen or fifteen with her butterscotch hair in a ponytail
and that same silly grin. The other girl in the picture was a
chunky redhead of about the same age with a double chin,

bright eyes, and a small potbelly. The youngsters had linked
arms and were mugging for the camera. Something about the
redhead's crooked smile was familiar.

"Sorry, Sister." Heidi's voice startled her.

Mary Helen looked up. Heidi, pale and swollen-eyed,
leaned against the bathroom doorjamb. "Are you feeling better?" Mary Helen asked.

Heidi nodded. "I'm sorry to keep you waiting, but every
time I touch—"

"Then don't touch anything," Mary Helen said. "In fact,
don't even look. Just put on your walking shoes and get something for the rain. Let's go!"

Obediently Heidi moved around the bedroom like a
robot.

"I was about to call out the militia," Eileen announced
when they finally joined her in the lobby. Heidi's color was
coming back, but Eileen didn't miss the red eyes. "Are you
feeling all right, dear?" she asked.

"She's feeling much better," Mary Helen answered, anxious to get Heidi into the fresh air.

Wordlessly, the trio skirted the plaza and rounded the
corner onto the Calle de San Francisco. The street was narrow with the College of Medicine on one side and, on the
other, a hodgepodge of small shops and cafés still closed for
the midday break.

Oblivious of the wind and the impending rain, they
walked toward the Convent of Saint Francis, where a carved
monument commemorating the life and works of the famous
saint of Assisi loomed large in the church plaza.

Their silence was becoming strained, at least for Sister
Mary Helen. There were so many questions she wanted to ask
Heidi. Whom had Lisa left the bedroom with on Friday afternoon? What had they done last night? When had Lisa left the
room and why? Last and probably least important, why had

Heidi brought an old snapshot with her on the trip? Mary Helen searched for a question or a remark to break the unnatural quiet. Before she could think of one, Eileen came to the rescue.

"Well, look at that!" Eileen exclaimed, pointing into a shopwindow crowded with souvenirs. A garish replica of the cathedral made into a barometer was dead center.

A little inane but a start!

Heidi stared at the trinket with little enthusiasm. The tiny barometer, set where the cathedral door should be, forecast rain. "And it works," Eileen said brightly.

Heidi gave a wan smile and studied an array of postcards on a wire stand just inside the shop's closed door. "I promised my cousin Doreen I'd write," she said, nodding toward the display. "Maybe I should buy one."

"The shop opens again at sixteen hundred." Eileen indicated the hours posted on the door.

Mary Helen watched Heidi count the time on her fingers. "Four o'clock," she said triumphantly.

"Is that Doreen's picture I noticed in your room?" Mary Helen asked, not wanting to let slip a perfect opening.

Heidi frowned. "What picture?"

She was either genuinely puzzled or the best actress Mary Helen had seen in a long time.

"In the drawer of the armoire. I just happened to notice a snapshot," she hurried on, hoping not to sound as if she had been intentionally snooping. "I picked up some of Lisa's things while you were in the bathroom."

"That picture!" Heidi's hazel eyes lit up in a rush of understanding. "That's not mine. That's Lisa's."

It was Mary Helen's turn to be puzzled.

"Lisa always carries that picture with her. It was taken years ago when we were still best friends," Heidi explained. "When Lisa was at her ugliest, at least that's what she says—

said." Heidi's face blanched as she corrected herself. "Before she got thin and glamorous. The only thing she didn't change was her crooked tooth. She would have, but her mom couldn't afford it.

"She said it reminded her of what she was like and what she never wanted to be again." Heidi gave a hollow little laugh. "She kinda liked to rub it in, you know?"

Mary Helen was afraid that she did know. At least she could well imagine Lisa's being quite impervious to other people's feelings. During their short acquaintance Lisa had appeared shallow and callous, flirting as she had with the men in the group and leaving Heidi alone on the first afternoon.

"By the time we walk down to the Convent of St. Francis, look around and walk back, all these shops will surely be open," Mary Helen said. Her mind rattled around for a way to introduce the topic of Lisa's whereabouts on the afternoon in question. She need not have bothered.

"Speaking of Lisa, God rest her," Eileen began in a nononsense tone of voice, "whom did you say she left the room with yesterday afternoon?"

Heidi blinked repeatedly. Either she's having difficulty remembering or she has something in her eye, Mary Helen thought impatiently.

"When I was in the shower, you mean?"

Eileen nodded.

"Why do you want to know?"

Great, Mary Helen thought, watching Heidi's mouth form a pout. Fine time for her to turn into a prima donna.

"We want to know"—Mary Helen was glad Eileen included her—"so that we can get a handle on Lisa's movements prior to her death."

Astonished, Sister Mary Helen stared at Eileen. Good night, nurse! What is she reading? She sounds like something right out of a police procedural.

Heidi's eyes lit up again. "Like real detectives," she said obviously thrilled with the concept.

Eileen, avoiding Mary Helen's eyes, gave a businesslike nod. "Just like them," she said in the thickest brogue Mary Helen had heard in a long while.

"It was Neil Fong," Heidi blurted out.

I should have bet money, Mary Helen thought. It made perfect sense. Dr. Fong came to the nuns' bedroom door by mistake with his silly Polaroid snapshot, then went in search of Lisa. When he did find her, they went for a walk, perhaps, stopped for a cup of coffee or a glass of wine, which was, of course, why Rita Fong was cold and distant toward him at dinner.

As the trio neared the end of the street and the imposing monument of St. Francis, a group of Japanese tourists swarmed over the plaza in front of the convent. At some silent signal, they clustered around a small woman holding up a red flag.

"About the year 1214 St. Francis of Assisi came to Compostela on a pilgrimage and was inspired to build a convent here for his friars." The red flag lady began first in flawless English, then switched into Japanese.

This is going to be a lengthy tour, Mary Helen thought, searching the area for a quiet spot, someplace to sit and talk. With a scrape and a creak, the wooden doors of La Perla Café unfolded. Perfect!

"How about something hot to drink?" she suggested.

The proprietor stood in the open entrance, scanning the sky. Mary Helen followed his gaze. Rain clouds piled up into an ominous mound. Any moment now it would pour. She hurried the other two toward a small round table.

"Ah, señoras." The proprietor greeted them warmly and called over their order to a countergirl. *"Tapas?"* he inquired hospitably.

Heidi looked blank. Eileen leafed through her pocket dictionary while the man waited patiently. Finally she shrugged and said, "Why not?"

"I hope we don't discover 'why not?,' " Mary Helen said, watching the proprietor hurry away to help the countergirl.

Within moments, he reappeared with three steaming cups of *café con leche*, as well as a plate full of thick, cold squares of Spanish omelet topped with asparagus and tomato slices.

"Where was your faith?" Eileen asked, smiling at the man and scooping up a square.

When he left, Sister Mary Helen hunched forward. "If we plan to be detectives, we are going to have to act like detectives," she pronounced in her firmest voice.

"How do you mean?"

Was Heidi frightened? Mary Helen softened her tone. "I mean that we must not let any detail slip by us. Everything you remember is important, Heidi. In fact, your memories are essential."

Heidi's bottom lip began to quiver.

Eileen shot Mary Helen a warning glance. "What Sister means"—she patted Heidi's chubby hand—"is that we'll help you try to remember as many details as possible. You just relax and do the best that you can. We will start by asking you some questions."

"I'll try." Heidi's voice was tentative.

The gentle ripple of rain against the café windows provided a soothing background for their whispered conversation.

"Did Lisa say anything when she returned yesterday afternoon?" Mary Helen began.

Heidi looked blank.

"From her walk with Dr. Fong?" Eileen prodded.

Heidi brightened. "Only that he was a drag. She did say

that she was sorry she left me alone. I was really mad when she got back to the room, and I told her so, too. It was my trip, you know."

Mary Helen did know. Heidi had mentioned it several times.

"I guess I was screaming because she told me to be quiet." A dark cloud of anger passed across Heidi's plain face. "But I wouldn't be quiet. I'm real sick of Lisa telling me stuff like she knows everything. You know what I mean?"

Mary Helen nodded, studying Heidi. "Carries anger as the flint bears fire." Strangely Shakespeare's words jumped into her mind.

"Anyhow, when I finally got so mad I stopped screaming and started to cry, Lisa said that she was sorry."

"What else did Lisa say?"

"Nothing. We just hugged and made up, like we always do."

Mary Helen figured as much. Obviously Lisa had had Heidi down to a system, although she doubted that Lisa had realized how deep and genuine her friend's anger really was. The pattern was probably set while they were still toddlers and continued until . . . It was difficult to think of Lisa as dead. It was harder still, dead or not, to think well of her.

"At dinner it certainly seemed as if you two had buried the hatchet," Eileen said cheerfully.

Mary Helen grimaced. Not into each other, I hope. She tried to shake the image of Lisa's open skull, blood snaking across the raspberry lamé.

"Tell us about last night, Heidi, everything that you can remember." Eileen encouraged the young woman, loath to drop her line of questioning.

Much to Mary Helen's chagrin, Heidi did just that. She regaled the nuns with everything that happened during the entire evening. She chronicled every morsel they ate, every drink they drank, and every witty thing, however insignificant, that Pepe said.

When Heidi finished, Sister Mary Helen knew few more pertinent facts than when the girl had begun: The Bowmans were the first to leave the public room. The Fongs left next, with Rita very angry. That was probably the loud arguing in the hallway. Before long the DeAngelos followed. Pepe and María José had quarreled, with Pepe returning to dance the evening away. She had not known about the midnight walk around the university, although she suspected that Pepe and the two girls were the three o'clock gigglers.

"Then there was the note under the door," Heidi added as an afterthought.

Eileen and Mary Helen bolted upright in their chairs. "What note?" they asked in unison.

Heidi frowned. "Only an old note for Lisa. Someone shoved it under our door."

"Who was it from?"

"I don't know." Heidi's slit-eyed glance was almost cunning. "She told me it was from an 'admirer,' but I don't think it was."

"Why not?"

" 'Cause she wouldn't let me see it and she acted kinda mad when she read it."

"Mad?" Pumping Heidi was becoming as tedious as playing pickup sticks.

Heidi shrugged. "Yeah, kinda. She tore it up in little pieces and flushed it!"

"Did Lisa say anything about meeting someone early this morning?"

Heidi shook her head.

Dead end! Mary Helen felt deflated. No name. No note. No nothing! Surely the note was from the murderer. He or she had planned a rendezvous with Lisa, a rendezvous that angered Lisa. Then why had she gone?

"You slept soundly the rest of the night?" With one of those half questions of hers, Eileen picked up the trail.

"Yeah."

"You heard and saw nothing else?"

"Not until Pepe knocked on my door this morning. Lisa's stuff was all over the place, and her bed was empty. I was half asleep myself when Pepe told me that she was . . ." Heidi's eyes began to fill.

This was exactly what Mary Helen was hoping to avoid. "Let's not forget your postcard for your cousin." She grasped at a straw.

With much counting of pesetas, they settled their bill, and Mary Helen jotted down the amount in her travel diary to study later. She was curious to know just how much they had spent on *tapas* and coffee. With so many zeroes, it was difficult to tell.

Outside, the rain had stopped as suddenly as it had begun, leaving the buildings and streets with a silver glistening. The impressive Convent of St. Francis forgotten, they began the walk back to the *hostal*, window-shopping as they went.

Sister Mary Helen scarcely saw the trinkets on display. Her mind whirled and spun, plucking at the details of their trip. Three short days ago Eileen and she were in San Francisco, their fellow *peregrinos* unknown. And less than a month ago, Santiago de Compostela and its Holy Year the farthest thing from their minds. And now?

She replayed all that Heidi had related. Surely the answer was there if she just knew where to look. And there was something else, another question she'd wanted to ask, but it hung at the edge of her mind just beyond her reach.

With a fistful of postcards, Heidi emerged from a small curio shop, Eileen right behind her. Mercifully she held only a single card. She must have noticed the expression on Mary Helen's face.

"We had better send the nuns one at least," she said defensively.

"We'll get home before it does," Mary Helen answered.

"Thank God for small favors." Eileen slipped the postcard into her purse.

By the time they reached their bedroom, Mary Helen was exhausted. The time change, her lack of sleep, and today's tensions were catching up with her. After kicking off her shoes, she spread out on the high, canopied bed, feeling like a beached whale.

At the desk Eileen chewed the end of her pen and stared down at the postcard. "What can we say that isn't a lie if they find out what happened and we didn't tell them, yet doesn't tell them what happened if they never find out?"

It took Mary Helen's tired brain a few moments to untangle the syntax. "Oh, what a tangled web we weave,/When first we practice to deceive!" she said with her eyes closed.

"I know what." Eileen ignored the allusion. "I will just say, 'We are having a very interesting time,' and I'll underline *very*."

Mary Helen's eyes smarted. The room was quiet now that Eileen had written the postcard and climbed atop her own bed for a short rest. Mary Helen heard her steady, rhythmic breathing. The velvet window drapes billowed out in the breeze. Everything was so still. Mary Helen's eyelids grew heavy, pulling her toward sleep.

With a start she remembered the question that had been eluding her. She tiptoed to the telephone and dialed Heidi's room.

"Hello." An eager Heidi picked it up on the first ring.

Ah, youth, Mary Helen thought sleepily. "Heidi, I was just wondering. On the plane, after the turbulence, when we all were going off to sleep, I remember hearing Lisa go toward the back of the plane. I think someone went with her. Do you have any idea who?"

"Why do you want to know?" Heidi asked. She sounded almost belligerent.

"As we discussed before, it's just the detective thing." Mary Helen's patience was strained.

After a momentary pause Heidi spoke. "The teacher. You know, Roger. He went back after her."

"Are you sure?"

"Sure, I'm sure. I sat behind him and his wife. I saw him go, and I saw his wife get up and look where he went. She was mad," Heidi added with malicious pleasure.

Odd duck, this young Heidi, Mary Helen thought, replacing the receiver. She tiptoed back to her bed, pulled the comforter up over her feet, and closed her eyes. Actually both young women were odd ducks, she thought. The professor, the doctor, Pepe, even Bud Bowman—Lisa had gone after them all. Did she have a need to vanquish men? And if so, why?

And butterscotch Heidi—very young for her age, an innocent, really, with a streak of what? Meanness? That seems too strong. Orneriness? Something like that. She doesn't miss a trick either. She knows exactly where Lisa was and who was with her. Actually Heidi makes an excellent detective. Unless, of course—Mary Helen caught her breath—unless she is the villainess.

Nonsense. She jockeyed into a more comfortable position on the high bed. The girl simply has an uncluttered mind. Fuzzy with drowsiness, Mary Helen tried to unclutter her own mind. A little snooze before dinner would do her a world of good.

"Mordre wol out, certein, it wol nat faille." Unexpectedly those long-forgotten words and their source came to her.

The Canterbury Tales, "The Prioress's Tale." The human mind is a gift of Memory, the mother of Muses, and its power has no bounds, Mary Helen thought, muddling the ancient philosophers. And it was the last thought she did have as she mercifully fell into a deep sleep.

♦

"I guess nobody's home at Gallagher's." Kate Murphy held out the telephone receiver so that her husband could hear its hollow ringing. Immediately interested, the baby stopped banging his plastic keys on the high chair tray, turned his head, and listened, too.

"Too nice a day for anyone to stay home." Jack poured what remained of his morning coffee down the kitchen sink. "You know, hon, we should go somewhere—Golden Gate Park, the Marina, out to the beach. Even out in our own backyard. Right, buddy?" He picked up little John, who gurgled in agreement.

Jack carried him over to the kitchen window, and together they looked down on the overgrown tangle of flowers and weeds, the remains of a once-well-tended garden.

"On second thought," he said, "maybe we should skip the backyard."

Kate winced. She had promised herself that she'd do something about that garden during her maternity leave, but somehow she never quite managed.

Just as she was about to hang up, she heard someone knock Gallagher's receiver off the hook, then fumble for it with butter fingers.

"Hello." Dennis Gallagher's voice was groggy.

"Are you still in bed, Denny?" Kate asked, glancing up at the kitchen clock.

"Where the hell else would I be at this hour of the morning on my day off?"

"Sorry." She hoped she sounded contrite. "You're not sick, are you?"

"No, I'm not sick. I'm just dead. And what the hell is so all-fired important that it can't wait for a decent hour?"

"I wouldn't call ten o'clock exactly indecent." Kate tried to sound reasonable, but Gallagher cut her off.

"What the hell do you want, Murphy? And it better be good!"

This was not going at all well. Kate wanted a favor, and this was not the way to get it. She tried the humble approach. "Sorry I woke you, Denny. Why don't you go back to sleep and I'll call you again in an hour or two?"

"Too late now," he said, then sighed dramatically. "What is it you wanted anyhow? Everybody's all right, aren't they?"

Kate caught the note of concern in his voice. Good, he was softening up.

"Yes, thanks. Everyone here is fine, but you'll never guess who I've heard from."

"Jeez, Kate, first you wake me up out of a sound sleep. Now you want to play guessing games? Damn it, who called? This better be good."

"A couple of hours ago, actually at the crack of dawn"— she dropped that tidbit hoping he'd feel fortunate—"I received a call from a Comisario Ángel Serrano. He's with the police in Santiago de Compostela in Spain."

Gallagher was quiet. Good. She'd hooked his interest. "An American tourist, a member of a group originating here in the city, was murdered in his jurisdiction. Serrano is pretty convinced that another member of the tour is the perp, and he needs some background information on these other members. You know, the usual stuff." Without a twinge of guilt, Kate skipped the fact that she had volunteered to get Serrano the information.

"A police commissioner from Spain called you at home? Why the hell would a police commissioner call you and not another police commissioner, may I ask?"

"It's somewhat of a long story."

"I've plenty of time," Gallagher said, his tone dangerous.

Kate cleared her throat. "Actually I received two calls from Spain. The commissioner called early this morning, and around midnight last night I received another call from—you'll never guess who. Our old friend Sister—" That was as far as she got.

"Sister Mary Helen," Gallagher roared. Kate held the receiver away from her ear. "What in the hell is that old busybody nun doing mixed up with murder, again? See what I mean, Murphy? It never fails. I swear, she's getting to be a regular goddamn Sister Mary Typhoid Helen."

"She didn't commit the murder," Kate said, but Gallagher was off and running.

"Honest to God, Kate, I hope this time they lock her up and throw away the key. She—neither one of them, and I assume that her sidekick Sister Eileen is with her, has any business at all going out of the country in the first place. Jeez." He exhaled a long, sad sigh. "We're all going to hell in a handbag. You know as well as I do that nuns should be home in the convents, praying their beads, and minding their own goddamn business."

"What in the world bit you?" Kate heard Mrs. G's voice ask from the background.

"It's those goddamn old nuns again."

"Dennis Gallagher, I hope you're not talking to Sister like that. If you are, give me that phone this instant. And if you aren't, stop it anyway. What kind of example is that for the children?"

"The children? What children? The children don't live here anymore, thank God, unless you just brought one of them home with you from the grocery store. And if it's up to me, I say let's keep it that way."

"You old coot, you don't mean one word you're saying."

"I mean every goddamn syllable of it. Every time our kids and their kids come near here, they eat us out of house and home. Don't they have houses of their own? It seems to me we're always helping one or the other of them to get their own place. Why can't they stay in it?"

Gallagher had switched to another of his pet peeves, and Kate decided she had caused enough damage for one Saturday morning. "Denny," she shouted into the fracas, "shall I call you back with the list of names that the commissioner wants you to check?"

"No," he grumbled. "I'm wide-awake now. Might just as well let me write 'em down. But remember I'm off this weekend, so I can't promise anything until Monday at the earliest. When's this tour scheduled to come home anyway?"

"A week from today, I think."

"With the time difference, this guy might have the thing worked out before I get him the info." Gallagher gave a loud yawn.

"That's true." Kate tried not to let her disappointment show in her voice. Actually she was surprised by it herself. She hadn't realized how much she wanted to get involved in this case.

"Jeez, if this Serrano guy can't figure it out in a week, he might put the whole goddamn bunch of them back on a plane."

"Then does it become our problem or the feds?" Kate wondered aloud.

Gallagher perked up. "Our problem? Do I take it you've decided to come back to work?"

"I haven't decided anything yet."

"Tell Kate I said hello," Mrs. G called from the background.

Saved! Kate thought and quickly began to pronounce and spell the names of each member on the tour. She threw in Jose Nunez, aka Pepe, and Señor Carlos Fraga, owner of the Patio Español, for good measure. Not wanting to give Gallagher more fuel for his tirade, she purposely omitted Sister Mary Helen and Sister Eileen, but he couldn't let it slide.

"And the nuns? Doesn't the poor unsuspecting slob want background on those two screwball friends of yours?"

"Friends of ours, Denny." Kate felt her own temper fizzing up. It felt good. It had been too long since she and Denny had had a real screaming fight. Maybe that was part of what she missed about her job. "Friends of *ours*! Let's not forget how helpful those two old screwballs have been," she shouted. "I don't know if we'd have done nearly as well solving those murders without them."

"I'd liked to have had the chance to try," Gallagher growled, but Kate knew it was more a matter of having the last word than of meaning it.

When she finally hung up, Kate walked over to the kitchen window and stood beside Jack and the baby.

"Ma, ma, ma." Little John pointed to a red-throated hummingbird treading air. "Ma," he screeched, watching it dart across the back porch and down toward the yard.

"Maybe the kid's going to be a naturalist." Jack put his free arm around Kate. "Just as soon as he gets you and the bird straight, hon, there's no telling where he'll go."

"Very funny." Kate watched the hummingbird stop, start, then dive into their small, narrow yard. And what a mess it was, she thought guiltily. The weeds shone green, and the square, seedy plot of grass was gray. Forlorn fuchsia plants drooped with red and purple dancing ladies, and dusty rhododendron and camellia bushes barely clung to life.

"Our yard is a disgrace," Kate muttered, putting her head on Jack's shoulder. "We're probably the talk of the entire neighborhood."

Immediately Baby John began a game of peekaboo, using his father's head as a shield.

"What should we do?" Kate bobbed out. "Boo!"

"About what?"

"About the backyard, pal. Boo!"

"Get a shade for this window?"

Baby John giggled. Jack looked pleased. "This guy's got a great sense of humor," he said, planting a noisy kiss on the baby's cheek.

After lunch Kate and Jack, at Kate's insistence, tackled the backyard. Kate decided to weed, while Jack mowed the lawn or what was left of it, trimmed the edges, and turned soil. He unearthed the remnant of a tiny oval fish pond, slimy with decaying stems of water lilies.

Little John crawled and scooted along behind Kate, babbling, investigating rocks and twigs and pointing with glee at the earthworms that crawled out of the broken dirt. Finally, worn out, he lay down on the cool cement walk and fell asleep.

Gently Kate moved him to a blanket under the shade of the overhanging porch. She felt like joining him.

"Want to quit?" Jack squatted down beside his wife.

"I'm pooped," Kate admitted. "How about you?" Her arms and legs were beginning to burn, and dirt was caked under her fingernails. Her stomach was queasy, probably from working in the heat.

"Tomorrow we're going to feel muscles we didn't even know we had," Jack said. "It's got to be five o'clock somewhere. How about a drink?" Taking Kate's hand, he helped her up, then gathered up the baby, blanket, blades of dried grass and all.

They had just settled down in the living room when the front doorbell rang—once, twice, three times before Jack reached the door. "Ma!" he said, doing an admirable job of sounding glad to see his mother. "What brings you?"

"What brings me?" Loretta Bassetti bustled into the entranceway, her soft, full cheeks flushed with the heat. "Jackie, go out to the car. I've been cooking all day long. It's in the backseat."

"Hi, Loretta," Kate called with as much enthusiasm as she could muster. "Come on in and sit down. We've been gardening."

"It's about time!" Loretta said without even looking at Kate. Instead she went directly to the playpen, where John still slept soundly. "Why isn't my precious grandson in a bed like other children?" she asked in a stage whisper. "Why is he sleeping in this cage full of stuff?"

"What did you bring us?" Kate asked, reminding herself that Loretta meant well.

"How about an old-fashioned?" Jack called from the kitchen.

"Homemade ravioli, a little salad, and garlic bread. Put the ravioli in the oven, Jackie. Keep it hot," she shouted, "and, yes, I'll take you up on that offer of a drink."

John stirred in the playpen. The piquant aroma of tomatoes and garlic and basil floated down the short hallway, and Kate realized how hungry she was.

Loretta accepted the old-fashioned but refused the invitation to join them for dinner.

"It's good for a little family to be together," she said and, with a *salute*, sipped her drink.

Kate bristled. "Little family" sounded so patronizing, as if they were munchkins playing house.

"We've had about as much togetherness today as any

little family can handle," Jack joked, and showed his mother a blister on the palm of his hand. "I mowed the lawn."

"What lawn? Last time I looked out your kitchen window, it looked like a hayfield. Maybe what you needed was a scythe."

"It wasn't that bad, Ma."

"Ha! My friend Mrs. Molinari, who lives around the corner, says your backyard is an eyesore for the whole neighborhood." She glared accusingly at her son.

"I told you so," Kate muttered.

"What else does Mrs. Molinari say?" Jack asked.

"She says that I've got the most beautiful baby grandchild in the whole world"—Mrs. Bassetti moved toward the playpen—"and that's why I'm still friends with the old buttinsky."

Baby John stirred in his crib, eyes fluttering open at last. His grandmother could resist no longer. "Come to your Nonie," she cooed.

To Kate's relief John recognized her immediately, smiled, and held out his arms to be picked up.

Mama Bassetti rocked the contented baby. "If Kate ever decides to go back to work—and I don't know why in the world she would, after all, what kind of son did I raise that can't take care of a wife and one child?—you cannot leave this precious baby with strangers. Can they, sweetie?"

Much to her delight, John answered, "Na, na, na."

"Sweet Mother of God." Mama Bassetti was wide-eyed. "Did you hear that, Kate, Jackie? My sweet boy is saying my name."

"Strike the naturalist," Jack mouthed to Kate. "Put in diplomat."

♦

Once again Kate was having trouble falling asleep. She heard the grandfather clock in the downstairs hallway strike eleven, eleven-thirty, midnight, and the quarter hours in between. Although her body was tired and heavy, a faint discomfort kept her from dozing off. Not that she was sick, exactly, but she wasn't just right either.

Kate rolled into a more comfortable position. Maybe she had eaten too many ravioli for dinner or maybe Mama Bassetti's crack about leaving the baby with strangers was making her uneasy. Although she refused to be baited by her mother-in-law, finding the right person to care for John was a big factor in her decision. So she really had not decided whether or not to go back to work. She didn't miss it, most of the time. Granted, if she was honest, she had felt exhilarated when Mary Helen called.

Sister Mary Helen. Kate wondered how the old nun and her murder investigation were doing. Maybe I should give her a ring, she thought, counting ahead on her fingers. About eight-thirty in the morning in Santiago. A new day had begun. Mary Helen was probably already up.

Too bad, Kate thought, then felt guilty. Was she really disappointed that she couldn't rouse an old woman in the middle of the night? Turn about is fair play, she reasoned, counting the hours again. If I called around dinnertime . . .

I really am sick. Kate gave the pillow a cranky punch. Some pagan philosopher whom she'd studied at Mount St. Francis College said that "Revenge is always the delight of a mean spirit. . . ."

Revenge isn't too Christian either, she thought, waiting for the grandfather clock to strike again, especially revenge on a nun. But in this exhausted, sleepless moment, it did sound very, very sweet.

SUNDAY, OCTOBER 10

TWENTY-SEVENTH SUNDAY IN ORDINARY TIME FEAST OF ST. FRANCIS BORGIA, CONFESSOR

♦

The sharp, insistent ring of the telephone pierced Mary Helen's dreamless sleep. As she pulled herself up from the blackness, she heard Eileen shuffle across the bedroom.

"Hello," Eileen called into the receiver. Rather cheerfully, Mary Helen thought, for the middle of the night.

After a few "yesses" and a noncommittal "no" or two, Eileen hung up.

"Who was on the horn?" Mary Helen asked, her voice hoarse.

"None other than our esteemed tour guide, Señor Pepe, with good news. At least, I think it's good," Eileen added tentatively, and sat on the edge of the canopied bed.

"Good or bad, couldn't it wait until morning?"

"It is morning, old girl. Eight-thirty, to be exact."

"You're fooling." Mary Helen rose on one elbow. The sudden motion brought on a wave of nausea and made her aware that her head ached with exhaustion. A heavy sadness hovered on the edge of her consciousness. It took her a moment to recall why she was so tired and sad. It took her a moment to remember that Lisa Springer was dead.

"What's his news?" she asked, hoping that the police had found Lisa's killer and that he was a demented maniac on a wild, unfathomable spree. Not that being killed by a maniac made Lisa any less dead or her murder any less tragic. It was just more palatable, somehow, more excusable than realizing that a perfectly normal-appearing person, one you'd had dinner with the night before, was a cold, calculating murderer. Despite the warmth of her bed, Mary Helen shivered.

"We had better be up and about." Eileen crossed the room. With a tug, she drew back the velvet window drapes. Dark clouds shifted across the leaden sky.

"Pepe said that there is Mass in a cathedral chapel at nine," she said, "and that at ten-thirty the *comisario* is allowing us to continue part of our tour."

"Which part?" Mary Helen asked.

" 'The visit to La Coruña' "—Eileen read from the trip brochure—" 'a lovely seaside city built on a narrow point jutting out into the Atlantic.' "

"Sounds cold," she said.

"Was that where we were supposed to go today?" Mary Helen asked.

"Not really," Eileen hedged. "Today we were scheduled for an in-depth tour of the cathedral, but as you know . . ." Her voice trailed off.

Mary Helen did know, and like an aftershock, the knowledge was more vivid and grim than she wanted to admit. Her memory conjured up Lisa with purple lips and a deep, thick welt across her throat, the thin streaks of blood slithering down the raspberry lamé.

Her stomach lurched, and for a long moment she was afraid she was going to be sick. She had found Lisa's body, and for some inexplicable reason she felt guilty about it.

"Are you feeling up to today, old dear?"

The unexpected sympathy in Eileen's voice made tears sting Mary Helen's eyes. Unable to speak, she simply nodded and padded toward the bathroom.

Oh, good! Mary Helen thought, hearing Eileen get on

the phone to the restaurant and order *café con leche*. A long, hot shower followed by a strong cup of coffee! The combination should bolster her courage. Relieved, she turned on the water and let the biting stream pour over her.

As uncontrollable tears splattered down her face and merged with the gushing water, she realized that today she was going to need all the bolstering that she could manage.

♦

"Tío, I insist!" María José pulled herself up to her full height and gave her head a determined toss that made her seem taller than her five feet. The fluorescent light in Ángel Serrano's office at the police station caught the magenta highlights in her dark hair. He stared at the strange color combination, silently wondering what it reminded him of. Doll hair! he thought triumphantly, motioning his niece to the chair on the other side of his desk.

"Sit down, Ho-Ho." He tried to sound soothing.

"Please, do not talk down to me, Tío." Folding her arms, she refused to sit.

Wearily Ángel stood and came around the desk. His eyes smarted with fatigue. "How am I talking down to you?" he asked.

"By calling me that ridiculous, childish nickname."

Ángel apologized. Loosening his tie, he ran his finger around his shirt collar. He must ask Julietta to do something about this starch. "María José," he began as patiently as his chafed neck allowed, "I cannot—repeat, cannot—send you on this American tour bus as an undercover officer."

"Is it because I am a woman, Tío?" Her chin protruded in a small, stubborn V.

"No, Ho—" He caught himself just in time. "No, María José. It has nothing to do with your being a woman."

"Then why?" she demanded.

Ángel shrugged. "It is because you are not a policeman."
María José bristled.

"Excuse me, police person. You are my niece."

"That's easy!" Her dark eyes danced. "You can deputize me!"

Ángel moaned aloud. "You are watching too much North American television," he said. "This is not the Wild, Wild West, nor is it Madrid or even Barcelona. This is Santiago de Compostela."

"Regardless, Tío," María José interrupted, "there must be some way we can handle this. Do you use undercover officers?"

"Undercover officers!" He exhaled loudly, hoping she'd realize that she was getting on his already stretched nerves. "I've been up all night, *hija*, searching the cathedral, soothing Canon Fernández, appeasing the mayor, talking to that insistent reporter from *La Voca de Galicia*." He stopped for breath and glared at his niece for effect. "I have not been home since dinner yesterday, and now you want me to think about an undercover officer?"

He did not tell her that he had already told Julietta that having given out assignments to his men, he was on his way home for breakfast and a few hours of sleep. Ángel knew that by the time he arrived she would have drawn him a hot bath and prepared his favorite soup, *caldo gallego*. His mouth watered at the thought of the thick, comforting soup full of potatoes and fresh spinach. He yearned for it and for round, pleasant Julietta.

"Tío?" María José interrupted his daydream.

His Julietta was the ideal wife. How, he wondered crossly, had his family spawned the little spitfire that stood defiantly before him? She had always been headstrong, but now she was getting out of hand. His sister, Pilar, was hopeless in controlling her. Once this tourist murder business was finished, he must talk to his brother-in-law.

"María José," Ángel began firmly, "as you know, we have very little crime in Santiago, therefore very little need for undercover officers. The officers I do have will be able to—"

"Who will be able to?" She cut him off. Her mercurial eyes blazed. "Esteban Zaldo? Ha!" She did a perfect imitation of the large, muscular policeman leering. "Will anyone let something slip in the front of such a sinister face? Don't you see, Tío?" Frustrated, María José collapsed into the chair she had refused. "I am the best one to do this. The Americans already know and trust me. Pepe and I have a relationship."

Ángel cringed at the word. "Relationship? What relationship?"

María José's face didn't even color, although she averted her eyes from his. "Friends, Tío. We are merely friends."

Her voice gave away nothing. Ángel scrutinized her face, hoping it was true. Surprisingly, María José's face was inscrutable. Good asset in police work, he thought in spite of himself.

Actually, as reluctant as he was to admit it, Ángel did think María José's plan had some merit. It was unorthodox, but so was murder in the cathedral's sacred crypt. Strange times call for strange measures.

"Are you afraid of what the mayor will say, Tío, if he finds out?" Again, María José intruded on his thoughts.

Ángel shook his head. The mayor was the last person he was afraid of.

"It's Mama then, isn't it?"

Ángel was astonished. His niece was right on the mark! He couldn't help laughing. "María José," he said, "our mayor's wrath pales before that of my sister, Pilar, were I to put you in danger."

"Then I'll talk to Mama myself!" She shot up from the

chair. "She'll understand, Tío. I know she will and she'll give her permission."

"No, no, no!" Ángel put up his hands as if to block a blow. Of course, Pilar would give permission. She indulged her only daughter shamefully. It was he who would get the phone call, the deluge of abuse.

"Are you afraid of your own baby sister?" María José asked in disbelief.

Ángel nodded. It was less humiliating than trying to explain to his niece that her mother drove him crazy, and his rank as *comisario* notwithstanding, when Pilar started her endless verbal barrages, Ángel visualized himself grabbing his sister by her skinny chicken neck and wringing it.

A mischievous grin played at the corners of María José's mouth. "If you don't want Mama to know, Tío, then let's not tell her."

For a long moment Ángel considered the pros and cons of Ho-Ho's plan. On the one hand, she was trusted by Pepe Nunez and the American tourists. She was eager, observant, and, if this morning was any test, downright persistent.

On the other hand, she wasn't a police officer. She could be in danger. He'd ask Zaldo to follow the tour bus at a discreet distance. His sister, of course, would never approve, but what she didn't know wouldn't hurt her.

His eyes burned from lack of sleep, and his muscles ached. Even if his niece didn't discover anything useful, she would be out of town and out of his hair for the rest of the day. Best of all, as soon as she left, he could get home to Julietta and his soup.

"Go, Ho-Ho," he said. "Look for slips, attitudes, random remarks, anything that might give me something to go on. When you come home tonight, give me a full report."

María José's dark eyes sparkled. "I will, Tío, and gracias!"

"And remember, *hija,* not one single word to your mama," he called to her fleeing back.

With a great yawn, Ángel Serrano turned off his office lights, but not before he had checked his calendar. He made a note of the exact date of his brother-in-law's return.

♦

A compact silver and red tour bus with "Pulmantur" printed in script down its side was parked outside the Hostal de los Reyes Católicos. Pepe Nunez stood beside its open door. His face was no longer ruddy, but the color of French vanilla ice cream, with blue circles, like bruises, under his eyes.

"*Buenos días,* Sisters!" He tried to give the nuns an enthusiastic smile, but somehow the enthusiasm fell just short of his eyes.

By contrast María José, his "special assistant," was bubbling. Her magenta-rinsed hair was drawn back and fastened at the nape of her neck with a bright red scarf that matched the red in her woolen herringbone sweater. The heavy sweater and the slim black woolen slacks the girl wore reminded Mary Helen that the day would most likely be cold and wet.

She turned to Eileen. "Should we bring our umbrellas?" she whispered.

"I brought them and our Aran sweaters." Eileen handed one of each to Mary Helen. "I don't mean to be acting like your caretaker, old dear, but you are walking around in an awful fog this morning."

Eileen was right. She was.

"Come aboard, Sisters," María José called from just beside the driver's seat. "We are about to begin our trip to La Coruña, one of Galicia's showplaces, where you will enjoy the view from its famed Tower of Hercules."

She sounds like a circus barker, Mary Helen thought,

pulling herself up the steep steps into the tour bus. At least the girl's trying to make things pleasant, and I should shake off this awful pall. It's perfectly silly.

She smiled at María José. It is not—repeat not—my fault that Lisa Springer was murdered, she chided herself. I simply found the body. I did not commit the crime. And it is ridiculous to imagine that anyone is blaming me.

With about as much confidence as the Christians must have felt when they met the lions, she threw back her shoulders and took a deep breath. "Good morning," she called cheerfully. Six pairs of hostile, accusing eyes met hers, and her greeting fell like a disturbed soufflé. Only butterscotch Heidi had the good grace to smile.

"Hi," Heidi said, her one-note greeting fading into a symphony of uncomfortable silence.

Mary Helen dived into the first empty seat and stared out the wide-view window onto the puddle-drenched Plaza del Obradoiro. Eileen followed quickly.

"I was right," Mary Helen whispered. "They are blaming me." She shivered. "Much more of this, and I'll know how the lepers felt."

Eileen let out an exaggerated sigh. "Now don't go getting paranoid on me. What in heaven's name makes you think they're blaming you?"

"For one thing, no one is speaking."

"You should be grateful! You do remember how they spoke to one another yesterday?" Eileen's gray eyebrows shot up like two question marks. "And what a strained, silent affair dinner was?"

Mary Helen did remember. It gave the expression *cold war* a new meaning.

Eileen patted Mary Helen's icy hand. "Let's just ignore them and enjoy ourselves. If any one of them is blaming you for anything, it's because that one is guilty and afraid you'll discover it," she announced with near-papal infallibility. "So buck up!"

Mary Helen stared at her friend in disbelief. "Why doesn't that make me feel better?" she asked in an as "bucked-up" a tone as she could manage.

The ride could not have been quieter if it had been taken by a busload of Trappists on retreat. Mary Helen stared out the window at the passing countryside full of fog-shrouded pines. Fresh yellow-green fern hugged the ground amid bright spots of red and pink carnations. As they sped along, Eileen's few attempts at chitchat fell as swiftly and surely as a SCUD missile.

"Will you look at that?" Twenty or so minutes into the trip Bud Bowman loosened up and pointed out the window at road workers in orange. "Just like the Cal-Trans workers back home," he said, and waited for a friendly comment.

When only Eileen's "Right you are, Bud," rose from the group, he shrugged and contined to stare out the broad window in silence.

All at once Mary Helen was angry. It was 67 kilometers to La Coruña, no sense making it feel like 567. Eileen was right. She'd enjoy this trip no matter what. Deliberately ignoring the hostility, she decided to concentrate on María José's commentary.

With superhuman effort, María José rose above the prevailing gloom and kept up a running monologue. She talked about the wide *autovía* with its special new tar surface that made rain disappear. She pointed to palm trees brought home as status symbols by sons gone to South America. She talked about La Coruña's "widows of the sea." Some husbands had drowned; some had sailed away to the Americas.

The two nuns oohed and aahed in all the right places. María José obviously took courage from their attention. When the bus stopped at the toll plaza, she joked about old highway bandits being replaced by new ones. This got a rise out of Bud.

Virtually unannounced, a gentle rain began to fall. Long wipers swished slowly, rhythmically across the front windows of the tour bus. Passing cars shot sprays of water against its sides. When the large windows were so fogged up that it was impossible to see out, María José gave up her spiel.

"My friends, it is time to play some Galician folk music," she announced, feeding a cassette tape into the recorder on the bus's loudspeaking system. She slipped into the seat next to Pepe Nunez.

The lively melody filled the bus with its energy. Bagpipes and tambourines combined to give it a Celtic flavor.

"You'd have to be dead not to tap your feet to this one," Eileen said. With a valiant try she managed to get some sporadic clapping going, but this, too, was doomed.

For lack of anything better to do, Mary Helen slipped her travel diary out of her pocketbook. On a blank page she wrote down the date and "Quiet trip to La Coruña." After a moment she added, "67 kilometers. Among the longest in my life."

After what seemed days, the tour bus pulled into the parking lot circling the Tower of Hercules. It took its place in the row of other tour buses.

María José rose. A morose-looking Pepe stood behind her. "This, my friends," she said, "is the famed Tower of Hercules." María José hopped down from the bus and waited until the whole group straggled out behind her.

The persistent rain continued, and they huddled under umbrellas. Pepe pulled the bus door closed with a final determined swoosh, as if to say, "Like it or not, we're seeing this tower."

The large, square granite lighthouse loomed above them,

high and lonely. The wind off the Atlantic caught in the umbrellas.

"We'll catch our death of cold out here," Bootsie complained, stamping her feet for warmth and, Mary Helen suspected, for effect. Her husband put his thin arm around her shoulder and drew her under his umbrella.

"This is a warm rain." María José put out her small hand to feel it. "You will not catch cold from Galician rain, and you will surely not melt." Her eyes, black as flint, dared anyone to disagree.

Damp and chilled though she was, Mary Helen had to admire the young woman's spunk. María José was determined to go through with this tour no matter what. Mary Helen couldn't help wondering why. After all, this was Pepe's group. He was the one who should be taking charge.

"Can't we at least move into the tower and get out of this rain? My wife is freezing." Professor DeAngelo turned his back on María José and spoke directly to Pepe. Obviously the professor thought that Pepe should take charge, too.

"Of course," Pepe said meekly, and whispered something in his assistant's ear.

With an angry toss of her head, María José led the way to a narrow wooden door painted glossy shamrock green. It was the entrance to the Tower of Hercules. A graying woman in a raincoat huddled on the granite threshold, offering souvenirs. She kept them dry in a white plastic bag.

When Mary Helen made the mistake of looking interested, the woman dug in her bag and pulled out a tawny replica of the tower made into a key chain. She dangled it within Mary Helen's reach.

"Who don't we like enough to give them this?" Mary Helen whispered to Eileen, who rolled her gray eyes.

Unfortunately the woman interpreted the whisper and the look to mean that they wanted to bargain.

"Fifty pesetas." The woman bounced the charm up and down. "Fifty!" She held up the five thick, calloused fingers of her free hand.

"She knows a soft touch when she sees one," Eileen said, and slithered through the open door while Mary Helen counted out the coins.

The stone interior was even colder than the parking lot. As María José pulled her woolen sweater around her, her eyes dared anyone to complain.

"The Tower of Hercules is the last Roman lighthouse still standing in the world," she said. Her breath hung on the freezing air. "Legend tells us it was built by Brehogan, the Irish chieftain, before he sailed for home. Later it was restored by the Roman emperor Trajan, who was born in Spain. It is one hundred four meters above sea level, and it still works. The four large lights can be seen for forty miles."

"And I don't want to hear that you are related to the Brehogans." Mary Helen slipped the key chain into Eileen's pocket.

"The steps to the top of the tower are narrow, and they can be slippery," María José said, "but the view is well worth the climb. If, however, you have difficulty climbing because of an infirmity or because of old—" She must have noticed Mary Helen's glare because she stopped right there.

"We'll lead the way." Rita Fong spoke up. "Coming, Neil?"

With her husband in tow, Rita pushed her way through to the staircase. Mary Helen and Eileen brought up the rear.

"This is going to be a long day," Mary Helen whispered to Eileen.

"As they say back home, old dear, it only seems that way!"

Not only was the staircase narrow and slippery, as María José had cautioned, but Mary Helen found that it was also steep, winding, and very dark. She'd counted thirty-eight steps when her thighs began to ache. By forty-eight both her legs were trembling. By fifty-eight steps her breath was coming out in "short pants," as old Sister Vincentia was wont to joke.

"Enough," she puffed, leaning against the stone wall.

"Thanks be to God," Eileen puffed back.

"I figure the view's the same at the bottom as at the top, only not quite so high."

"Absolutely! Furthermore, we'll still be alive to see it." Turning, Eileen began the descent.

Slowly, carefully, with one hand on the tower wall, Mary Helen followed. Between the dimness, her bifocals, and the irregular stone steps it was difficult to make her way down. Cautiously she felt each step with her toe before placing her foot on the worn stone.

"Are you coming?" Eileen called. She had turned a corner, and Mary Helen was unable to see her.

"Don't worry," she called back. "I'm right behind you. I'm just taking my time."

Sister Mary Helen put her foot forward, hunting in the shadows for the edge of the next step. She had just found a foothold when she felt a sudden grab at her pocketbook. Startled, she swung away, trying to hold on to both it and the slippery wall, to keep her feet steady, to regain her balance.

Before she could, the blow came—quick, sharp, deliberate, throwing her off center. Mary Helen's stomach lurched. She bumped against the wall, rolled a little. Her foot missed the next step. She let out a squeal and instinctively threw up an arm to protect her glasses. Her knees went weak and watery. Her hand reached out to nothingness, and she felt herself tumbling forward. She was falling forever.

She smelled the faint odor of musk as two strong hands caught her. A heavy ring cut into her arm as they pulled her close. Trembling, she buried her head into a shoulder, breathing slowly, deeply, until she was able to speak.

"Thank you," she said looking up into the concerned eyes of Pepe Nunez.

"What happened, Sister?" he asked.

"I'm not sure," Mary Helen said, still unsteady. "I must have slipped."

"Careful now." Pepe's grip was firm. He stood sideways on the step ahead of her and offered his arm. Arm in arm, one step at a time, the two of them reached the narrow green door.

"What happened?" Eileen's usually ruddy face was ashen. "I thought I heard you shout. Are you all right?"

Mary Helen nodded. She still felt too shaky to speak.

Much to her relief, Pepe insisted that the two nuns sit in the bus until the others returned.

Eileen's eyes pinned Pepe. "What happened?" she asked, with a hint of the brogue.

"She missed her footing," Pepe said simply. Mary Helen knew better than to think that would satisfy Eileen.

Once they were seated, Eileen examined Mary Helen's scraped knuckles and the stone burns on the palms of her hands. She pulled up Mary Helen's skirt hem to check her knees for scratches. Amazingly, not even the nylons were snagged. "Are you sure you are all right?" she asked.

"I'll probably have a few bruises tomorrow, and observations to the contrary, my knees have melted and I don't know if my heart will ever beat slowly again. Other than that . . ."

"Which is only half of what could have happened if Pepe—" Eileen checked Mary Helen's hands again. "What did happen to you anyway? Did you miss the step?"

"You won't believe it. I hardly can believe it myself. But I think someone tried to steal my pocketbook, then pushed me."

Eileen's eyes shot open. "Did you see who it was?"

Mary Helen shrugged. "I didn't see or even hear anyone behind me."

"Why, in the name of all that's good and holy, would someone want to do that?"

"I don't know. Unless it's what you mentioned before."

"Glory be to God"—Eileen's brogue was thickening—"what is it that I mentioned?"

"That one of our fellow 'pilgrims' is guilty of murder and is afraid that I'll discover which one."

"Be honest with me, old dear. Do you have the faintest idea who it is?"

"Not a clue," Mary Helen said, suddenly exhausted, "not a single clue."

Both nuns were startled to hear a throat cleared in the back of the bus. When they boarded, the bus seemed empty, but the seat backs were high, and it was possible that a short person was seated.

"Who's there?" Eileen called in a high, nervous voice.

"Only María José," a voice called back, and the small, energetic woman popped up. The seat back came to her collarbone. "I have seen the tower dozens of times, so I thought I would sneak a catnap." She smiled.

Mary Helen studied the girl. There wasn't a hint of sleep in her bright eyes. If she wasn't sleeping, what in heaven's name was she doing in the bus? And exactly how much of their conversation had she overhead?

Before she could ask either question, Cora's head appeared at the door. "I thought for sure I'd be the first one back on the bus. These old legs gave out about halfway up," she said, smiling at the two nuns. "You, too?"

Mary Helen nodded for the both of them.

In ones and twos the others began to dash back to the coach. The rain stopped as suddenly as it had begun, but the wind off the ocean whistled and wailed among the parked buses.

"That's everyone," Pepe announced with an air of relief. He shut the wide door with a swoosh. The windshield wipers made a dry, rubbing sound against the glass.

"Now, to our delicious lunch," he announced, "at the Hotel Sol Coruña."

Before anyone could comment, María José pushed a cassette of flamenco music into the tape deck. With castanets clicking, the bus drove along the sea green Ensenada del Orzan past a park filled with roses, magnolias, palm trees, and magenta and glowing yellow dahlias. On a space of lawn, the hands of a gigantic clock made entirely of flowers pointed to one-thirty.

The hotel dining room was expecting them, and there was no delay. The thick, hot chick-pea soup seemed to soothe Mary Helen, and from where she sat, it was having a somewhat similar effect on several others in the group.

"Please pass that bread," Bootsie asked politely.

Cora actually smiled a cautious smile and did.

Although the professor remained distant, he was not altogether rude when Neil asked how he'd liked the view from the tower.

The unsquelchable Bud asked Eileen, "How the heck did the Irish get into Spain?" and they were off and running while the others picked small, treacherous bones from their white fish.

The ride home was predictably quiet. Worn out from the climb and heavy with food, the bus passengers took on a siesta air.

Sister Mary Helen stared dreamily at the swiftly passing countryside and tried to get her mind off the incident in the tower. To distract herself, she forced her thoughts to Francis

Borgia, the nobleman saint whom the Church honored this day.

She strained to recall all she knew about the man who was born in this rugged land just after Columbus discovered America. Years later, when his wife died, Borgia joined the newly founded band of Jesuits and sent their first missionaries to the New World.

Studying the squat, granite dwellings along the roadside, Mary Helen wondered if the saint might have galloped past these very houses on his way from Santiago to La Coruña. Interesting question, she thought, and pulled her travel diary from her pocketbook.

"Find out if F. B. ever preached in Galicia," she scribbled.

Having exhausted her knowledge, not to mention her interest in Francis Borgia, Mary Helen tried to concentrate on the changing scenery, thick groves of pine giving way to waving pampas grass. It was futile. No matter what she tried, her mind crept back to the dark, narrow stairs at the Tower of Hercules.

She had neither seen nor heard anyone behind her, had only felt the sudden grab, the push. Was it her imagination? Could she have imagined two such things?

The tumble was real enough. Thanks be to God that Pepe had appeared. Where had he come from so suddenly? The young man was a riddle. He was charming most of the time and even an able tour guide. Yet his uncle clearly had no use for him. "A bum" he called him. Was shiftlessness alone the reason?

Where had Pepe gone Friday night after he left the girls in their room? Could he be the one who had left the note for Lisa? Something about a note fluttered on the edge of Mary Helen's mind, just out of reach.

Pepe couldn't be the guilty party—or could he? She

leaned toward Eileen. "Do you think Pepe murdered Lisa?" she whispered.

For an instant Eileen looked startled. "Sh-sh, he'll hear you," she said, shaking her head. "I don't think so. He doesn't seem the type."

"What type is that?"

"It's the type he's not," Eileen pronounced with certainty. "He's a mite too charmingly dull." She thought for a moment. "He's more likely to bore someone to death with that savoir faire of his than actually to kill them."

Clearly not listening, Mary Helen stared out the bus window. "What motive would he possibly have?" she asked.

"That, too," Eileen agreed.

Mary Helen fell back into her thoughts. Motive! That was the crux of the matter. What motive could any of them possibly have? Like Chaucer's famous pilgrims, they were "a companye/ Of sondry folk, by aventure y-falle/ In felawshipe. . . ."

Mentally she ran through the laundry list of tour members: Cora and Bud Bowman, Roger and Bootsie DeAngelo, the Fongs, pert, little María José. Each of them had just met Lisa. Or had they?

Only Heidi admitted to knowing her before the tour. Could Heidi, her childhood friend, have hated her enough to kill her? And if so, why?

The motive, like the October sun behind mounds of dark, ominous rain clouds, lay hidden.

◆

Refreshed after his bath, his dinner, and his siesta, Comisario Ángel Serrano sat in his cramped office at the police station, thinking. The top of his desk was covered with papers. With one pudgy finger he pushed them around until he uncovered Victor Morales's report.

When the need arose, Dr. Morales, who taught at the Facultad de Medicina, acted as Santiago's medical examiner. On those rare occasions when his services were called for, Morales filled out his report as if he were addressing a class of backward third formers; that suited Ángel fine. At least the doctor's findings were stated clearly. Now, if he would only do something about his handwriting.

Squinting, Ángel skimmed the details. Morales was a stickler for details. "Lisa Springer, female, 5'8"," etc., etc. He skipped to the cause of death. With interest, he read and reread it.

"The victim," Morales had scribbled in his cramped hand, "had a gash on the left side of her skull just above the left ear. The size and shape of the wound fit the size and shape of the corner of the sacred crypt of St. James. Several strands of the victim's hair were found on said corner. Strands of hair were also found on the ground below the tomb.

"Although the blow to the head rendered the victim unconscious, the actual cause of death was strangulation. The victim was caught from behind with a ———." Morales had left a blank where a weapon should have been inserted.

"The victim's neck," he wrote, "has a thick bruise across what is commonly called the Adam's apple. This bruise is wider in the middle, tapering to become very narrow on the ends.

"I have no idea what the weapon was," Morales confessed. "It appears to have been soft, maybe padded."

Closing his eyes, Ángel leaned back in his chair and rested his heels on the edge of his desk. On the stage of his mind he tried to reenact the scene.

Lisa meets her assailant in the crypt. They talk. Realizing his intentions, maybe fighting off his advances, she turns to run. The murderer grabs her by her flowing hair. That would account for a few strands of hair on the floor. He pulls her so hard that she falls backward. She hits her head on the corner of the crypt. The blow stuns her. The murderer sees his opportunity, grabs for his weapon, and strangles her with something padded.

Ángel slammed forward in his chair. Padded? Wouldn't any murderer worth his salt bring along a wire or a rope if he intended to strangle his victim? Maybe this murder was not premeditated. Perhaps it was caused by the emotion of the moment. He grabs for something, anything, that is handy. Maybe something belonging to the victim, herself. What do men or women—let's not forget women—wear that is padded?

In an effort to concentrate, Ángel closed his eyes again, rested his chin in the palm of his hand, and tried to visualize Julietta's half of the closet. Actually Julietta's three-quarters of the closet.

What of his wife's was padded? Hangers, pads in the shoulders of her dresses and her blouses. Neither was handy or the right shape. A belt perhaps? Would a belt be padded and tapered at the ends? He would have to ask her. A tie for a blouse? Not padded, not even the right shape. For that matter, a man's tie, doubled maybe?

"Tío!" María José's shrill voice startled him. He felt a strong gust of cold air as she burst open the door.

"Wake up!" she shouted.

Ángel did not open his eyes until he was sure that his temper was under control. "I am awake!" He forced the words through clenched teeth. "I am thinking, Ho-Ho. You have heard of thinking, I assume." He hoped his sarcasm was not lost on his niece. Apparently it was.

"Tío!" She was all but dancing with excitement. "Let me tell you what happened." She perched on the corner of his desk.

Shaking his head, he raised his hand to silence her.

"First, María José, in this office, we knock." His tone was deliberately icy. "We wait until someone says, 'Pase!' before we burst in. Finally, we stand until we are invited to be seated; then we use a chair, not the edge of the desk."

"I am sorry, Tío," she said, totally unrepentant. She jumped down from the desk and planted a loud kiss on the top of his bald head.

Quickly Ángel wiped his crown with his handkerchief. "Don't ever do that in here again!" he shouted, making a mental note to tell Julietta how lipstick came to be on his hankie. Smoothing down his sparse gray tonsure, he moved across his office and kicked the door shut.

"What if someone had seen you? Do you want to make me the laughingstock—"

"No, Tío," she interrupted. "I want to tell you why you were so wise to send me on the bus."

Frustrated, Ángel sat down. His annoyance began to evaporate as María José told him of overhearing the conversation between the two nuns on the bus.

"She said that someone grabbed her purse, then shoved her?" He was incredulous.

María José nodded, her eyes wide with excitement.

"And she didn't see or hear anyone?"

"No one. Only Pepe, who caught her."

"Are you sure?"

"I am positive!"

"By the way, María José, why did you stay on the bus instead of going into the tower with the others?"

"I made up an excuse, Tío, that I had seen it dozens of times and that I wanted to nap."

"But what is it that you really wanted to do?" he asked, instinctively dreading her answer.

María José gave a broad, charming smile. "I wanted to

look through the things the group left on the bus and see if I could find something suspicious."

Ángel puffed out his cheeks, a telltale sign that he was getting angry. He let his breath out slowly through a small hole he made with his lips. Surely his niece watched too much American television. "María José, do you know that you could have been caught and accused of—"

"But, Tío," she interrupted. Another bad habit, he thought. "No one caught me."

"No matter. It is not what I sent you to do. If you intend to work with me . . ." As soon as the words left his mouth, Ángel wanted to bite his tongue. He stared at her. Her eyes danced.

"Did you find anything?"

Laughing, María José shook her head, then glanced at the large clock on his office wall. "It's nearly seven o'clock, Tío," she said. "Mama will be beginning to worry about where I am. You and Tía Julietta are coming for Sunday dinner, and I promised her I'd be home to help."

"Go, Ho-Ho. Heaven forbid that we should upset your mother. And remember, not one word of this to her. Not one word of this at dinner!" He shook his finger for emphasis.

Nodding, María José opened his office door.

"Before you go, let me ask you one question."

María José's eyes were alert.

"What could a woman be wearing that is padded?" he asked.

"A bra, Tío!" Giggling, María José turned on her heel and left the word to echo through the squad room.

"Have you no shame?" Ángel roared to her retreating back. He puffed out his cheeks, again, and glared around the room, daring any of his officers to laugh. Discipline must be maintained. All eyes averted his. The glass in his office door rattled from his bang.

Safely back in his office, Ángel fell into his overstuffed chair, pushed back, and began to chuckle. You stepped right into that one, my lad, he thought, feeling foolish.

He got out of the chair and walked over to the narrow window facing the Avenida de Rodrigo del Padrón, where he caught a glimpse of his niece's small figure threading her way down the street. That bizarre hair color made her easy to spot even in a crowd.

Whatever else one could say about María José, Ángel admitted, she was no ordinary young woman. And she wasn't easy to ignore. Then, again, neither was a migraine headache.

♦

When they were finally back in their hotel room, Sister Eileen was the first to speak. "I have been mulling over this whole mess," she said, "and I've come to a decision."

Sister Mary Helen could tell by the tilt of her friend's chin that they were in for trouble. "What decision?" she asked cautiously.

"We've an old saying back home. . . ."

Mary Helen groaned.

Impervious, as always, to Mary Helen's reaction to her bits of wisdom, Eileen continued.

"You'll never plow a field by turning it over in your mind," she announced, then let the words dangle like bait.

"Meaning what?" Mary Helen asked, more for form than content. She knew exactly where Eileen was heading.

Eileen searched the side pockets of her suitcase until she found a brand-new tube of antiseptic cream. "Lucky I remembered this." She handed it to Mary Helen, then plunked down in one of the overstuffed velvet chairs and kicked off her shoes.

From the looks of things, Eileen's plan was to be long and detailed. Mary Helen followed suit. After a slight struggle with the screw top, she dabbed small squirts of cream on her scrapes.

"According to our itinerary," Eileen began, "this evening we are invited to a cocktail party in the Grand Salon, after which"—she read from the brochure—"we are 'free to enjoy northern Spanish cuisine in one of the many excellent restaurants in this city.' "

"When does the 'plowed field' come in?" Mary Helen asked, eager to see if her hunch was correct.

Eileen blinked. "Oh, right," she said. "As you well know, old dear, *in vino veritas!*"

Mary Helen finished the thought. "So, this evening at the cocktail party, after our group has enjoyed their *vino*, we mingle and dig for the *veritas?*"

Eileen nodded. "Exactly," she said with a satisfied grin that reminded Mary Helen of a first-grade teacher whose Bluebird Reading Group had just conquered *See Spot Run.*

"What we need here is a motive," Eileen said. "We need to discover who in this group had a reason to want Lisa dead. And we'll never do that unless we take action. Which was my point."

Mary Helen raised her palms to show Eileen the abrasions.

"Ouch!" Eileen made a sympathetic face.

"You do realize that one of this group is a murderer?" Mary Helen asked.

"We don't know that for sure. Besides, we will never find out which one it is unless we discover a motive. Somebody besides Heidi, who does not seem like a murderer to me, must have known Lisa before."

"And how do you propose to find that out?"

"You sound like a regular Devil's Advocate." Eileen let out an exaggerated sigh. "But I can tell by that look, my friend, that you are dying to question these people."

"I don't want to be dying because I did," Mary Helen said in a feeble attempt both to save and to adjust her face.

Without any further discussion, they split the group. Mary Helen was to interrogate the DeAngelos and the Fongs while Eileen concentrated on the Bowmans, Heidi, and Pepe. They flipped a peseta for María José, and the lot fell to Mary Helen.

♦

The music of a string quartet filled the Grand Salon and provided a tranquil background for the hum of conversation. Mary Helen was surprised to find the room crowded. Apparently several tour groups had been invited to cocktails simultaneously. Good, she thought, tossing a thumbs-up at Eileen. Their maneuvers wouldn't be so obvious.

Feeling as if she had painted a smile on her face, Mary Helen wove her way across the room toward the DeAngelos. The couple, wineglasses in hand, stood together like matched mannequins. Only the shifting of their eyes gave them away.

From a distance Bootsie was striking: tall, straight, and slim with a dress of cobalt blue silk that trapezed down from her broad shoulders into flattering folds. The color matched her eyes and exaggerated their size. Her fingers sparkled with rings, and a jeweled comb stood out against the shoe polish black of her hair.

It was only as Mary Helen drew nearer that the signs of age appeared. Tonight neither the dim light of the room nor the heavy layer of makeup hid the creases that time and temperament had drawn around Bootsie's tight mouth and at the corners of her frosty eyes.

Next to her stood Roger, lean, hollow-cheeked, bearded. Except for his eyes, which were a little too close to his nose, he was the perfect television stereotype of a professor.

Mary Helen half expected to smell the soft leather smell

of elbow patches. Instead, as she drew closer to the couple, she smelled the unmistakable odor of stress.

The waiter passed with a full tray, and Mary Helen accepted a glass of wine. To set the stage for casual cocktail chitchat, it was best to be armed with a cocktail.

"Good evening, Bootsie," Mary Helen called cheerfully. "Don't you look lovely this evening!"

"Why, thank you, Sister," Bootsie drawled, with a stiff little smile that went no farther north than her nose.

"And how are you, Roger?" Mary Helen smiled up at him. "Tired from our outing?"

Roger DeAngelo, momentarily distracted by his own thought, hesitated as if to ponder her question.

"A little," he said finally.

Better than a grunt, Mary Helen thought, but not much. "You are a professor, I know," she said, "but I don't remember your mentioning what your subject is."

"History." Roger gazed down his nose at her.

"What a coincidence! That's my field, too. Where did you study, Roger?"

"University of Southern California."

"USC! I did my graduate work there, too," Mary Helen said with genuine astonishment, then noticed the horrified expression on his face. "But long, long before your time," she added hastily, in case he thought that she thought they were contemporaries.

A sticky silence followed. This conversation was going nowhere. One word at a time and I'll be here all night! she thought, turning back toward Bootsie. Her mind did a quick search for a question that demanded at least a sentence-long answer.

Bootsie's bright red mouth was pursed into what looked to Mary Helen like the adult version of "Lock your lips and throw away the key."

The couple was visibly relieved to see a waiter appear with a white towel in one hand and a bottle of wine in the other.

"Señor? Señoras?" He offered the bottle.

Quickly both DeAngelos extended their glasses for a refill. Smiling, Mary Helen declined. She needed to keep her wits about her.

Maybe the problem was that there was not yet enough *vino* to produce the desired *veritas*. Later she'd come back to the DeAngelos.

Excusing herself, Mary Helen searched the room for the Fongs. She spotted Rita first. The tiny woman was talking animatedly, almost nervously to a young fellow from another tour group.

Neil hung behind her, apparently enjoying the conversation, although he wasn't actually participating. Instead he surveyed the room from over the rim of his half glasses. Like Argus with the hundred eyes, Mary Helen thought, moving toward the trio. Unlike Argus, the giant, however, Neil Fong was a short, slight man.

Just about my height, she thought, easing up beside him.

"Hello, Sister." He gave her a genuinely friendly grin.

Mary Helen was encouraged. So far this interview was more promising than the last.

Rita stopped chattering long enough to introduce Mary Helen to the young man, who was quickly developing the haunted look of a captive. He extended his hand, and after a sinewy grasp that made Mary Helen's palm sting, he slipped into the crowd.

Without warning all of Rita's energy was unleashed on Mary Helen. Almond eyes darting, Rita began to babble about her family, about her education, about her job.

Within minutes Mary Helen knew that Rita Fong was a fifth-generation San Franciscan, that her great-great-great-grandfather had been brought from China to labor on the Central Pacific Railroad, that she and Neil had known each other since childhood, that both had attended the University of California in Berkeley, and that they had married while Neil was still in school.

She knew that the couple had four children of high school and college age, that they actually lived not in San Francisco but down the peninsula in Burlingame, and that Rita worked because she liked to, not because she had to. She even knew that Neil was distantly related to Edsel Ford Fong, the stand-up comedian, who once had worked as a waiter at Sam Wo's in Chinatown.

To Mary Helen's way of thinking, none of these facts seemed remotely like a motive for Lisa Springer's murder.

"Before you came on this tour, did you happen to know any other members of our group?" she asked when Rita stopped for breath.

Rita shook her head. The coarse black curls that were cleverly piled on the crown of her head wobbled precariously. "No one," she said, her eyes suddenly wary. "Why do you ask?"

"No reason, really. It's just that we are all from the same area, a rather small area, really, and it just seems likely that we might have some connection." Her explanation sounded feeble, even to herself. It was obvious from the amusement in Neil's eyes that he wasn't buying it at all.

"Sister, doing your own police work can be dangerous," he said softly.

Mary Helen felt her face flush. She was sorely tempted to flutter like a heroine in a Victorian novel and ask, "Whatever do you mean, Doctor?" Instead she opted for the honest approach. "Was it that obvious?"

"Direct questions out of context usually are, even to Rita." He turned toward his wife.

Rita shot him a "don't-push-your-luck-with-those-smart-remarks" look and latched on to an unsuspecting middle-aged woman who had unwittingly brushed shoulders with her.

Neil blinked several times. "Rita has a tendency to talk a lot when she's nervous," he said in a soft voice. Obviously he did not want his wife to overhear.

Not that Mary Helen blamed him. If Rita talked that incessantly when she was nervous, imagine her tirade when she was angry.

"She told you everything but our Social Security numbers and my weight." He held out his glass to a passing waiter.

Again, Mary Helen declined. "Why is your wife so nervous?" she asked.

"For the same reason we all are." Neil's dark eyes, sharp as needles, stared over the rims of his glasses and fastened on her. "Because one of us is a murderer," he said in a tone that turned Mary Helen's spinal cord to ice. "And only one person knows which one."

Excusing herself, Mary Helen headed for the door with the word *Damas* inscribed in the center of a large brass cockleshell. It was a two-room affair, part lounge, part lavatory.

Still reeling from Rita's barrage and Neil's single sentence, she sank down on a small, overstuffed couch that ran along one wall. The couch and two matching chairs, set across from an enormous mirror, formed an intimate "conversation group," should any of the *damas* wish to gossip in the bathroom. Flushing toilets and running basins provided a watery background for all conversation.

Glad to be alone, Mary Helen dug through her pocketbook for Eileen's cream and Anne's travel diary. Her palms stung, and the cream soothed them. That done, she opened the diary to jot down some thoughts, not that she'd forget, but sometimes when things are fresh . . . "Evasive," she wrote next to the DeAngelos' names. "Stonewalling—possibly a better word."

With a swish of cold air, the lavatory door swung open and Mary Helen was aware of a person approaching her. The first thing in view was a pair of black shoes. She knew they must be fashionable, but to her they looked for all the world like something Minnie Mouse would wear. The feet were small and splayed.

Mary Helen's eyes climbed up the black leotards to a swirling, voluminous black cashmere skirt and fitted top. An enormous fringed challis scarf, a riot of teal and red paisley print and black hound's-tooth, was draped across one shoulder and knotted on one shapely hip.

When Mary Helen finally reached the face, she was not at all surprised to see María José.

"Hi, Sister," the girl chirped happily, her breath smelling of wine. "You are just the one I am looking for." She sank down on the couch beside Mary Helen, pausing for a long moment to examine herself in the mirror and tuck a few strands of magenta hair back into her tight French braid.

"Me? Why are you looking for me?" Mary Helen asked when María José's attention shifted back to her.

"To see how you are feeling. My uncle—" She stopped abruptly. Her face colored. Obviously she had let the last two words slip. At last the *vino* theory was paying off.

"Your uncle? Who is your uncle?" Mary Helen asked.

María José's eyes avoided Mary Helen's steady gaze. Her lips moved as if she were practicing an explanation but having very little success making it sound plausible. Finally, with a resigned sigh, María José laid her head against the back of the couch and closed her eyes. "The *comisario* is my uncle," she said in a voice so low that Mary Helen nearly missed it.

"Ángel Serrano is your uncle?" Mary Helen was surprised. For some reason she had not thought of the *comisario* as a family man. Once she did, her mind clicked, and several small pieces snapped together. It explained why his face had registered surprise on Saturday, when he found María José among the tourists in the hotel's catchall room, and why she had never returned. Undoubtedly he'd sent her home. And it accounted for her actions today. He had asked her to go along on the trip, then stay behind in the bus and look for clues.

"Are you working with the police?" Mary Helen asked. Her direct question was jarring, she knew, but time was a-wasting. The cocktail hour would soon be over, and she wanted to get back to the DeAngelos.

The pleased expression on María José's face answered her question. A wannabe, Mary Helen thought, recognizing a kindred spirit.

"I had a difficult time convincing my uncle to let me go along today on the tour bus," María José began, a note of triumph in her voice, "because I am not a police person."

Mary Helen did not miss the emphasis on the nonsexist title.

"But now he is happy that I did, or else he would never have known that you were accosted in the tower." Her dark eyes sparkled with excitement.

"You told him that?"

"I overheard you say so when you reboarded the bus today. And that Pepe caught you."

"What did your uncle say?"

"He huffed and puffed about my not doing as I was told, but I knew from the look on his face that he was glad for the information." She glanced at her watch. "Soon they will miss me at home." Leaning forward, she took Mary Helen's hands. Turning them over, she frowned, and a little round column of concern formed between her eyebrows as she examined them. "We will find whoever did this," she promised earnestly.

"How do you know Pepe?" Mary Helen asked.

Startled by the change of subject, María José let go of Mary Helen's hands. "Actually, I never met him until we sat next to each other on the plane from Madrid to Santiago."

"You mean you met him on the day we arrived?"

María José nodded. "I was flying home from a visit with my cousins in Madrid, and Pepe's seat was next to mine. We started talking, and very soon into our conversation he told me about leading an American tour group to Santiago and knowing very little about the city. I told him I was a native, and before I knew it, he asked me to go along on the tour as a consultant. It sounded like an unexpected opportunity to try out the tourist business, and what, I thought, could possibly be the danger?"

Mary Helen was flabbergasted. "What did your uncle say to that?"

María José's eyes clouded. "My uncle, my whole family really do not take me very seriously."

No small wonder, Mary Helen thought, what with sudden business alliances with perfect strangers. Not to mention the magenta hair.

"They think that I am just headstrong, going through a phase." María José's nose rose in the air until her chin jutted out in a determined V. "But, Sister, I am a Galician woman. Galician women are strong and resolute. We possess white magic."

We could use a little of that all right, Mary Helen thought.

"You do trust me to help you, don't you?" The young woman searched Mary Helen's face.

For some inexplicable reason Mary Helen did. She sensed that somewhere between the Minnie Mouse shoes and the magenta braid was a backbone of cold, solid steel. She knew from experience that that kind of determination and stick-to-it-iveness produced a magic power all their own.

When Mary Helen finally returned to the cocktail party, the noise level had risen in direct proportion to the alcohol intake. It was difficult to hear the stringed quartet. She searched the crowd for the DeAngelos, but they were nowhere in sight. It was just as well, Mary Helen thought. Her hip and knees were beginning to stiffen.

Finally letting the waiter refill her wineglass, she carried it with her upstairs.

◆

Sister Mary Helen was surprised to hear the bath water running. "Eileen, it's I," she called, closing their bedroom door behind her.

The door to the bathroom opened a crack, and a billow of steam softly scented with lavender poured out into the room. "I'm just out of the tub." Eileen's voice rose above the sound of running water. "I took a chance you'd be right behind me, so I ran one for you." The faucets screeched off, and Eileen came out of the bathroom. "Why don't you jump into the tub and I'll order us room service, and when we've settled, we can—"

"I am not an invalid, you know!" Mary Helen snapped. Despite the soreness in her back, she had no intention of giving in.

Eileen's eyebrows and shoulders shot up simultaneously. "Invalid? Who said anything about an invalid? Did I say, 'hobble or crawl to the tub'? Did I say, 'I'll help you to the tub'? If I remember correctly, I said, 'jump into the tub.' Does that sound like I think you're an invalid? I don't know about you, old dear, but I've had a long and nerveracking day, and I am bushed. So you do whatever you want." Tired, angry tears welled up in Eileen's eyes.

"I'm sorry," Mary Helen said, regretting her impatience. She smiled meekly at Eileen, who refused for the moment to smile back. "Thank you for thinking of me," Mary Helen said, and for the first time since lunch she really looked at her friend. With a stab of guilt, she noticed that beneath the flush from the tub, Eileen's face was pale and small pouches had formed under her eyes. She looked absolutely exhausted.

"I'll be out in a few minutes," Mary Helen mumbled, and made her way like a medieval penitent to soak in the hot tub.

◆

After a few prickly moments, smoothed over by steaming bowls of *sopa de crema de espárrago,* crusty bread, assorted pastries, and a bottle of aromatic white wine, the two old nuns settled down peacefully to work.

"Neither Bowman holds much promise as our murderer." Eileen tried unsuccessfully to stifle a yawn. "They are your ordinary run-of-the-mill 'small-business-makes-good' story. Bud never went to college, worked as an electrician, bought his own shop in Daly City, invested wisely, and now buys Cora, who is, by the way, his first and only wife, expensive jewelry."

"So that's why she was wearing emeralds and diamonds on Friday night."

Eileen nodded. "Fortieth wedding anniversary gift, Cora told me. She worked as his bookkeeper for years. They have one son, and now that he can easily take over the business, Bud wants to travel.

"They are nodding acquaintances of Carlos Fraga because they eat at the Patio Español once or twice a month. They never heard of any of the others before they won the prize, and if Cora is to be believed, they never want to hear of them again once it's over. Maybe they'll even give up the Patio Español.

"Bud told me they should have started with Club Med,

but Cora couldn't pass up the free trip." Eileen yawned again. "Dead end number one," she said.

"Did you learn any more about Heidi?"

Eileen shook her head. "If you ask me, the girl is becoming a bit unglued. She's very distressed about Lisa's murder, I'm sure, but to hear her talk tonight, she was more concerned about how angry her mother will be. Why would her own mother be so angry?"

Mary Helen had no idea.

"She makes no pretense about liking Lisa and is very relieved that a police matron packed all her belongings and took them away."

"Do you think by some remote chance she could be our murderer?" Mary Helen wondered aloud.

Eileen closed her eyes, apparently deep in thought. She looked so drained that Mary Helen wondered if she'd dropped off to sleep.

"No." She paused. "Although I have no reason to say that. She is just not enough."

"Not enough?" Mary Helen was genuinely puzzled.

"You know, angry, but not angry enough. Jealous, but not jealous enough. Shrewd, but not shrewd enough. Crazy, but not—"

"Enough! You've made your point. To your way of thinking, she's dead end number two. What about Pepe?"

"As I told you on the bus, I'd never cast Pepe in the murderer's role, yet he does put a new spin on the word *enigma*. Charming, with a scoundrel of sorts hidden not far below the surface. The well-traveled man of the world with that touch of a Spanish accent."

"Could be a combination of listening to his uncle and to *I Love Lucy* reruns on the tube." Mary Helen refilled both wineglasses.

Eileen smiled. "I'll wager he's gone no farther from home

than Yosemite." She sipped her wine. "He did attend college. Even though he wears that ostentatious signet ring, I doubt if he graduated. 'All show and no go,' as the girls say. He admires and appreciates his uncle, but we both are well aware of the other side of that story.

"Yet after all I've just said, he really has no apparent motive. He claims that he never met Lisa before this trip, and I believe him. So although he may not be a complete dead end, he is, at best, a cul-de-sac."

Mary Helen agreed. "Do you know who else he never met before?" she asked.

Eileen shook her head.

"María José!" Wasting no time, Mary Helen told Eileen about the Fongs, most likely dead end four, the disappearing DeAngelos, and, saving the best until last, the deadest end of all, María José.

Relief washed over Eileen's tired face. "I don't know why, but having someone even remotely connected with the police along on that bus with us makes me feel better." She yawned so hard that her eyes watered. "Let's call it a night," she said.

Mary Helen pushed herself up from the chair. Her knees were stiff, and a spot on her left shoulder felt sore to the touch. "I don't know why it makes you feel better after what happened today." She grinned at Eileen. Still contrite for her earlier peevishness, she added, "But there must be an old saying back home to cover it."

"Indeed, there is," said Eileen, who recognized true repentance when she heard it. "A trout in the pot is better than a salmon in the sea."

♦

Not ten blocks away Comisario Ángel Serrano was having a sleepless night. A sliver of moonlight cut through a small opening in the heavy drapes and lay across the bedcovers. Beside him in the light, he watched Julietta's stomach move up and down, up and down, in deep, contented sleep. He tried to match his breathing to hers but failed.

Frustrated, he rolled onto his side. Despite his best efforts he kept replaying the account of the Americans' trip to La Coruña. He could not block it from his mind.

María José was so certain that the old nun had been accosted. Maybe she was exaggerating. First thing tomorrow he would check with the Sister. If his niece had embellished the story, he would personally go over to his sister's home and throttle María José. And his sister, Pilar, too, if she objected. The pleasure of the thought embarrassed him. What violence for a peace-loving man! But Pilar did that to him.

If he were honest, María José's observations were helpful, if one considered knowing that a killer was on the loose and disposed to kill again helpful. He, Ángel Serrano, must prevent it. One murder in Santiago, American or no, was quite enough.

To find the murderer, he must first find the motive. That was obvious, yet he knew so little about this group of Americans. That was what made it difficult.

The clock in the downstairs hallway chimed two. The time difference was driving him crazy. It was still Sunday in San Francisco. He must wait for Monday to arrive there. He must wait until this Kate Murphy had an opportunity to pull up information. Wait, while a murderer was on the prowl. He was not good at waiting.

Ángel kicked his feet out of the bedcovers. Sleep! He needed sleep. Tomorrow he had a whole day to get through.

His stomach complained. Pilar never serves enough food, he thought testily. Maybe he was hungry. Maybe that was why he could not sleep.

Cautiously Ángel tiptoed down the stairs, avoiding the

steps that creaked. No sense waking up Julietta, too. He opened the refrigerator door and peered into the covered bowls, hoping to find some leftover soup.

"What in the world is worrying you?"

Ángel jumped and waited until his breath caught up.

Silent as a spider, Julietta had followed him downstairs and now, in only her nightgown, stood in the door frame of the kitchen. Her long dark hair flowed freely over her shoulders and covered her breasts.

"It's this American murder case and María José," he said. "I cannot sleep."

"Sit down," Julietta said, and bustled past him.

He watched her deftly heat his soup to a perfect sipping temperature, butter a slab of soft bread, and pour him a tall glass of milk.

While Ángel ate and talked, Julietta listened and nodded encouragingly. When he finished, Ángel felt much better.

It was only as Julietta, holding firmly to his hand, led him back up the creaky stairs that he realized that once again she had simply agreed with him. How wise this wife of his was and how fortunate he was to have her.

With a surge of love, he grabbed her full hips. Moving her hair, he kissed the nape of her neck and smelled the fresh, clean scent of lilac.

monday, october 11

feast of st. maría desolata torres-acosta, foundress

♦

Clenching her teeth, Sister Mary Helen eased out of the high, canopied bed. Her legs were stiff, her shoulder and back ached, and there was a purple bruise the size of a fist on her hip.

"How are you doing this morning, old dear?" Eileen sat in one of the velvet chairs studying the room service menu. "They say you will feel better if you move your sore spots, you know."

"Who says?" Mary Helen groused.

"Undoubtedly someone who never bounced off the walls at the Tower of Hercules."

Mary Helen, her whole body tense, sat on the edge of the bed, examining her hands. "I look—and feel—more like I played for the Forty-niners yesterday," she said with a twinge of homesickness. Why in the world had they ever decided to take this blasted trip?

No sooner had Eileen ordered room service than someone rapped sharply on their door.

"That was surely speedy." Eileen moved toward it.

Mary Helen's heart jolted. Too speedy. She slipped into her bathrobe. "Who's there?" she demanded, and was relieved to hear the clipped British tones of Comisario Ángel Serrano.

With perfect courtesy, the *comisario* excused himself for

disturbing them, asked a few perfunctory questions about their comfort, and then, refusing a seat, zeroed in like an expert marksman on the reason for his call.

"I am here because I am concerned about your safety," he said. His sharp black eyes roamed the room as if they expected to find danger lurking under their unmade beds. "My niece, María José, tells me that you are aware of her identity. She also reported to me that you were hurt during yesterday's outing."

Mary Helen held out both her hands, determined not to show him any more.

"Heaven knows what might have happened if Pepe hadn't been there to catch her," Eileen added.

"Where were you, Sister?" He focused on Eileen. She blinked at his unexpected question.

"I was ahead of Sister Mary Helen—on the way down, that is. I had turned a corner and momentarily lost sight of her. All I heard was her cry out."

"Did Pepe pass you on his way up?"

Eileen shook her head. "No one passed me," she said. "Sister and I were the cow's tail of the group."

"Then how did Pepe happen to stop Sister's fall? Did he grab you from behind?" Ángel's eyes leaped to Mary Helen.

"I think so," she stammered, remembering the terrifying sensation of free-falling. "I fell forward. I had my eyes covered. Instinct," she added deliberately. She didn't want him to imagine for a moment that it was cowardice. "I felt hands grab me. Pepe must have spun me around. It happened so fast, so unexpectedly, that I wasn't aware of anything except the faint musky smell and two strong hands grabbing me."

A sharp knock at the door startled her.

"That must be room service," Eileen told the comisario, who was suddenly alert.

The waiter wheeled in a table and miraculously produced three chairs. It took some doing, but Ángel was finally induced to join them.

"Only café!" he said, pouring about an inch of coffee into his cup, then filling it up with hot milk. "My wife is after me to reduce." Inhaling, he tried with no apparent success to pull in his little round belly.

After two deep swallows he placed the empty cup back on the saucer. "Today, Sisters"—he was back to business— "you go to La Toja with your tour. It is about fifty-six kilometers to the south. I will once again send María José on the bus. Do not take any chances. If you sense anything out of the ordinary, you are to notify her. Officer Zaldo will drive behind the bus as a backup."

Mary Helen's mouth went dry. "Am I to assume that you think we are in some sort of danger?" she asked, having trouble getting her tongue around the words.

"Not at all, Sister. I am assuming that yesterday was a freak accident. I am, however, taking no chances. I was going to cancel this trip, but since I have no way of knowing that the murderer is one of your group, I have decided to let it go on as scheduled."

After the *comisario* had left, Mary Helen and Eileen sat for a few moments in an uneasy silence. Even after a night's rest, Eileen's face was pale and strained. "Do you think one of our group is the murderer?"

"I don't know." Mary Helen tried not to let her own panic show. "Who had a reason to kill Lisa? When we know that, we'll know—"

Eileen studied her pensively. "Something is bothering me, rather like an itch that I can't reach," she said.

"What is it?" Mary Helen broke off the corner of a croissant, piled it with berry jam, and popped it into her mouth.

"It's Lisa herself. We know very little about poor, dead Lisa. Heidi told us that she'd changed in college. But we are not sure from what to what. Where did she go to college? Another thing, don't you think that picture business is odd?"

"What picture business?"

"That picture you found in their room. How many people do you know that take a 'before' picture of themselves on a trip to Europe?"

"One, to date," Mary Helen admitted.

Eileen's gray eyes narrowed. "There is something there that is very, very"—the word eluded her—"peculiar," she said at last.

The sharp ring of the phone caught them by surprise. It was María José reminding them that the Pulmantur bus would pull into the Plaza del Obradoiro and meet them in front of the Hostal de los Reyes Católicos in about twenty minutes.

"What's our plan for today?" Eileen asked while they gathered up their coats, umbrellas, and pocketbooks.

"Why don't we switch? You try the DeAngelos, and I'll see what I can pry out of Heidi." A shooting pain in the small of her back made Mary Helen flinch.

"What is it?" Eileen hadn't missed her grimace.

"Nothing really. I must have knocked against something in the tower."

"Let me see."

"There is probably nothing to see."

Eileen insisted on looking anyway. She sucked in air. "Ouch," she said.

"What is it?" Mary Helen was impatient to tuck her blouse back into her skirt.

"You have a nasty-looking bruise in the small of your back." Her cold fingers touched the spot lightly. "About the size, shape, and, I daresay, color of a ruby seedless grape."

"That is about where I felt the jab yesterday," Mary Helen remembered. "Could it be from someone's thumb or a knuckle?" she asked.

"A thumb, a wide knuckle, or perhaps—" Eileen's brogue was thickening.

A sudden draft of cold air across her back made Mary Helen shiver.

"Perhaps," Eileen said thoughtfully, "it was made by someone's heavy ring."

The two nuns were in front of the *hostal* before any of the other tour members or even the bus arrived. At ten o'clock in the morning the Plaza del Obradoiro already was crowded with what looked more like tourists than townsfolk.

To the left of the cathedral, three young men wearing woven panchos, and with the traditional chullos of Peru covering their heads and ears, huddled together near the door to the archbishop's palace. One played a drum, one a guitar, and the third blew a plaintive melody on a reed flute.

Starving students, Spanish style, Mary Helen thought, before her attention was caught by a bevy of young nuns descending the cathedral steps. Their blue habits set them apart from the regular churchgoers.

There was something refreshing in the way they were laughing and teasing one another, something that made her yearn for her own nuns. For the second time that morning Mary Helen felt a wave of homesickness.

"Let's vow that if we get out of this mess, we will never leave Mount St. Francis College again," she said, but Eileen raised her hand.

"Vow to whom?" she asked. "God certainly isn't going to buy that one!"

Eileen was right, of course. It was simply the stress of the situation. Mary Helen jerked her thoughts back into line. Today she must summon up all the energy she could and begin to solve this mystery!

The nuns in blue hurried across the plaza toward where

Eileen and she stood. Eileen had noticed them, too. "I'll wager it's a feast day of some sort," she said.

Mary Helen racked her brain. Today the hours of the office were seasonal. Nectarius, a third-century bishop, was noted but certainly not celebrated. "What feast day?" she wondered aloud.

From Eileen's frown, Mary Helen knew that her friend was dredging up some little-known fact from that phenomenal memory of hers.

"There's a Spanish order called Handmaids of Mary or Servants of Mary. If I remember correctly, twenty or so years ago, Pope Paul the Sixth canonized their foundress."

"How in the world do you remember that?"

"Because her name was María Desolata something or other, or Soledad in English. I remember thinking at the time about the California mission being named Soledad and wondering where Junípero Serra had pulled that name from—"

"Let's just ask them," Mary Helen cut in. She had followed Eileen's labyrinth about as far as she intended to go.

Fortunately one of the young nuns spoke passable English. By the time the other members of the tour group finally assembled, Mary Helen and Eileen stood amid a sea of nuns in blue, learning more than they needed to know about St. María Desolata Torres-Acosta, who, indeed, had been born in Madrid and had founded the Handmaids of Mary to serve Spain's poor.

When he spotted them, Bud Bowman laughed and pointed. "Birds of a feather," he said.

Mary Helen smiled politely at his attempt at good humor. It was all she could do, however, to keep that smile in place when she overheard Bootsie snip, "Or you could say, 'Water seeks its own level.'"

As the group boarded the bus, an umbrella of rain clouds was moving in to cover the remaining few patches of blue sky.

Pepe swooshed the door shut, and a tense silence enclosed them all. Couples isolated themselves from the others not only by their silence but by space.

Pepe, realizing that Heidi was alone, slid into the seat next to her. Drat it, thought Mary Helen who, once the bus was under way, had fully intended to slide in next to the girl. The trip would take the better part of an hour. Surely in that amount of time she'd have been able to pump out some information.

María José cradled the microphone. *"Buenos días, per-egrinos."* Her dark glance darted around the bus. "I see that everyone is with us," she said, "so near, yet so far away." She motioned the DeAngelos to move up closer to the rest of the group.

Reluctantly they complied, only to have the Fongs move to another seat. When they did, the Bowmans shifted, too. María José watched in astonishment as the couples jerked from seat to seat.

Crazily, Mary Helen was reminded of the little square computer disks jumping around on Shirley's screen when she pushed the "clean up" command. Shirley and her computer! At the thought of her faithful, efficient secretary, yet another wave of homesickness tumbled over Mary Helen.

Tough up, old girl, she chided herself. Soon this will all be over. And "the sooner the quicker," as old Sister Donata liked to say. A soft rain washed the tour bus as it pulled onto the wide highway leading south to the island of La Toja.

Healthy green countryside spread out over low hills. Vines with leaves the color of deep red wine grew up from the stony ground. Pink roses and brilliant yellow and tangerine dahlias climbed up rock walls.

"Look at that." Eileen pointed to the narrow dirt road that ran alongside the highway. Two middle-aged women rode a donkey. A third walked behind, balancing a tub of freshly cut lettuce on her head. To their left, parked in a stone carport, looking for all the world like an anachronism, was a bright red Opel!

"You'd think they'd carpool," Eileen said, turning her attention back to María José, who had once again taken up the microphone.

"The west coast of Galicia offers some of the most beautiful scenery in all of Spain," María José declared. "We are on our way to the resort paradise of La Toja."

Mary Helen chanced a quick glance around the bus. "From the looks on the faces, you'd think she just said that we were on our way to the Inferno," she whispered to Eileen.

"This whole pretense is an inferno to someone," Eileen remarked wisely. Mary Helen agreed.

Undaunted by the general gloom, María José explained that rias were the inlets cutting deep into the shoreline. In this part of Galicia the estuaries seemed to go on forever.

Like a genuine tour guide, she reminded them all to look again for the *hórreos* set on six stone pillars and that if in a ria, they saw a strange kind of raft with a hut on it, these contained cages and were mussel beds.

As the bus wound along the corniche road to La Toja, even the gloomiest of the group was lifted by the beauty. The salty smell of the ocean filled the bus. Gigantic waves surged against the cliffs, and the Atlantic stretched in silvery splendor to the horizon.

The bus pulled into a paved lot and parked beside a row of other tour buses. María José straddled the aisle. "We will meet at the Gran Hotel in three hours for our lunch," she said with a smile. "In the meantime, have fun. There is the beach. Souvenir stalls. Snacks. Anyone who wishes can come with me to La Toja Cosméticos to buy some black *jabón* or soap."

"Black soap?" Eileen made a face.

"It's really excellent for your complexion," Bootsie said in a slightly superior tone.

When they finally disembarked from the bus, the day had turned almost balmy. An expanse of blue sky dotted with tiny cotton-ball clouds faded into the shimmering ocean.

"Do you mind if I join you?" Cora asked.

Mary Helen did. Her task was to pump Heidi, but how in the world could she refuse anyone's attempt at companionship?

"Not at all," she answered. While she waited for Cora to catch up, Eileen scurried ahead. Bud, beating a quick retreat toward the beach, waved.

"Bud hates shopping," Cora said pleasantly. "He says that he married me for better or for worse, but not to go shopping with."

Mary Helen snickered.

"It was funny about the first four thousand times he said it." Cora, shading her eyes against the sun, located her husband on the shore.

"He's watching the fishermen," she said. "He should be good for at least two hours."

Two hours of shopping! For a fleeting moment Mary Helen was tempted to follow Bud's example. Unfortunately she had her task before her.

"Heidi is alone," Mary Helen said. "Maybe we should ask her to join us." She turned to find the girl, but Pepe already had her in tow, and Heidi appeared happy to be there.

Pepe swaggered along talking softly, and Heidi's giggle floated on the sea breeze. Mary Helen was aware that none of this escaped Cora.

She scouted the crowd to see how Eileen was faring. The DeAngelos, following María José, strode along a treelined road at a fast clip. Eileen, walking as quickly as her short legs allowed, tailed them. The four, like a line of quail, zigzagged toward the black *jabón*.

Content that Eileen, at least, was making progress, Mary Helen resigned herself to Cora.

They sauntered by a flea market of stalls in companionable silence, examining shells, handcrafts, and the myriad trinkets on display. Mary Helen bought several inexpensive key chains with spiny murex shells dangling from them. These she'd bring home to the other nuns.

Understandably Eileen and she had been so preoccupied with the events of the last few days that they had almost completely forgotten about souvenirs. Not that the nuns would expect gifts under the circumstances. But with any luck at all, this whole thing would be solved before they left for home and the nuns never need know that there were circumstances!

Cora filled her shopping bag with T-shirts, lace mantillas, brightly painted ceramic plates, dolls dressed in Galician costumes, and several things that Mary Helen was unable to identify.

"Will you be able to carry all that?" she wondered aloud.

Cora stuffed in yet another set of painted napkin rings. "That's what Bud is for," she said.

Sated at last, Cora pointed down the road toward La Toja Cosméticos. "Let's give that soap a try," she said, and Mary Helen agreed.

As they strolled along, several Gypsy women, arms loaded with bargain souvenirs, tried to sell their wares, but even Cora had tired of shopping.

"Are you sleeping well?" Cora asked, putting her heavy bag on the ground for a rest.

"Pretty well," Mary Helen said. "Why? Are you having trouble?"

Cora's watery blue eyes focused on her, and she put her

hands on her broad hips. "How can anyone sleep well after what's gone on?" she asked. "Aren't you afraid we're all going to be murdered in our beds?"

"Not really." Mary Helen fudged a little. "Whoever murdered Lisa, and we don't know for sure that it was one of our group, must have a motive. People don't kill without a reason."

Cora looked doubtful.

"Even serial killers have a reason, twisted though it may be."

Cora's expression moved from doubt toward terror.

"Not to say we have a serial killer in our midst," Mary Helen added hastily. "I was just making a point," which even she was beginning to lose.

"Heidi did it!" Cora blurted out.

Mary Helen couldn't believe her ears. "Heidi? What makes you think Heidi killed Lisa?"

"She had plenty of reason. Did you notice how much attention that young man Pepe was paying to Lisa? And today do you see he's with Heidi? Mark my words, she is enjoying his attention."

"Everyone enjoys attention," Mary Helen conceded, "but to kill for it? I'm not sure about that."

Narrowing her eyes, Cora gave it some thought. "Then Bootsie did it!" she said.

"What reason does Bootsie have?" Mary Helen was beginning to get used to Cora's blunt accusations.

"Plain as the nose on my face," Cora said. "Jealousy! Did you see how Lisa flirted with all the men. Even my Bud, the old goat. And if you ask me, that Roger enjoyed it."

"Roger is a college professor," Mary Helen reasoned. "Over the years lots of young women must have developed crushes on him. Bootsie must surely take them all with a grain of salt. If she murdered every coed who was attracted to her husband . . . Well, you see what I mean."

Cora nodded. "Rita! It must be that little Rita then. You know, Sister, she's tiny, but I'll bet that with all that exercise she does she's a lot stronger than she looks."

"What do you think is Rita's motive?"

"Did you notice that her husband the doctor—"

"Dentist," Mary Helen corrected absently.

"If you ask me, that Neil was interested in lots more than Lisa's teeth. Did you notice that her front one here"— Cora pointed to her own gapped teeth—"was crooked?"

Mary Helen nodded, amazed at all that Cora did notice.

"They were cootchie-cooing when we all were in the airport in Madrid."

Mary Helen frowned. All she could remember about the Madrid airport was Rita taking Polaroids. "Rita wanted us all to move together for her pictures." Mary Helen tried to bring some reality back into the discussion.

"So now she has it on film." Cora smirked. There was a hard glint in her watery blue eyes. "Did you notice that at our dinner on Friday they were barely speaking?"

Mary Helen did remember. She also remembered that Neil had whispered his apology for disturbing her in her room. Was he trying to keep his wife from overhearing? Had he actually been on his way to meet Lisa Springer when he stumbled into their room instead?

She hesitated to encourage Cora. "Surely they'd only had a misunderstanding," she said. "That happens in the best of families."

"That little Rita has a very hot temper, which we've all seen. Right?"

Mary Helen didn't deny it. The whole group, after all, had seen Rita's temper. Cora gloated. A quick breeze ruffled her waxy yellow hair. She smoothed it down with her fingers, then picked up the heavy shopping bag.

"Heidi, Bootsie, Rita. Why is it that you've only named women as the murderer?" Mary Helen asked.

"Because Lisa was a woman that only another woman would kill." Cora gave a complacent smile.

And like Chaucer's Wife of Bath, Mary Helen thought, in my "owene grece," she leaves me to "frye."

As they neared the *jabón* store, Mary Helen spotted Eileen. She was coming out of the building alone, carrying a large black and gold bag. "I guess I won't need to go in," Mary Helen said to Cora, pointing to the bag. "Sister Eileen looks as if she shopped for the two of us."

With a uninterested grunt, Cora headed like iron to a magnet toward the cosmetics store.

Mary Helen, her mind reeling backward and forward through Cora's conversation, waited on the lawn for her friend.

"Wait until you see this." Eileen opened her bag. It was filled with three-bar boxes of soap, done up in black and white. "They were on sale. I've a bar for each of the nuns, I think. The only catch is we need to give this bar to someone who doesn't know Spanish." Eileen pointed to the middle bar in each package. It was clearly marked "Gratis!" on a pale yellow band. "If I'm not mistaken, that means 'free,' " she said.

"How did it go with the DeAngelos?" Mary Helen asked. She was hoping that one of them had accomplished something besides shopping.

"Elusive as all outdoors." Eileen rolled her eyes. "And they could not get rid of me fast enough. Bootsie bought some cosmetics. I watched her do that. I turned away to look at something, and when I turned back, she and Roger were gone with not so much as a by-your-leave."

Across the road Mary Helen noticed an empty bench shaded by a lush chestnut tree. Eileen looked tired. She surely was ready to sit down. "Let's go over there. . . ."

The revving of a motorscooter engine drowned out the rest of her sentence. Several hundred meters down the road two Gypsy women, dressed in somber black dresses, straddled the machine. Brightly colored scarves were wound around their heads like babushkas. At this distance it was impossible to tell their age, although there was a middle-aged thickness about them.

The engine whined, and with a kick of the stand, the driver opened up the throttle. Small whirlwinds of dust and gravel trailed the scooter, which accelerated, sweeping down the road toward them. The women struggled against the velocity for balance.

Eileen gripped Mary Helen's forearm. The bike was gaining speed. Mary Helen spun in fear. It was roaring directly toward her. This couldn't be happening. Eileen shrieked as the scooter cut away from the road and onto the grass. Stunned, Mary Helen felt strong, thick fingers ripping at her arm, at her purse, locking her wrists with their hold. The screeching motorscooter shivered with the force.

As she fought against the pull, Mary Helen's reflexes took over. Slamming, tugging, twisting, she wrenched back her purse, pulling the woman's torso with it.

The woman lunged. Mary Helen felt fingers dig into her hair and yank. With a quick twist she was thrown to the ground.

Shouting a shrill curse, the driver floored the motor. The scooter rattled, then bolted off the grass, bounced onto the road, and in a burst of speed skimmed away toward the sea.

"Mary Helen." Eileen, near tears, crouched down beside her.

María José ran across the lawn. "What happened?" She was panting. "Are you two all right?"

Eileen folded down onto the grass. She began to shake. "Two women on a motorscooter tried to run down Mary Helen." Her brogue was so thick that María José was straining to comprehend.

"What they wanted was my pocketbook."

"What in the name of God do you have in this thing?" Eileen grabbed the offending purse.

"Are you all right?" María José asked, her voice crackling with tension.

Mary Helen's neck felt stiff. Her scalp burned. A dull headache was on its way. "I'm really fine," she said, trying to prove it by smiling. "Where is Officer Zaldo?" she asked. "Maybe we should notify him."

María José sat down on the grass next to the two nuns. "Our fine Officer Zaldo is in the hotel having his lunch," she said with disgust.

Sister Mary Helen started to laugh. "Typical," she said. "Even in Spain you can't find a policeman when you need one."

For some reason, which she was never fully able to explain, she crumpled forward, put her hands over her face, and began to cry.

♦

Kate Murphy sat alone at her kitchen table, feeling lonely. There was really no reason for it; at least, that was what she had been telling herself since Jack's mother had picked up little John about half an hour ago.

Today was to be her day. She had scheduled an eleven o'clock appointment with René to get her hair cut. She fingered the straggly red pieces curling around her neck and over her ears, trying to remember when she'd last had a haircut. Regardless, she certainly needed one.

At her mother-in-law's insistence, Kate had also made an appointment to have her fingernails done. She never, or almost never, had her fingernails done. She didn't really like to have a perfect stranger fiddling with her nails. Why had she allowed herself to be persuaded?

Kate stared morosely into her coffee mug. Jack had made the coffee this morning, and it was so weak that she could make out the bottom of the cup.

"She who must be obeyed," the mug said. Jack knew that she enjoyed "Rumpole of the Bailey" and Rumpole's wife, Hilda, to whom the cup referred. Nonetheless, Kate was piqued when she found it with her Christmas presents. The mug, more appropriately, should have gone to Jack's mother. Loretta Bassetti meant well. Kate knew that. But some days, like this morning, she was hard to take.

The doorbell had rung impatiently, and Loretta bustled into her house before Kate was even dressed.

"Today is Monday," Loretta announced as though Kate might have forgotten. "You do remember that this is to be your day, and I'm taking my favorite grandchild . . . my only grandchild," Loretta added, making it sound like a condemnation, "off your hands."

I like him on my hands, Kate wanted to say, but she knew Loretta would be hurt.

A thin ray of morning sun cut across the tablecloth and landed on John's empty high chair. A petrified lump of oatmeal still lodged in the corner of its tray. Like the lump in my stomach, Kate thought, going to the sink for a sponge to clean it up.

She was not surprised that Loretta had missed the corner in her hasty cleanup. It was as if she were impatient to whisk the child away.

John's little mouth turned down when Loretta, not she, began to feed him his mush, and Kate was afraid he was going to cry. But Loretta made choo-choo noises and zigzagged the spoon like a runaway train until both John and Kate stared at her in amazement.

When the spoon finally connected with his mouth, John giggled and Loretta puffed with pride. "He just has to get used to his old Nonie," she said in a falsetto voice that made the baby giggle again.

Why? Kate wanted to ask, but she knew the reason. Mama Bassetti had set it forth on several occasions, which didn't stop her from saying it again this morning.

"If you should choose to go back to work"—Jack's mother used the same tone of voice that she'd use to say, "If you should choose to rob a bank" or "to take drugs"—"you cannot leave this precious baby with just anyone."

Kate felt her temper rising. She had no intention of leaving John with "just anyone."

Mama Bassetti's tirade held no surprises. This morning it ended where it always ended: "A child belongs with family. I'm family. It's only natural that the precious baby stays with me."

"That doesn't seem fair. . . ." Kate protested, as she always did.

"Fair, shmair!" Loretta waved a plump hand as if to dismiss all arguments. "This is not some labor dispute we are talking about. This is my baby!"

"This is *my* baby," Kate said aloud to the half-empty coffee mug. She fully intended to ask Sister Mary Helen and Sister Eileen for baby-sitter suggestions. Surely they'd know some student or alumna to recommend.

She realized she was running out of time. In just one week she was expected back at work. Why hadn't she asked them before they went to Spain? She avoided the answer, which was obvious to any pop psychologist. Some part of her did not want to go back to work, while another part of her did. By not making a decision, she was making one, of sorts.

I really do intend to ask the nuns, she protested to herself. They have a beat on nearly everyone who ever passed through the college's hallowed halls. Some woman must be into child care. Kate refilled her mug with coffee and sat back down to brood.

What if they were detained in Spain? She didn't have a good feeling about Spain. Actually she wasn't feeling good about anything today, period. She couldn't put a finger on why the nuns in Spain worried her. It was just one of those intuition things. Wouldn't Gallagher throw a fit if she said that to him!

Kate glanced up at the kitchen clock. Her old partner should be at his desk by now. She'd call to prod him on.

"Homicide," Gallagher roared into the telephone.

"Not having a good day already, huh?" Kate asked.

"Damn right! Not even noon, and my stomach is killing me! And do you want to know why?"

"No," Kate said.

Gallagher ignored her. "Your friends in Spain, that's why."

"What happened?"

"First thing this morning, Mrs."—Kate heard him fumbling through the papers on his desk—"Mrs. Mabel—there's no mister—Springer, mother of the victim, Lisa Springer, was in my office tearing my ear off. She wants the SFPD to get her daughter's body back for a decent burial."

Kate's stomach sank at the thought of having to claim your child's body. "You can't blame the poor woman, Denny," she said.

"I didn't blame her, Katie-girl, at first. Hell, I felt sorry for her. It's got to be tough. She's a skinny little thing, and she's raised three kids, single-handed. Worked her butt off. I was only trying to explain that Spain is out of our jurisdiction, that the American Embassy would handle it.

"Then she starts mumbling about being a taxpayer and demanding that we arrest the killer. I'm still patient. Like a saint, if you ask me. I explain again that the crime falls into the jurisdiction of the U.S. government and the Santiago police.

"Now, Mrs. Mabel Springer is as tiny and timid-looking as milk toast, but it turns out, Katie-girl, that she is anything but. She starts hollering in a high, skinny little voice, cussing out everyone, beginning with our esteemed mayor, his board of supervisors, the chief of police, the Department of Public Works, and me.

"Goddamn, if she wasn't the bereaved mother, I'd have hauled her in. Finally she refuses to budge until I've called somebody. Did you ever try to get through to somebody in an embassy?"

Kate admitted that she hadn't.

"If you did, you'd know it's easier to get ahold of the Ayatollah Khomeini."

"He's dead, Denny."

"You get my point, Katie-girl. By that time I'm raving as bad as Mabel is." He let out an exaggerated sigh. "Anyway, why did you call? Are you coming back to help me unravel this mess?"

Kate felt her stomach lunge again. "You know I'm not due back yet. I have a week left to decide. I was just checking in with you to see how things are going with that list of tour members I gave you on—"

"Lousy," Gallagher burst in. "If I'd quit getting interrupted—"

"Right," Kate said. "I'll let you go. It's just that I don't have a good feeling about the case."

"Who does?" she heard Gallagher shout before he slammed down the receiver.

Kate rinsed her cup and set it on the drainboard to dry. Trying to put aside her inexplicable feeling of dread, she went upstairs to run her bath.

A wave of nausea washed over her when she started to dress. She felt hot and sticky. Maybe she was coming down with something. Impossible! she thought, examining her flushed face in the dressing table mirror. She was just warm from the tub. Once she was out in the fresh air, she'd be fine. It was as good an excuse as any, however, to cancel her nail appointment, and she did before she left for René's.

♦

Impatiently Comisario Ángel Serrano waited all day for a decent time to place a phone call to San Francisco. The tour bus would return from La Toja soon, and he wanted as much information as possible about its occupants before it arrived.

All around him he heard the sounds of his small police force changing shifts. Members of the day shift were clearing off their desks as an even smaller skeleton crew was settling in for the night.

When he thought he could wait no longer, Ángel called Kate Murphy's number. He let the phone ring twenty times. When no one answered, he cursed himself for delaying so long and slammed down the receiver.

Next, he tried Carlos Fraga.

"Hello," a man's voice answered on the second ring. Ángel noted the heavy Spanish accent.

"Señor Carlos Fraga, *por favor*," he said.

"This is he," Fraga answered in flawless Spanish. Ángel's spirits rose. Not only had he reached Pepe's uncle in America, but they could speak without Ángel's searching his memory for the unfamiliar English words.

After Ángel explained who he was and why he was calling, he noted that a certain reluctance crept into Fraga's voice.

"My nephew is basically a good boy," Fraga assured him. "He would never harm anyone."

"I am not accusing him of murder," Ángel told him. "I just want some background information on him."

"Pepe is my wife's sister's boy," Fraga whispered into the receiver.

"And you cannot talk right now?"

"*Sí, señor,*" Fraga answered quickly.

"Your wife is listening?"

"*Sí, sí, señor!*"

"Is there another number where I can reach you?"

Happily Carlos Fraga gave him the number of the Patio Español. "I will be there in less than ten minutes," he said.

Fifteen minutes later, when Ángel was finally reconnected, he could hardly stop Fraga from talking.

"Ay, that Pepe," Fraga said angrily. "He is my wife's sister's only child, spoiled, shiftless, and, I regret to say, señor, he is"—Fraga switched to English—"a bum."

"What exactly do you mean by that?" Ángel asked, wondering if he had translated correctly.

"A bum is a bum is a bum!" Fraga shouted. "The boy—no! He is no longer a boy. He is a man of thirty. He has no steady work, no real job, no responsibility, but, always, always, a scheme. 'A deal,' he says. And his deals always lead nowhere but to trouble!"

"If he has no job, what is he doing leading a tour group in Santiago?" Ángel asked.

"*Dios mío!*" Ángel envisioned Carlos Fraga holding his head. "That is the latest and, señor, the most expensive of his deals, at least for me. He promises Pulmantur that he will organize a Holy Year pilgrimage for ten to Santiago. They advance him some money. It is September, and he still has no pilgrims. Pulmantur wants him to produce or give the money back. He can do neither.

"Suddenly, señor, it is my problem. I tell my wife's sister, 'Let them put him in jail! Good riddance!' My wife gets into it. She calls me 'heartless,' then stops speaking to me at all. In the end, señor"—Fraga's tone was martyred—"what can a man do?

"I run a contest at my restaurant. Fortunately two nuns have entered, so I can pull their names for a tax write-off, at least. The rest I just choose, fair and square. There are two young girls on the trip. Maybe, I hope, when I see them, maybe my nephew will get to know one of them and settle down. Better yet, maybe he will find some nice rich Spanish girl and settle down in Spain. But no! He can't do anything right! Now he is involved in murder." He gave a pitiful sigh.

"You say that this is your nephew's latest scheme. There were other schemes?"

"Ah, señor. Once the dumb ox sold advertising for a throwaway paper. Of course, I had to take a full page, but I was his only customer. To get more, he offered so many specials that not only did the paper lose money, but he lost his job and his paycheck to make up the difference."

Ángel chuckled, and Fraga picked up steam. "Another time he and a friend invented a can crusher. They were going to make a million. Of course, I had to buy one for the Patio Español. The crusher not only crushed the can but held on to it so tightly that it took three of my busboys and the cook to pull the can loose! My sister-in-law has two thousand of these crushers in her basement next to boxes of see-through drainpipes. Who in his right mind, I ask you, would pay good money to see dirty water go through a drainpipe?"

Ángel had heard enough of Pepe's escapades. They were

foolish, granted, but not criminal. This call must be costing his department a fortune.

"Do you think, Señor Fraga, that your nephew Pepe would be capable of murder?" he asked bluntly.

There was a long silence. "I am sorely tempted to answer yes, Comisario. That is one way to be rid of the bum for good, but in all honesty, I must say no."

"Why is that, señor?"

"Because poor Pepe could not be a murderer. He has neither the brains nor the gumption!"

By the time Ángel hung up he had begun to feel that his niece, María José, was not so bad after all. Since you can choose only your friends and not your relatives, he was grateful that Divine Providence had not saddled him with a Pepe.

Long shadows began to fill his small office. Before he left for home and supper, he decided to try Kate Murphy once more. When he had the information from her, he would be able to relax and enjoy his meal.

He listened to the ringing and was about to hang up when someone grabbed the receiver.

"Hello," a woman answered breathlessly. He recognized Kate Murphy's voice.

"Did I catch you at a bad moment?" he asked.

"Not at all." Kate sounded happy to hear from him. "I just came through the door and the phone was ringing. I'm glad it's you. How are the Sisters doing?"

"Sister Eileen is fine," he said, "but Sister Mary Helen has had a rather unfortunate incident." He told her about the nun's near fall in the Tower of Hercules.

"Is she hurt?" Kate asked.

"Shaken, of course, but not really hurt."

"Oh, good!" He heard the relief in Kate's voice.

"Has your friend been able to find any information on the other tourists?" Ángel asked hopefully. "As you can see, it is becoming even more imperative that I find something, anything at all, that will help me discover who has a reason to kill Lisa Springer and who, now, has a reason to want to harm the good Sister."

"Inspector Gallagher is working on it today. It's still too early here in San Francisco for him to have found any real leads." Kate paused, and Ángel wondered why she was hedging. "There is something that perhaps I should have told you before," she said finally.

"Anything would be helpful."

Quickly Kate Murphy told him about Sister Mary Helen's role in helping the police department solve several murders. "To anyone who reads the Bay Area papers, and I assume all your suspects are from the Bay Area," she said, "the old nun is notorious. And I might add, she may present a real threat."

The back of Ángel's neck prickled. He had sent the nuns off on a tour to La Toja with María José in command. Officer Zaldo was trailing, but if they were, as this Kate suggested, in real danger, would Zaldo be aware of it? Had he, unwittingly, facilitated a second murder?

He must call Julietta, tell her not to wait supper—his stomach rumbled in protest—then go right to the *hostal* to await the bus's return.

"Comisario? Are you still on the line?"

"*Sí*, Inspector Murphy. What you have just told me has taken me by surprise." He tried to keep the anger out of his voice. If this case was to be solved quickly, he needed her cooperation. "I wish I had known this sooner," he said.

"Why is that?" Kate sounded anxious.

"Because I have allowed the Sisters to go on another tour today."

Kate sucked in her breath. "I am sorry!"

Ángel's temper waned now that he was not alone in

feeling guilty. "Those things happen," he said with more lar-
gesse than he felt. "Would you advise me to put the Sister,
maybe both Sisters, into protective custody?" He heard her
laugh echo down the phone lines.

"That would be like trying to hold two tigers by their
tails," Kate said. "More trouble, Comisario, than it's worth."

"What, then, would you suggest?" Ángel used his most
formal tone. He liked being taken seriously, especially when
he was hungry.

"I'd encourage you to collaborate with her. Rather, with
the pair of them," Kate said. "They are uncanny when it
comes to ferreting out the guilty party. And I, Comisario,
have learned from experience that they make much better
friends than enemies."

"Collaborate with nuns on police work?"

"I know it sounds bizarre," Kate said gently, "but I promise you, you won't be sorry."

Sorry? Ángel thought, replacing the receiver and quickly
picking it up again to call his wife. What is sorry is my police
force. I have few enough officers to cover the students, the
usual tourists, and the residents; none, *por Dios*, to spare. Of
necessity, my team must be made up of Esteban Zaldo, María
José, two old nuns, and me.

Despite the seriousness of the situation, Ángel had to
laugh. It was like those old-time American comedians. What
were they called? The Keystone Kops. All his bunch lacked
were nightsticks, the Black Maria, and, of course, the high-
crowned hats.

◆

By the time the Pulmantur bus pulled up in front of the
Hostal de los Reyes Católicos, the rain had stopped. Banks of
lights flooded the cathedral. They shimmered across the slick
flagstone Plaza del Obradoiro, illuminating the entire area.

Sister Mary Helen was surprised to see Ángel Serrano huddled in the arched doorway of the hotel. With his hands in his pockets and his tan raincoat wound around him for warmth, the *comisario* might easily have been mistaken for a plump relief carving, set in the stone facade.

She wasn't the only one who'd spotted him. Before the door of the bus opened, María José was waving frantically. Officer Zaldo, who had tailgated the bus all the way back from La Toja, jumped from the patrol car, leaving his door swinging open.

At first glance Mary Helen thought Ángel looked strained. Now with both María José and Zaldo surging toward him, she was sure of it. His color drained. His shoulders tensed. Beneath a worried frown, his sharp eyes roamed the bus windows. If she wasn't mistaken, he was relieved to see her. Could the news of the Gypsies and the purse snatching have traveled so quickly? If not, what was wrong?

Before the bus door snapped shut behind its last passenger, Comisario Ángel Serrano had herded the two nuns, his niece, and Officer Esteban Zaldo into the hotel manager's office. They stood in a silent knot in front of the large hand-carved desk.

"The manager kindly offered his accommodations for privacy," Ángel said. He pointed at chairs for Zaldo to move from the wall and set around the desk.

Mary Helen felt a twinge of sympathy for the manager. From the telltale bits of paper still strewn across the desktop, his offer might have been more forced than free. What is so urgent? she wondered.

With cold courtesy, Ángel invited them all to be seated.

"Is something wrong, Comisario?" Mary Helen could restrain herself no longer.

He raised his hand. "One moment, please, Sister." He turned his head.

Oh-oh! Mary Helen thought, doing a quick examination of conscience. Something is stuck in his craw. Unable to surface any recent guilt, she focused her attention where his was, on his niece.

"What is it you are trying so frantically to tell me, María José?"

As if a sluice gate opened, a swift and mixed channel of Spanish and English poured over the room. María José deluged her uncle with every detail of Mary Helen's "accident" in La Toja.

"And while this happened"—she glared at a red-faced Zaldo—"your officer was having his dinner!"

Ángel's dark eyes moved toward Esteban Zaldo, whose whole body stiffened to attention in his chair. "Even policemen have to eat," Ángel said with unexpected sympathy.

Flipping her magenta hair, María José turned to face Ángel, but his attention was still on Zaldo.

"Did you notify the La Toja police, Esteban?" he asked in Spanish.

María José switched to the role of an interpretor.

"Sí, Comisario." Zaldo's trim mustache scarely moved when he spoke.

"And what did they say?"

"That the snatching of purses from tourists is becoming common among Gypsies. And that they will be on the look-out for two women on a motorscooter, although this is common, too."

"Then that is perhaps all it was," Mary Helen said when María José finished the translation. "A common occurrence." Common or no, the ordeal had worn her out. She wanted nothing more than to forget all about it and go to bed. She pushed herself up from the chair.

"Please, Sister, one more moment. There is something I need to talk to you about."

Here it comes! Mary Helen readied herself for combat. Whatever is bothering him has something to do with me, and it's on its way!

"Today I had a conversation with Inspector Kate Murphy."

Mary Helen felt her face flush. Beside her Eileen shifted in her chair. Zaldo stared in baffled silence.

"Why didn't you tell me that you—and your work with the San Francisco police—are notorious?"

"Even if it were true, Comisario, that is hardly the first thing one says about oneself."

"Sister"—anger clipped his words short—"I never would have allowed today's trip to La Toja if I had realized."

Mary Helen's back went up. Baloney! she thought. You wanted us all in one place. Maybe you even hoped something would happen to give you more to go on. Their eyes locked.

"You see how you reacted to the news?" Her words every bit as clipped as his. "Would you have told you if you were I?"

She watched a small storm fight its way across Ángel's round face. Fortunately for both of them he began to grin. "Your point is well taken, Sister," he said.

Happily Mary Helen felt the tension fall away. Fair is fair, she thought. "To be completely candid," she began with a stab of compunction, "Sister Eileen and I are doing a little inquiring on our own." Still somewhat unsure of her ground, she emphasized the word *little*.

Taking her cue from Mary Helen, Eileen moved forward in her chair. "We divided the group in half," she said, "to see if we could discover a motive."

Ángel blinked with surprise but recovered quickly. "Good." He sounded almost enthusiastic. "The quicker we solve this thing, the better for us all. Motive, as you say, is indeed the key."

With a few words he dismissed Officer Zaldo, who looked

relieved to be on his way at last. "María José"—Ángel pulled a blank sheet of hotel stationery from the desk drawer—"write everything down for us."

With the skill of two old schoolmarms the nuns quickly outlined the information they had gleaned.

"The Fongs," Mary Helen began, and waited until María José scribbled down the name. "Neil is a dentist. Rita teaches aerobics. Four children. They live outside San Francisco in Burlingame. Claim never to have met Lisa before this trip. No apparent motive. She is talkative. He is the quiet, unassuming sort who doesn't miss much."

Ángel brightened. " 'He thinks too much: such men are dangerous.' Oxford!" he said, and gave a triumphant laugh at his ability to remember Shakespeare.

"Very good!" Eileen said appreciatively, then took up the litany. "The Bowmans, Cora and Bud."

María José wrote.

"Successful small business. One grown son in the business now. Did not know Lisa. No apparent motive."

"Cora, however, thinks a woman did it," Mary Helen said.

Eileen's eyebrows shot up in surprise.

"She told me at La Toja today that she suspects Heidi, Bootsie, and Rita, in that order, of committing the murder."

"What did she give as a motive?" María José glanced up from her paper.

The *comisario* frowned at his niece. "Ho-Ho! I ask the question, you write." He turned to Mary Helen. "What did she give as a motive, Sister?"

"Jealousy in all three cases."

"Hmm." Ángel hummed to himself thoughtfully.

Mary Helen cleared her throat. She hoped they'd soon call it a night. Everything, including her throat, ached. Especially her head. "The DeAngelos, Bootsie and Roger. He is a history professor. Did you find out which college?" she asked Eileen.

"Redwood, a small Marin County community college."

"And Bootsie. We both found her very tight-lipped."

Ángel frowned at the term.

"Noncommunicative, almost elusive."

He nodded his understanding.

"Nervous, too, I'd say," Eileen added, "but a wealth of information on *jabón*!"

Mary Helen closed her eyes, trying to remember whom they'd left out, then popped them open again. Too dangerous, she thought. I'll drop right off to sleep.

"Let's not forget Heidi," Eileen said.

Mary Helen nearly had.

"The girl is quite distressed about her mother's reaction to the murder," Eileen began. "She makes no pretense about liking Lisa. That is, liking her recently. Yet she didn't seem to hate her enough to kill her."

"And let's not forget Pepe." Mary Helen was glad to reach the end of the list. Actually they had tried to pump María José, but under the circumstances it seemed foolish to say so.

"In popular parlance, Pepe is what you call a flake."

The *comisario* looked puzzled again, and María José translated. "His uncle concurs," Ángel said, beaming like an aging cherub.

María José glanced at her notes. "I know that Cora named the three women on the tour as having a motive. But doesn't strangulation seem more like a man's crime than a woman's?" She put down her pencil and flexed her fingers to relax them.

Her uncle shrugged. "What makes you say that?"

"Because a woman would have to be very strong to hold down her victim, especially a young, strong one."

"Are you telling me that women are the weaker sex?" he baited her.

The young woman's eyes blazed. "Of course not," she snapped. "It just seems physically more suitable for a man."

Quiet settled over the manager's office like the night-cloth over Sister Angela's canary cage, leaving each one to brood on his or her own thoughts.

"Where does all that information leave us?" Ángel broke into the silence.

"With the same basic questions and no answers," Mary Helen said. Oh, to be upstairs in bed!

"Perhaps things will be clearer after a good night's sleep." Eileen sounded hopeful.

A sharp rap on the door startled them all. Zaldo was back with a sheaf of papers for the *comisario*.

"*Gracias*, Esteban." Ángel took the papers and, once again, dismissed the officer.

"Now that we have all decided to collaborate"—his eyes twinkled as though he had made a great joke—"let me share some information from Dr. Morales's report on the cause of death." He scanned the papers.

With her last spurt of energy, Mary Helen perked up.

"According to the doctor," Ángel began, "the victim's head hit the corner of the crypt. Hmm . . . she was rendered unconscious. Then strangled. So, Ho-Ho, we could have here an equal opportunity murderer."

María José refused to bite.

"The weapon, garrote, tool, whatever you choose to call it, is as yet unidentified. The bruise it made is about two inches wide in the center, narrower at each end, and it is perhaps padded. Does anything come to mind?" he asked after a silence.

At the moment the only padded thing that came to Mary Helen's mind was her pillow.

"It is a strange bruise for a strangulation," he said.

"Sister Mary Helen has a strange bruise on her lower back," Eileen blurted out. Mary Helen could not believe her ears.

Ángel reddened. "What sort of bruise do you have, Sister?" He avoided her eyes.

"Three bruises about the size of American dimes." Eileen riffled quickly and apparently unsuccessfully through her traveler's dictionary trying to find the Spanish equivalent.

"Put that thing away," Mary Helen snarled, then smiled sweetly at the *comisario*. "I'm sure they are from that tower business," she mumbled, not sure what she'd do if he asked to see them. "From someone's knuckle or thumb perhaps."

"Or a ring! A large, round ring stone!" María José's eyes danced. "Maybe our killer is a woman after all."

Unexpectedly a gentle rain began to patter against the window.

"Enough for tonight," Ángel said, levering himself up from his chair.

Mary Helen heard his stomach growl.

María José smirked. "Is Tía Julietta saving your supper?" she asked.

Ignoring her, Ángel bundled himself into his raincoat and checked his watch. "I will meet with you all here tomorrow morning at ten." He glanced around to see if all agreed. Anyone who didn't was too tired to object. "Sleep well," he called. "Tomorrow with fresh minds things will be clearer."

♦

From their bedroom window Mary Helen watched Ángel and María José cross the nearly vacant Plaza del Obradoiro together. Halfway across, she brushed his cheek with a kiss, and without many words, they headed in opposite directions.

The steady rain glistened in the floodlights and washed

down the ancient stone buildings, the cars, and the pedestrians alike. It cleanses the whole world, Mary Helen thought as she watched a single drop slither down the glass pane.

"What are you looking at?" Eileen asked from her bed.

"Nothing. Just watching the rain. 'The silver hosannas of rain.' Do you remember where that's from?"

Eileen grunted a no. "You must be asleep on your feet," she said. "Get into bed, old dear, before you catch your death."

The rainwater made a low, steady trickle against the stones. Mary Helen leaned out to pull shut the window. A cough floated up from the floor below. Someone else was watching the rain.

Déjà vu! Mary Helen thought. Like last Friday night when all this started, when she'd thought she saw someone on the cathedral steps. She squinted into the watery darkness. Tonight, strain as she might, she was positive that those cathedral steps were completely deserted.

tuesday, october 12

feast of
Our Lady of the Pillar
Spanish National holiday

♦

The ragged ring of the telephone woke Sister Mary Helen. She sat up quickly. Too quickly. The blunt edge of an ax split her head, or at least that was how it felt.

The second ring woke Eileen. "Who in the world?" she said, fumbling toward the phone.

Mary Helen fell back against her pillow and listened to the one-sided conversation. "Good morning to you, Comisario . . . Yes . . . Oh? . . . Yes . . . Fine."

"What was that all about?" With one eye open, she watched Eileen crawl back under her covers.

"That was the *comisario*. He forgot to tell us that today is a national holiday in Spain."

Mary Helen tried to remember the date, but the effort only made her head ache more.

"It's the Feast of *Nuestra Señora del Pilar*," Eileen said. Her accent was improving. A few more weeks and she'll be able to pass for a native, Mary Helen thought, then wished she hadn't. The idea of being detained in Spain sent her stomach into a spasm.

"Our Lady of the Pillar," Eileen translated in a sleepy voice. "If I remember correctly, there's a shrine in her honor in Saragossa with a miraculous statue of the Virgin. Tradition says that St. James himself built the original shrine at the request of the Blessed Virgin." Eileen's brow puckered. "So you see it's all of a piece."

"What's the 'pillar' part about?"

The questions slowed Eileen down, but not for long. "The statue sits on a pillar, hence the name," she said with so much confidence that Mary Helen believed her.

"And the whole country takes the day off?" she asked.

Eileen yawned. "Yes, and isn't that grand? The *comisario* called to tell us that there is a special Mass in the cathedral at ten. They will use *el botafumeiro* to incense the church, and he thinks it is something we ought to see. What I think is that he'll be there and wants to keep an eye on us. Anyway, he'll meet us here after Mass, which should be about eleven-thirty."

"What time is it now?" Mary Helen asked, but Eileen had fallen back to sleep. With superhuman effort, Mary Helen raised her head and studied the clock. Thank God, she thought, sinking into her pillows. We have another hour.

◆

The nuns were the last of their group to arrive at the cathedral. When María José saw them, she waved to them to join the others at the foot of a gloriously carved pillar. Like a mother bird, she gathered them in a tight little nest around her.

Mary Helen shivered. Cold and dampness emanated from the stone. When María José began to speak, her breath came out in little clouds.

"Today, *peregrinos*, you will witness one of Santiago's unique sights," she said. Her dark eyes danced like a child's as she began her narrative.

By contrast the *peregrinos* themselves looked as pale and stony as the statues surrounding them. Actually the faces on the statues showed more animation.

The cathedral filled quickly. An odd mixture of the faithful and the curious spilled through the Pórtico de la Gloria into the main body. Sister Mary Helen strained to hear María José's voice, which was nearly drowned out by a Japanese tour guide, red flag aloft, giving her spiel.

"Speak up, please." Roger DeAngelo's eyes flicked around the group, then returned to the speck he was studying on the granite column.

Although María José frowned with annoyance at the request, she did raise her voice. "*El botafumeiro* is a huge censer that dates back to the Middle Ages," she shouted over the Japanese guide, who turned up her volume, too. "It began because hundreds of pilgrims slept in the cathedral, and they smelled. It perfumed the great naves and purified the air. Incense was thought to be a germ killer.

"*El botafumeiro* weighs fifty-four kilos—one hundred and nineteen pounds," she translated quickly. "And it stands this high."

Mary Helen peered around Cora's shoulder to see where María José's hand was. She held it about three feet from the ground.

"That's what you call a king-size incense burner," Eileen whispered. "Just think what our Sister Anne could do with it."

Mary Helen grimaced at the thought.

"Eight men called *tiraboleiros* swing the censer." María José toned down her voice as if she were about to confide a secret that she didn't want the Japanese to hear. "When Alfonso the Third was king, the bishop of Santiago was accused by three men of our village of nefarious crimes too ugly to be announced."

"Nefarious?" Heidi wrinkled her nose.

"Vicious," Eileen whispered, "very wicked."

Like any good gossip, María José paused to let her listen-

ers' imaginations run wild. "The king," she said as confiden-
tially as if it had happened last week, "ordered the bishop
thrown to a wild bull. Of course, the bull knew our bishop
was innocent, so instead of charging the good man, the bull
placed his head in the bishop's hands. The king was furious.
'You and all your offspring,' he thundered at the accusers, 'are
sentenced to perpetual servitude in the cathedral which you
have shamed.' It is the descendants of these three families
who still swing *el botafumeiro*."

Head held high, María José inched her charges down a
crowded side aisle toward the main altar. The organ thundered. A fugue soared into the arches, filling the gigantic
nave and drowning out any attempt at conversation.

As the group approached the sanctuary, someone
touched Mary Helen's forearm. "Good morning, Sister." It
was Ángel Serrano. He was sitting just behind what looked
like a pewful of dignitaries. "How are you this morning?" he
asked.

"Fine," she said, anxious not to lose the others in the
packed crowd. Their leader had apparently hit a small bottle-
neck, so Mary Helen had time for a quick introduction to
Serrano's wife. Small, round Julietta was a woman with a
friendly face. The kind of person you'd enjoy having a cup of
coffee with, Mary Helen thought.

"This is my sister, Pilar." Ángel pointed to the woman
on the other side of Julietta. Thin and wiry, Pilar was the
antithesis of her brother. An astonishingly large white orchid
was pinned to her angular shoulder.

"It is my sister's birthday and feast day," Ángel said by
way of explanation.

The crowd loosened, and Mary Helen, afraid that she
would lose sight of the back in front of her, waved a hasty
good-bye.

"Quickly, stand here." María José ushered them into a

space just behind the altar rail and beneath the ornate pulpit. The Japanese tourists bunched in beside them. Despite their objections, the two nuns were shuffled to the front of the group. "You are shorter than most of us," Bootsie said. "We can see over you."

"And we can see what to do," Bud Bowman said, which Mary Helen thought was probably closer to the truth.

With a long, loud chord, the organ signaled the procession. Amid the scuffing of wooden benches and kneelers, the throng rose to greet it.

First came the altar boys in lacy surplices, carrying tall candles in silver candlesticks. Behind them a steady stream of priests in shimmering brocade chasubles decorated with the cockleshell of St. James flowed down the center aisle. They were followed by the monsignors in white and gold and magenta and more delicately embroidered shells.

Finally, the archbishop of Santiago de Compostela entered the cathedral with Canon Fernández at his side. Carrying his curved, golden crozier in one gloved hand, the archbishop blessed the crowd with the other as he moved down the main aisle. In his jeweled miter, pectoral cross, and cockleshelled cope ablaze with gems, he looked taller and mightier than he ever could hope to in his plain black suit. With his golden cope waving behind, the archbishop swept on to the baroque sanctuary, where he blended in perfect harmony with the gilded altar.

Meanwhile, two short, balding men in bright crimson cassocks approached the sanctuary. On their shoulders they bore a long, thick pole, and from the pole hung an enormous silver-plated censer, the famed *botafumeiro*.

The hushed crowd watched six more crimson-clad men rush around the sanctuary. One unfastened a thick hemp rope from its hook on a nearby pillar and brought it to the middle aisle. One end of the rope was attached to a complicated-looking series of pulleys on the ceiling. The other end was quickly lashed to the huge iron loop attached by chains on top of the censer.

A haunting organ melody filled the church. Spellbound, Mary Helen watched the eight red-robed men grasp the rope and pull it taut. They tugged. The censer rose several feet off the ground. The archbishop, flanked on either side by priests holding back his cope, stepped forward. He lifted the lid and ladled incense onto the hot coals. With a metallic rattle, the lid fell back into place. Smoke circled and curled around the enormous thurible. Gingerly the archbishop gave it an initial shove down the transept.

At some silent signal the eight men pulled the rope, and with a jerk el botafumeiro rose just above the upturned faces of the crowd. In a rhythm perfected by time, they strained at the thick hemp until the censer, like some giant smoke-throwing pendulum, began to swing across the breadth of the cathedral. At first its arc was shallow, but with each pull the height and momentum grew until it seemed to take on a life of its own.

Higher and higher it rose. Faster and faster it swung, spitting out sparks and throwing clouds of incense. Before Mary Helen's astonished eyes, the censer soared toward the ceiling, then fell like a missile of silver, cutting across the dim cathedral, perfuming the air as it flew. Each pull propelled it close to the roof. There it hesitated, trembled, then roared down again, whizzing past with sickening speed until it flew out level with the ceiling some ninety feet above.

Mary Helen sucked in her breath. The next pull of the rope would surely send el botafumeiro crashing through the roof. Just as that seemed certain to happen, the impetus was imperceptibly checked, and inch by inch, the heavy, hot vessel began its descent toward the floor.

All around her Mary Helen heard her fellow pilgrims releasing their breaths, like a collective sigh of relief. A little prematurely, she thought, as the censer skimmed past her at what seemed seventy miles an hour. The thing could still do a lot of damage if the coals went sailing or if, God forbid, it hit anyone. She'd feel a lot better when it was safely on the ground.

"How do they stop it?" she whispered to Eileen.

"They grab it, I think."

"It's a frickin' Disneyland," Bud Bowman remarked irreverently.

Mary Helen covered her nose against the cloying incense. Head raised, she watched the huge *botafumeiro* climb fifty feet into the air. Someone bumped against her, not a gentle, accidental nudge, but a deliberate, hard push.

A hot streak of fear shot through Mary Helen. Her thigh hit the altar rail. She pushed back against the pressure, struggling to keep her balance, not to topple forward.

High above them, *el botafumeiro* trembled in space, hesitated, then plummeted toward the sanctuary. Mary Helen felt a second nudge. Harder, more vicious than the first. She was being pushed over the rail into its path. She tried to twist, to glance behind her. Stop! she wanted to shriek, but fear closed her throat.

The seconds seemed frozen; she was like an animal caught in headlights. She watched the huge censer, spewing sparks and smoke, speed toward her. Closer, closer. Eileen screamed and clutched at her, but Mary Helen felt herself teetering, off-balance, right into its course. Dear Lord, here I come in a blaze of glory, she thought crazily. Her whole body tensed for the collision.

The world stopped for a moment until Ángel Serrano's voice jerked it back into motion.

"Get it!" he shouted in Spanish. And one small red-clad figure lunged forward in a kind of flying tackle to grab the chains. With the echoing clang of metal, he hurled himself around the censer, and using his own weight and momentum, he brought the smoking *botafumeiro* to a abrupt stop, inches from where Mary Helen stood.

"Thank God, for the nefarious," she said, giddy with relief. It was the only thing she did say before she fainted.

◆

"I never faint," Mary Helen protested, removing a cold wash-cloth from her forehead. "I never even feel faint."

"Anyone would have under the circumstances," Ángel Serrano assured her. "I almost fainted myself."

Pale-faced, Eileen stood beside Mary Helen's bed with a glass of water. "Take these." She handed Mary Helen two white tablets, which she obediently swallowed.

"How did I get here?" Mary Helen wiped drops of water from her upper lip.

"Those dear little red-coated men carried you on a stretcher." Eileen peered down, her gray eyes swimming with concern.

"Those poor devils are really paying for their ancestors' sins." Mary Helen tried to act glib, but an act was all it was. Her insides were as cold and shaky as tomato aspic, and she felt that at any moment she might explode into tears.

"What did I just take?"

"Something to relax you," Eileen said, and, aware of Mary Helen's abhorrence of pills of any sort, added, "Probably just the Spanish version of aspirin."

"Do you have any idea who pushed you?" Ángel's face was drained of all color except for two bright red circles on his chubby cheeks.

"None whatsoever." Mary Helen took a deep breath. "Could it have been an accident?" But even as she asked, she began to shiver and to become conscious of the soreness in the small of her back.

"Too many accidents, I'm afraid, Sister." Ángel's eyes were hard.

"Who was behind us?" Eileen wondered aloud. "Everybody and nobody," she answered herself.

"I have questioned them all. Several times." Ángel sounded frustrated. "Everyone says the same thing. 'I did not do it, and I did not see who did. I was looking up.' They all were looking up," Ángel muttered. "The whole congregation was looking up."

"It's a good thing you weren't." Mary Helen patted his chubby hand. "Thank you," she said, feeling tears well up in her eyes.

Embarrassed, Ángel cleared his throat. "Rest today, Sister. I have put Officer Zaldo at your door. No one is to come in without his permission. If, after a rest, you feel like going out for anything, even to dinner in the salon, I implore you to take him with you."

When the *comisario* left, Mary Helen and Eileen eyed each other. "That was close, old dear, too close." Eileen's brogue was thick. "We have to figure out what you know or have that is making someone want to . . . silence you."

Mary Helen could barely summon up the energy to agree.

"Think, Mary Helen. Think of something, anything we can start on."

"I'll try," Mary Helen said, "but right now my mind is about two blocks beyond exhaustion."

"I'll bet it is." Eileen clucked. "Why don't you try to get some sleep? I'll think for a while."

Mary Helen struggled to keep her eyelids up, but they were too heavy. "Maybe if you flip on the television for a while, we'll get our minds off everything, and things will be clearer when we get back to them." She knew the sentence was circuitous, but she was too groggy to straighten it out.

With a click the television came on. Mary Helen lifted her eyelids for a second. Before her, cavorting on the screen, was Daffy Duck. Was he speaking Spanish?

"Is that our Daffy Duck?" she asked, her eyelids slipping shut.

"We're all a little daffy, ducky!" Eileen's voice sounded far away.

Only when she actually laughed at Eileen's horrible pun did Mary Helen realize what the white pills were: a sedative. She was whirling toward a deep darkness. They have given me a sedative.

♦

Head down, Ángel Serrano made his way through the choked streets of Santiago toward the police station. By a hair he beat a cloudburst into the front entrance.

"I do not want to be disturbed," he barked at anyone within shouting distance, then slammed the door for emphasis.

Ignoring a stack of messages on his desk, he dropped into his swivel chair, pushed it back, propped his feet on the desktop, closed his eyes, and tried to reconstruct the scene in the sanctuary. He wanted it clear in his own mind before he continued to question the Americans. When he spoke to them, none claimed to have known exactly what had happened.

"Maybe the smell made her dizzy," Cora said sensibly. "I was feeling a little dizzy myself."

Roger DeAngelo agreed, and Bootsie fluttered her thick false eyelashes to stress the point.

"The poor thing." Rita was sympathetic. "It scared me to see her slip forward like that. What if—" María José's face had blanched, and Rita knew enough to stop.

"Who was directly behind Sister?" Ángel had asked bluntly.

"I'm not sure," Roger said. "I was so busy looking up at that contraption I'm not sure who was directly in front of me. Besides, when that Japanese group squeezed in next to us, we all shifted."

"Could it have been one of them?" Cora asked hopefully.

Ángel knew that the picture was there somewhere in his brain. He must concentrate, remember where each one was standing. Remember how they shifted. The two nuns were in front, he was sure of that. Their tan Irish knit sweaters stood out in contrast with the bright colors surrounding them.

His niece, he remembered, ended up in front, too. Closest to the main altar. That made sense, since María José had led the group up the aisle and into the sanctuary.

He placed her there in his mind's eye, right next to Sister Eileen, but she did not look right. Something about the picture was off. Someone else, short, was between them. Heidi. That was who.

He remembered now. Heidi, with hair the color of caramel candy, was a contrast with Ho-Ho's magenta mop. Encouraged, he reconstructed the front line. María José, Heidi, Sister Eileen, Sister Mary Helen.

A sharp rap at the door broke his concentration. *"Pase!"* he shouted.

"Perdón, Comisario." An officer cracked open the door. "It is the mayor on the line. He has been trying to get you all morning."

"Tell him I am busy." Ángel waved the man away. "Busy thinking, if I ever get the chance," he added to the closed door.

"My niece, Heidi, the two nuns." Ángel reviewed the front row in his mind. "Next to Sister Mary Helen?" He con-

centrated, trying to see who was there, but the person remained a blank.

Now the back row, he thought, those behind. He remembered the round, placid face of Dr. Fong peering over his
half glasses at *el botafumeiro*. His face appeared between María
José and Heidi. Next to him . . . Ángel squeezed his concentration harder, hoping a face would appear.

A stiff rap came on his door.

"*Pase!*" he shouted angrily. The door opened, and the
archbishop's secretary, Monsignor Varela, strode into the office as if by divine right. With him was Canon Fernández.
The monsignor peered down his aquiline nose at the soles of
Ángel's shoes.

"Monsignor!" With a slam of his chair Ángel was on his
feet. "I wasn't expecting a visit from either of you. Why didn't
you simply call?"

The monsignor was tall and, in Ángel's opinion, thin
enough to hang on a clothes hanger. This morning his face
looked as if he had just found a flea in his hair shirt. By
contrast, the canon was a bantam of a man whose bluster kept
him perpetually rosy-checked.

"The canon tells me he has been calling all morning,"
Monsignor Varela said, "only to be told that you are busy."

"Indeed, it is true." Ángel frowned. "I have been trying
to reconstruct the whole series of events in my mind, to figure
out, you see, who had the motive, the opportunity, the
means."

"Figure all you please"—the monsignor's tone was superior—"but do it quickly. The archbishop is very distressed
with the events that have taken place during the past week in
his cathedral. I understand that your niece has been involved.
The archbishop is also very concerned and, I daresay, dis-
pleased about a young lady from our city being involved in
such a crime. We don't want to displease God's servant the

archbishop, so I urge you to solve this quickly." The monsignor didn't say so, but his tone implied "or else."

The canon, smirking like a satisfied tattletale, held open the door. With a flourish the monsignor swept out of the office, leaving Ángel mentally telling God's servant the archbishop what he might do with his distress, concern, displeasure, and, yes, his "or else."

"God, forgive me," he whispered, rolling his eyes toward heaven. "It's nothing personal to You! None of us can help our subordinates."

The clerics' visit ruffled Ángel's powers of concentration. He closed his eyes and rubbed his temples in an attempt to regain the scene. After several tries it seeped back into his mind.

In the front row he saw María José, Heidi, Eileen, Mary Helen, and someone else. Behind them, Neil Fong, someone tall, Bud Bowman's head over Eileen's right shoulder, Cora, someone else, and Pepe on the end. That made sense. Pepe would have brought up the rear.

An insistent knocking interrupted him again. This time Ángel walked to the door and opened it himself. He was glad he did. It was the bold young reporter from *La Voca de Galicia*, and he had no intention of letting the man get a foothold in his office.

"I am busy." Ángel's voice echoed through the entire floor of the building.

"The people have a right to the news," the reporter said quietly.

"What is your name, señor?" Ángel asked in a voice he hoped sounded threatening.

"Héctor Luna," the young man answered, totally unimpressed. "Have you any comment on this morning's near tragedy in the cathedral, Comisario?"

"No comment." Ángel tried to control his temper.

"Only twice in its entire history has *el botafumeiro* ever posed a threat to the congregation. Once in 1499 and again in 1622—"

"I know the history of *el botafumeiro*, young man. I knew it long before you were born and I don't need any upstart—"

Luna cut him off. "Is it true that your niece, María José Gómez, is helping you with your investigation?"

"Get him out of here before I'm the one taken in for murder," Ángel roared so loudly that two of his officers came running.

He slammed the office door and watched the small pane of glass rattle in its frame. What if word of María José's involvement should reach Pilar? There would be the devil to pay.

Ángel's temples throbbed, and his stomach churned. He checked his watch. No wonder! It was dinnertime. Picking up the telephone receiver, he called his wife and told her that he'd be home as soon as he was done thinking.

"Thinking, Ángel?" Julietta's voice was sympathetic. "You know you can always think better when you are full. What are you thinking about?"

Quickly he told her about trying to reconstruct the positions of the American pilgrims in the sanctuary, about those he could place in his mind and those he could not.

"Of course," he said, "the blanks are the DeAngelos and Rita Fong. I could ask them, but I want them to think that my eye was on them the entire time. It should have been, you know," he admitted to his wife.

"The Chinese lady was in the front row next to the Sister," Julietta said.

"Are you sure?"

"Sure, I'm sure. She had on a lovely silk dress that I'd die to fit into."

"And behind? Do you remember who was behind María José?"

"The woman with the too-black hair?"

"Bootsie. How can you remember that?"

"Because I thought both Ho-Ho and this woman should see my hairdresser Ricardo for a better coloring job."

"And on the far end behind the Sister?"

"Two men."

"Can you recall who stood where?" he asked, more as a credibility test than anything else. He had remembered Pepe was on the far end.

"Ángel"—her voice was teasing—"you know that I don't look at any man besides you."

"So now we know that one of the two of them shoved her, but which one had the reason?"

"Ángel, *querido mio,* anyone could have pushed her," Julietta reminded him gently. "Anyone with a reason and a long arm or a quick step. Anyone who took advantage of everyone else's distraction. You must admit all eyes were on *el botafumeiro.*"

"Enough, Julietta!" he said impatiently because he knew she was right.

"Come home." There was a subtle invitation in her voice.

"I have to call San Francisco. As you helped point out, the motive here is all-important. And I have some police detectives investigating these North Americans for me."

"Ángel, it is nighttime in San Francisco. Come home. Eat something. The time will go more quickly."

"What if the mayor calls or that newspaper reporter? Or if the canon comes looking for me, or, God forbid, what if the children drop by?"

"I have already taken care of that. I have pulled down the shades, locked the doors. If the phone rings, we will not answer. If anyone comes, we will pretend we are not at home. We will only be at home to each other," she said in a rich, husky, inviting whisper. "We will not be at home to anyone else, especially the children."

♦

Kate Murphy had just put John down for his afternoon nap when her telephone rang. Damn, she thought, glaring at it. If that is Mama Bassetti, I am not answering any questions about baby-sitters or work.

She stomped toward the telephone table. I know if I go back, I'll need someone to stay with John. I know I have to make a decision soon. Too soon, she thought, her neck muscles cramping with tension. If she intended to return to Homicide, she was due to report in on Monday!

"Hello," she barked into the receiver, and was pleasantly surprised and a little embarrassed to hear the crisp British accent of Ángel Serrano.

"I have some disturbing news, Inspector," he said. The long-distance wires snapped. "I am afraid that someone is making attempts on Sister Mary Helen's life."

"Is she all right?" Kate asked. Dread filled her stomach like a heavy meal.

"So far she is fine." Ángel's tone was urgent. "At the moment I have her under police protection, but I am most anxious that we identify this killer before we have another victim. That is why I am calling you, Inspector Murphy. Has your friend found anything?"

Kate had intended to nap first, then call Gallagher just before he quit at four-thirty. That way he'd have had the entire day to investigate, and maybe he'd be so eager to get home that he wouldn't question her about her decision to come back to work. But the *comisario*'s voice was so grave she changed her mind immediately.

"I'll call him right away," she said. "As soon as I've talked to him, I'll call you right back."

"Regardless of the time, Inspector." Ángel sounded relieved.

"Homicide," Dennis Gallagher shouted into the receiver.

"How are you doing on those tourist names I gave you?" Kate dived straight to the point.

"It's like pulling molasses," Gallagher said, happily mixing his clichés.

"The *comisario* just called me, and he's afraid someone is trying to kill Sister Mary Helen. So he wants as much information on these clowns as possible. And as soon as possible. What have you found?"

"What the hell is this world coming to? Killing an old nun!" Gallagher sounded as shocked and outraged as if he hadn't suggested it several times himself.

Kate heard him shuffling through papers. "Jose, aka Pepe, Nunez," Gallagher began. "Hispanic male, thirty years old."

"Skip the statistics," Kate urged. "Just get to the juicy stuff." Her pencil was poised.

"Our boy Pepe has a juvenile record. Nothing dangerous. Mostly disorderly conduct. Stuff like mooning in Golden Gate Park and peeing in the lagoon at the Palace of Fine Arts. He has a host of unpaid parking tickets. One of these days he'll find a Denver boot on his tire, but that's Traffic's problem."

Gallagher paused, and Kate heard him lighting his cigar stub.

"Haven't you given up that disgusting habit yet?" she asked.

Gallagher just blew smoke into the phone by way of a response.

"The Fongs," he said. "From our point of view, both Rita and Neil are clean as a whistle. Not even a parking ticket. He's a dentist with a small but lucrative practice on Judah Street. I called his office but got his exchange. I haven't had time yet, but I'll nose around, see if I can locate his receptionist or his dental assistant to get something about his character."

"I'll let you know, Denny, after I talk to Serrano, but if he's that squeaky clean, maybe there's no reason."

"The squeaky cleans can fool you, Katie-girl," Gallagher said, "and we got two more of them, Cora and Bud Bowman. He's an electrician. I went by his shop in Daly City and talked to his kid. Nice young fella, big, blond, worried about his folks. Far as I can figure, they are as average as apple pie. Been married over forty years. Worked hard at it and at the business, the kid says.

"Being married that long would keep them, at least him, out of trouble, if you ask me." Kate heard Gallagher rustle his papers. "I had to call Patio Español three times before I got ahold of Carlos Fraga. He's a busy guy, and to hear him talk, he'd be just as glad if they kept his nephew in the Spanish hoosegow for good."

"Why is that?" Kate asked.

"Because he thinks the kid's a pain in the butt, that's why."

"But that doesn't make him a criminal."

"Sometimes you wonder," Gallagher said pensively. "Kids, not cute little kids like yours, Kate, but kids change, and sometimes they drive you right over the wall.

"I took another shot at Mrs. Mabel Springer, the victim's mother, to see if she'd thought of anything. The poor lady seemed skinnier and mousier than before except this time I didn't fall for it. Once burned, you know—"

"Did she think of anything more?" Kate asked.

"No. When I got to the house, she was going through some old things of Lisa's. Pictures, yearbooks, you know."

"Doesn't she work?"

"Night shift," Gallagher said, "at San Francisco General. Anyway, she gave me some coffee, and she sort of seemed to want company. Showed me lots of pictures of Lisa. Speaking of kids who change, did that kid change!"

"What do you mean?"

"She went from a fat, redheaded kid in pigtails to a fat teenager to one gorgeous young woman with flowing red hair."

"What happened to change her?"

"Her mom said that it was after her freshman year in college. She got a scholarship to college. When she got there, something happened, her mom has no idea what, that made her decide to change, and you should see the results."

"What college?" Kate scribbled down Gallagher's answer on her pad. "Belmont?" she asked. "The Catholic college down the peninsula?"

"No." Gallagher hesitated, and Kate heard the sound of more paper shuffling.

"Here it is." He must have really worked to locate the place, Kate thought. "Belmont College. It's a small private college in Greensboro."

"North Carolina?" Kate was surprised. "That's a long way from home."

"According to her mother, the farther away the better. Not from the mother's point of view—the kid's. Lisa wanted a new start. Her mother says she dropped everything to go away, even her old friends like Heidi next door. They were inseparable since they were babies. That's why Mrs. Springer thought it would be good for them to go on this trip together. Then she wept like it was her fault, somehow, that the kid was killed. I stuck around for another cup of coffee. Then, since I was so close, I went next door to the Williams house. Did I hit pay dirt!"

"You mean you think Heidi may be responsible."

"What I mean is, I think it's a miracle that somebody in that house hasn't killed the mother."

"Why?" Kate tried not to sound disappointed. She was hoping for a quick breakthrough in this case.

"Because the woman is obnoxious. First of all, she's built like a Sherman tank. No, I take that back. She's built more like one of those balloon people they blow up and float in the Macy's Thanksgiving Parade on TV."

Kate had an instant and vivid picture of Mrs. Williams.

"Her name is Marvis. Marvis Williams. The husband is Malcolm. The missus keeps house, and Malcolm works at a bank within walking distance of home. Every noon he walks home for lunch, which Marvis cooks. And, from the looks of her, eats most of. So, when I rang their bell, I hit a doubleheader."

"They sound like something out of a fifties sitcom," Kate said.

"Except they aren't funny. Marvis may not look like a Sherman tank, but she acts like one. Malcolm apparently did not want Heidi—who is their only child, and they look like she was born late in their lives—anyway, he didn't want her to go to Spain. At all. Forbade it.

"But the poor guy, who looks more like Mr. Peepers than anything else, had no real say. The missus thought Heidi should go, and should go with Lisa next door.

" 'Lisa knows how to have fun,' the lady tells me. 'She went to college and is making a life for herself. I want our Heidi to get out and meet the right people while she's young. I want her to have a better life than I've had.'

"The husband's face and neck went beet red, and he gave her such a look that I was afraid he'd leave his bowl of chicken noodle soup and strangle her. 'Lisa Springer's kind of fun is not the kind I want my daughter to have,' he bellows.

" 'And what kind of fun do you have?' his wife yells. 'Heidi is my daughter, too, Mr. Perfect. Although you'd never know it. She's exactly like your mother. She can't cut loose, enjoy herself. Even when I get her out of this house and she goes to Spain, she screws up. I skimped around so she could have a few nice dresses and some spending money, and what does she do? She gets mixed up in a murder.'

"By this time Marvis's eyes are blazing, and her face is almost purple. 'Wait until I get my hands on that kid,' she says to the father. 'I'll wring her fat neck.'

" 'If anyone needs her fat neck rung, it's you, my dear Marvis,' he says as mean as you please. Only this time he is staring into the empty soup bowl.

"Right about then I excuse myself. I know either a donnybrook or a coronary is coming, and I don't want to explain to the lieutenant why I'm in the middle of the Williamses' kitchen when I should be working on my own cases."

"Sounds gruesome."

"They're a couple of showstoppers," Gallagher agreed.

"Did you get to the professor and his wife? What were their names?"

"DeAngelo," Gallagher roared. "What do you think I am? Some sort of miracle worker? It's only two-thirty, for crissake, and I'm not bilocated. I can do only one thing at a time."

"Does that mean no?"

"It means sort of. The professor teaches at Redwood College in West Marin. He's new there, and the secretary I talked to was real closemouthed about information. She wants me to talk to the dean or whoever and ask him about the guy. All she'd do was make me an appointment with the big mucky-muck, which is for tomorrow morning. I did manage to wres-

tle the name of the Faculty Wives' president from her. Bootsie is a member of the group. The president lady wanted to see
my credentials, so I decided to see them both tomorrow
morning, unless, of course, the lieutenant sees me first."

"You're great, Denny. The *comisario* will be thrilled to
get this background." Kate heard the baby fussing in his crib.

"It would have gone a hell of a lot faster if I had some
help," Gallagher wasn't able to resist saying. "Are you coming
back?"

Kate felt a tightness over her eyes. "I haven't decided,
Denny," she said.

"I wish you'd hurry up and make up your mind, Katie-
girl. The suspense is killing me."

"You'll know when I know," she said. "Promise."

"Not that I'm keeping track, mind you, but I think your
leave is up on Monday."

John let out such a wail that even Gallagher heard it.

Perfect timing, Kate thought.

"Sounds like wet pants to me." Gallagher said a quick
good-bye. And as in so many things, he turned out to be
right.

John, still pink and warm from sleep, sat in his high
chair, picking up Cheerios. "Na, na, na," he called to Kate,
who was at the kitchen sink, pouring them both glasses of
orange juice.

"Bye, bye, bye." He waved his small hand to get her
attention.

"As soon as you finish this, we'll go bye-bye." Kate stared
out the kitchen window at the brilliant October sunshine.
Across the yards a neighbor's sheets and pillowcases moved
like a fully rigged ship in the sparkling blue sky. On the horizon a bank of fog was in a tight roll somewhere near the
Farallon Islands waiting for sunset.

It was a perfect day to take the baby for a ride in his

stroller. She still had a tight pain over her eyes. Fresh air and exercise would do them both good. Maybe while we're walking, Kate thought, I'll be able to figure out exactly what to tell Comisario Serrano.

In the end the decision was easy. She told him everything, and a groggy Ángel was very grateful for the information.

wednesday, october 13

feast of St. Edward the Confessor, king of England

✦

"Are you awake yet, old dear?" Mary Helen heard Eileen whisper.

She was awake, but not awake enough to say so or even to open her eyes. She lay still, listening to the rain beat against the granite facade of the hotel and run in noisy streams off the gargoyles.

Today's rain was not the gentle, caressing rain of which Santiago boasted. It was a driving, drenching rain that threatened to soak everything in its path. A sudden, frigid gust of wind filled the room. Eyes still shut, Mary Helen heard the dull flap of velvet drapes billowing out into the bedroom. Crazily she longed for her own cozy room at Mount St. Francis, her own bed, her own pillow.

"I know you're awake." Eileen's voice was matter-of-fact. "Your breathing's changed. Do you hear anything?"

Without answering Mary Helen listened. A soft yet steady tap-tap came on the door. "I hear it," she croaked, "but I don't know if I can move yet."

Pulling her bathrobe around her, Eileen opened the door a crack. "Come in, dear," she heard Eileen say. Curiosity getting the best of her, Mary Helen opened one eye to see who "dear" was. It was María José.

"I am sorry to disturb you, Sisters, but my uncle has sent me to see how you are this morning."

"Is it morning?" Mary Helen pulled the covers up around her ears like a mummy.

"It is nine o'clock, Sister. Tío was afraid, when neither of you came to breakfast, that you were not feeling good this morning." Her dark eyes searched Mary Helen's face, which was all that was visible, for any outward signs of disease or disaster. "You are all right, aren't you?" she asked anxiously.

"I don't know. I haven't moved anything yet." And I don't intend to while you're standing there staring at me, Mary Helen thought.

Eileen must have perceived the stalemate. "Why don't you go downstairs to the dining room, María José, and bring us up a tray?"

"I could call room service."

Eileen, pretending she didn't hear, hustled the girl out the bedroom door.

Slowly, painfully Mary Helen sat on the edge of her bed.

"What are you feeling like this morning?" Eileen asked, helping Mary Helen hobble into the bathroom.

"Like I played halfback for the Forty-niners again yesterday!"

"And we won?"

Mary Helen flinched. "I'm in too much pain to care!"

"Should you see a doctor?" Eileen paged through her pocket dictionary, obviously in search of the appropriate phrase.

"Put that thing away," Mary Helen pleaded, "before we are in worse trouble than we are already. For all we know, doctor and undertaker may be only a mispronunciation apart."

Despite her soreness, both Mary Helen and Eileen were

up and waiting when María José returned with a busboy carrying the large linen-draped tray.

Mary Helen savored each mouthful of the strong, hot coffee and felt it roll all the way down. When she bit into the crisp, crusty roll, she realized how hungry she was.

Having refused coffee, María José sank down into a chair and watched glumly while the nuns ate.

"What's the matter?" Mary Helen asked when she finally swallowed the last corner of roll.

"Tío has canceled today's trip," she said. "He thinks it would be too dangerous."

"Where were we off to?" Eileen refilled both cups.

"Mount Santa Tecla to see the Celtic ruins. The place is steeped in history. There is a replica of an ancient hut and from the rugged mountaintop a magnificent view of the coastline of Portugal."

A rugged mountaintop! Inwardly Mary Helen shuddered. That's all she needed—a little shove into Portugal! No wonder Ángel Serrano was concerned.

"I am not disappointed about the trip. I am disappointed because I wanted to help Tío catch this murderer before he kills a second time."

"You have my support," Mary Helen said, trying not to remember that she was the aforementioned second victim.

"How do you intend to catch this person?" Eileen moved forward on her chair.

"I think I know who it is," María José said.

"Who?" Both nuns sat bolt upright.

María José narrowed her dark eyes. "Pepe!" she said.

Sister Mary Helen was surprised. He was the last one she would suspect. "Do you have some reason for saying that?"

"I have been thinking about it," the young woman said. In the bleached morning light María José's face was pale and strained with a hint of blue under her eyes. Mary Helen suspected that she was doing most of her thinking at night.

"Pepe Nunez is quite the Don Juan, you know." María José yawned as if to prove Mary Helen's suspicions.

"That makes him unscrupulous," Mary Helen said sensibly, "not a murderer. To be a serious suspect, he needs a motive, means, and an opportunity."

"He had the opportunity." María José stared at the old nun. "Last Friday night we were to go to the opening dinner together, and do you remember what happened?"

Friday seemed so far away Mary Helen had to think. Pepe had escorted Lisa and Heidi into the Salón Real. María José, blazing with anger, arrived alone. "Yes, I do remember, now that you mention it."

"I assumed from what he said earlier that he was to escort me, but instead he left me waiting and picked up the two young girls. We had a fierce argument afterward."

I can attest to that, Mary Helen thought, remembering their battling figures in the deserted plaza.

"Then we went our separate ways."

Mary Helen remembered that, too.

"Maybe as our tour guide Pepe felt obliged to be sure his charges were enjoying themselves." Eileen leaned forward and patted María José's hand.

"That's just what he told me." María José pulled thoughtfully on her lower lip. "Still, we cannot let men get away with this kind of behavior and suffer in silence."

As Mary Helen remembered the late-night scene, suffering in silence was not an issue.

"Women must insist on being treated with dignity. I was especially angry with Pepe because I had high hopes for developing a relationship."

"You just met the man!" Without thinking, the words slipped out of Mary Helen's mouth.

María José looked puzzled. "From the first we were simpatico or I never would have consented to be his assistant."

"I thought you told me that you viewed Pepe as a business opportunity."

María José grinned sheepishly. "Of course, Sister," she said, "but I am not one who refuses to mix business with pleasure."

No wonder her mother's thin, Mary Helen thought, grateful that she needn't raise a dichotomous daughter like María José.

"Getting back to your point." Eileen cut in with a tone of urgency that surprised Mary Helen. "Pepe had the opportunity to kill Lisa."

"But so did Heidi. So did I, for that matter." Suddenly all business, María José had switched suspects. "And I am afraid everyone else did, too."

Mary Helen agreed. "Each married person on the tour claimed to be with his or her spouse all night. Of course, all uncheckable alibis, making everyone's whereabouts uncertain."

"We are also uncertain about what was used to strangle Lisa," María José said.

The three sat in perplexed silence and listened to the steady rain. "It's the motive," Eileen said at last. "We must discover the motive. Why did someone kill Lisa, and why is someone trying to kill Mary Helen?"

A sudden wind rattled the windowpane, and Mary Helen's breath went shallow. "Why, indeed?" she said with a stoutheartedness that fooled no one.

María José stayed for only a few more minutes. Mentioning something about wanting to catch her uncle, she left.

Eileen seemed glad. "She's a nice girl," she said, "and she means well, but you need some rest and quiet. Maybe I'll order a pot of tea and you can spend the rest of the day in bed reading and napping. We need to wash out some things."

"It seems almost sacrilegious to stay in our room in Santiago. Shouldn't we be out viewing the famous statues and works of art?"

"Give it a rest," Eileen said, and dropped their nylon stockings into the marble sink. "Don't you have a mystery squirreled away in that pocketbook of yours?" she called over the sound of running water.

Obediently Mary Helen dug into her bag for the paperback and began to read.

With the stockings hung dripping from the shower rod, Eileen perched on the end of Mary Helen's bed. "While I was rinsing, I was thinking. What do you have in that purse?"

"What do you mean?" Mary Helen was genuinely puzzled.

"Obviously it is what the Gypsy ladies were after. And your purse may have been what someone wanted at the Tower of Hercules."

"But it doesn't explain yesterday and . . ." Mary Helen faltered. She could not yet think calmly about her near collision with *el botafumeiro*.

"Maybe, maybe not. Getting back to the Gypsies." Eileen smoothly changed the subject. "If I were a Gypsy, your pocketbook would be the last one I'd snatch."

"What's wrong with my pocketbook?" With inexplicable loyalty, Mary Helen felt that she must defend the battered old thing.

"Nothing. But there's nothing right with it either. It's not a designer bag or even good leather. Nor do you, no offense, old dear, dress as if you have money. If I were a thief, I'd go for Cora's purse first, then Bootsie's or Rita's. Do you see my point?"

"Absolutely!" Eileen watched expectantly as Mary

Helen shook the contents of her bag onto the bed. Passport, comb, wallet, pen, keys, used tissues, pocket calendar, loose pesetas, glasses' case, Anne's travel diary, and, with a thud, a second paperback mystery.

The two nuns scrutinized the lot. "That's it!" Eileen pointed to the diary. "It has to be. What have you written in it?"

"Next to nothing." Mary Helen flipped through the book showing Eileen the nearly empty pages. The two nuns stood in baffled silence.

Suddenly it struck Mary Helen like a dash of cold water. "Of course!" she nearly shouted. "It's not *what* I wrote in the diary. It's what someone *thinks* I wrote in it."

Eileen's gray eyes clicked to attention. "You're right! Who saw you writing in it?"

Mary Helen's mind sped back over the last five days. Saturday morning she'd written in it in front of Cora and Bootsie.

She'd jotted something down in the catchall room when all were present except Bootsie and María José. María José had stumbled upon her writing in the lounge. "Everyone," she said. "Everyone saw me write in the darn thing!"

"So we're back to square one." Eileen sounded disappointed. "I bet you're right anyway." She watched Mary Helen shove her things back into her pocketbook, then walked to the window and peered out at the black and bruised sky. Rain blew sideways in sheets against the magnificent buildings that framed the enormous plaza.

Mary Helen limped over and stood beside her. "I'm getting submarine fever," she said.

"How can you be?" Eileen asked. "We've been in our room for not quite one whole day, and part of the time we were asleep."

"You were asleep. I could not seem to doze off."

"You were snoring, old dear."

Mary Helen chose not to dignify the remark with an answer. Instead she stared out into the Plaza del Obradoiro, rain-soaked and deserted, much as it had been on their first night in the *hostal*.

Below them someone coughed and banged the window shut.

"Do you hear that, Eileen?" Mary Helen strained, hoping the cougher would cough again. "Whoever that is . . ."

"Whoever who is?"

"The person who coughed."

"That's Bootsie DeAngelo." Eileen didn't miss a beat. "She's been coughing like that all week. Haven't you noticed? It's more of a clearing her throat than a real cough. I think it's a nervous habit."

Chagrined, Mary Helen stared at Eileen. She'd noticed that little idiosyncrasy herself. Why had she failed to put it together? Was she losing her touch?

"Well, then, Bootsie was at the window the night I thought I saw someone on the cathedral steps. The night before I found Lisa."

Eileen's face fell, and her eyes narrowed. "I do not remember your telling me about seeing someone on the steps," she said crisply.

Quickly Mary Helen explained the *comisario's* concern. "So, if I did see the killer and the killer saw me, I wouldn't want to put you in danger."

"That makes no sense at all," Eileen snapped. "We are sleeping in the same bedroom. I am your constant companion on the trip. For the love of all that's good and holy, I already am in danger. It seems only reasonable that I should be told!"

"You're right," Mary Helen said. "I should have told you." She was too sore and too lame to argue.

"And since when are you so obedient to police officers?"

Obviously Eileen was not yet mollified. "Kate Murphy and Dennis Gallagher will be duly impressed."

"I wonder if those two were able to find out anything helpful about the other tour members." Mary Helen tried valiantly to change the subject.

Eileen stared.

"All right. If you must know, I didn't tell you primarily because I forgot."

"That makes me feel a great deal better," Eileen said with her usual smile. "How do you think we can ask Bootsie if she saw anyone when you can't tell anyone you saw someone?"

"I don't intend to." Mary Helen cut through the meandering sentence.

"You don't?" Eileen blinked in surprise.

"No! I think we tell the *comisario* about the cough in the window and let him deal with it." Mary Helen hurriedly threw on her clothes. "Get your raincoat, Eileen," she said, "and let's go."

◆

For the tenth time Comisario Ángel Serrano wondered if he should have insisted that the Americans be brought to the police station for interrogation. He had hoped that questioning them here in the hotel manager's office would create a false sense of chumminess and that one of them might slip up on a detail, anything that might give him a crack in this case.

Now he asked himself if the stark walls of the police station interview room might have put a little fear into them, let them know this was not just a cozy chat. Would the American Embassy take exception if he brought them all in? He didn't need any more officials on his tail.

Ángel loosened his tie and ran his finger around his tight shirt collar. He had been at this for more than two hours. His throat was dry, and his patience wearing thin. One of these Americans was the murderer. He was sure of that, but which one?

He had begun the morning with Jose Nunez, aka Pepe. After a few minutes of questioning, Ángel agreed with the man's uncle. Pepe had neither the brains nor the guts for murder.

He had partied until three o'clock on Saturday morning, fallen into a dead sleep, and not awakened until Sister Mary Helen telephoned him in his room to tell him she had found Lisa Springer's body.

At the word *body* Pepe lost all his color. For a few tense seconds Ángel feared the young man might faint. He sent Officer Zaldo for water and a brandy. Ángel figured that if Pepe had killed Lisa, Sister Mary Helen would have found his unconscious body right beside hers.

Next Ángel had met with the Bowmans, Bud first, then Cora. He questioned them about their whereabouts at the time of Lisa's murder in a dozen different ways and each time received the same answer. The Bowmans had had a nightcap in the *hostal* lounge, a brandy for each. Then they had gone directly to their room.

"Bud's not much of a dancer," Cora said, "and I was tired anyway."

Once in bed Bud fell right to sleep and didn't move until morning. Cora reported hearing a heated argument in the hallway shortly after she'd turned off the light.

Either the Bowmans had rehearsed their deception perfectly, or they were telling the truth. Ángel tended to believe that they were. He put the pair at the bottom of his suspect list.

He had a bit more luck with the Fongs. Rita stuck to her original story. "As I told you, Comisario, Neil and I were arguing about his drinking." Giveaway lines of tension pulled her mouth into a tight little grin. "Wine makes him sick. He is allergic to it. When I reminded him, he lost his temper, shouted, and stalked off. Before I could say 'I told you so,' he was in our bathroom throwing up and moaning about his head." Her black eyes shone like hard, polished jet. "I was disgusted, but he was in bed with me until morning."

Ángel found Neil Fong an interesting character and, in contrast with his wife, a very poor liar. Even as Neil repeated his original explanation, which concurred with his wife's, his face paled and he began to blink.

"Are you allergic to wine?" Ángel asked.

"Yes." Neil blinked repeatedly. "No."

"Is it yes or no? Your wife says you are."

"I know she does, but I'm not." Neil's glasses slipped down his nose.

It was difficult for Ángel to imagine this mild man losing his temper and shouting, but according to his wife and Cora Bowman, he had.

"Was that what you two were arguing about in the hallway the night before Señorita Springer was murdered?" he asked.

Neil's face froze. Ángel could almost see the man struggling with his conscience.

"No, it's not," Neil said at last, his voice a whisper.

Ángel's hopes soared. Was this the breakthrough at last? He tried not to pounce. "What was it then that made you shout at her?"

"Rita kept kicking me under the table all night."

"I remember you said that." Ángel's hopes plummeted like a roller coaster. He hid his disappointment.

"I said that, but I told you that it was because she wanted me to go to bed. That was not the real reason."

"What was the real reason?" Ángel held his breath.

"We were fighting about Lisa Springer."

"What about Lisa?" His surge of elation returned.

Neil Fong's eyes blinked at an incredible rate of speed. "Rita thought that I was flirting with Lisa. Rita always thinks I am flirting with other women. I love my wife, but she is a very jealous and a very suspicious woman. I have had to let several capable hygienists go because Rita thought that I had something going with them."

"And was she correct?"

"No. They were just nice women, easy to talk to and attractive."

"Do you have affairs with women?"

Neil Fong looked more astounded than offended. "Look at me, Inspector," he said. "Do I look like the kind of man dozens of women flock after?"

Silently Ángel studied Dr. Fong. He was a slight, short man with a flat nose, glasses, and a tendency toward baldness. Since he could think of no tactful way to say, "I see your point," Ángel said nothing.

"This time Rita got it into her noggin that I was going after Lisa Springer."

"Did she have a basis for her suspicions?" Ángel asked, then watched the doctor squirm. Once again he was calculating his reply.

"Did you go after Lisa Springer?" Ángel persisted.

All the color left Neil Fong's face. "I did spend some time with her while we were on the plane."

"Anything else?" Ángel was sure there must be.

"Friday afternoon, after we arrived, Rita wanted to bathe and nap. I needed some exercise. I decided to walk around town sightseeing. It's more fun to go with someone, so I invited Lisa to come along, and she did. She was company, and that's all."

Ángel said nothing.

Neil stared at him over his half glasses. Like a Chinese

Benjamin Franklin, Ángel thought. The silence lengthened. Neil made a tent with his long, thin fingers, then turned his stare to his fingernails and examined them minutely. Still, Ángel said nothing.

"I know you're waiting for me to say something about Rita," Neil said finally.

Actually Ángel wasn't. He thought that Neil might confess that he and Lisa had taken a small hotel room for the afternoon.

"Rita was very angry when I came back. Furious, actually. Accused me of God knows what. 'I'm a doctor, for God's sake,' I told her. 'Would I have sex with a girl I hardly knew?'

" 'Doctors, even dentists, know about condoms,' she shouts. 'And malpractice,' I shouted.

"My wife, you see, Comisario, thinks I was infatuated with that young girl."

"Were you?"

"Of course not! Attracted, yes. Infatuated, absolutely not. To be honest, Lisa didn't turn out to be much fun at all. She seemed preoccupied. And she had all the self-absorption of the young," Neil added.

"Did you tell this to your wife?"

"I tried. I could not convince her that we hadn't had sex. When she gets like that, there's no use."

"Like what?"

Neil Fong looked wary. "Rita did not kill that girl, if that's what you're getting at, Comisario. She's jealous and verbally abusive, unreasonable even, but she would never physically hurt anyone. She gets you with her tongue, but she would never harm anyone's body. She's practically a physical fitness freak, for God's sake." He shook his head furiously. "I know she didn't do it."

"How can you be so sure?" Ángel wondered: Did Dr. Fong protest too much?

"I was in bed with her all night."

"Could you have dozed off?"

"Not likely. After I was sick, and I was sick for quite some time"—Neil reddened—"I got into bed, and we spent quite a while making up, if you know what I mean."

"Then what your wife says is true? You were violently sick?"

"I was, but after I got rid of everything, I felt lots better."

Ángel nodded. "I see. Then you are allergic to wine."

Neil blinked. "The wine is not what makes me sick. It's the fighting. The tension wreaks havoc on my stomach. Much as I try to control it, up it comes." He smiled and peered over his half glasses at Ángel. "I guess if I'm allergic to anything, I'm allergic to Rita."

When Fong left, Ángel immediately crossed him off the suspect list. Too poor a liar. Rita Fong, however, was a different matter. Ángel guessed that she was high on her husband's list, too.

A sharp rap on the door startled him.

"*Perdón*, Comisario." Officer Zaldo stood at stiff attention.

"Come in, Esteban." Ángel hoped he sounded genial. For some reason Zaldo's military precision put Ángel's nerves on edge.

"Our next suspect has not yet arrived, Comisario," Zaldo announced. "Shall I bring you coffee?"

"Gracias," Ángel nodded. A cup of coffee would be perfect. "Who is our next suspect, Esteban?" he asked.

"Señorita Williams," Zaldo said with an air of importance that rankled Angel.

The *comisario* had just taken a mouthful of coffee when the door flew open, and María José burst into the room.

"I am sorry, sir." Zaldo followed her, his face crimson with anger.

"It is not your fault." Ángel waved aside Esteban's explanation and turned his eyes on his niece. "María José, what is the meaning of this?"

"Tío," she said, ignoring both men, "tell me again. What shape was the murder weapon? That may be what we can use to break this case. Something of an unusual size and shape that only one person owns."

Ángel could feel his temper fizzing up. "María José," he said, his voice dangerously low, "I am in the middle of interrogating suspects. You are impeding police business."

María José's face froze. "Impeding!" Her eyes were large. "How can I be impeding? I am trying to help." She shot Zaldo a contemptuous look. "I would think with help like—"

Realizing where she was headed, Ángel cut her off. "I have half a mind to ask Officer Zaldo to arrest you," he said. "Perhaps a night in the cells would teach you to think. It might even improve your manners."

"I am sorry about not knocking before I came in, Tío." she said, although Ángel suspected that she wasn't sorry at all. "I thought that someone should look into the weapon."

"You may go, Esteban, and thank you." Ángel dismissed his subordinate before his niece insulted him further.

"María José," he growled, "Esteban Zaldo is my deputy. He is the one who should be investigating murder weapons. How do you suppose—"

"Esteban Zaldo is a dolt!" She snapped off his sentence. "He is tall and strong and dumb. Since we were youngsters in school, he has bullied people."

"Esteban is not the criminal." Ángel's shirt collar chafed, and his coffee was getting cold. He struggled to keep himself in check. "You cannot burst in on a criminal investigation and insult my police—"

"Esteban probably did not notice." She cut in again.

"María José"—Ángel, fighting to keep his temper, gave

it one more try—"I want to get on with what I am doing. This afternoon, after dinner, we will meet—"

"After dinner?" She interrupted him for the third time, and Ángel Serrano lost his battle.

"Enough," he shouted at the top of his voice, shocking María José into silence. "You listen to me, young lady." He watched her back go up at his choice of address and waited, daring her to comment. Wisely she said nothing.

"I told you I will talk to you after dinner about the weapon. If you intend to be of help to me, the first thing you must do is obey orders. Is that clear?"

Her mouth clamped tight, María José nodded. Her eyes could have burned him.

"Dismissed!" he shouted. Amazingly she swung on her heel and left.

Ángel leaned back in his chair, closed his eyes, and tried to calm himself before Heidi Williams was ushered in. He must clear his mind, recapture his patience. He hated to lose his temper. It made him feel hot and sticky all over. María José had no business driving him to it. She had no business at all insulting a police officer. Above all, she had no business being smarter than one!

Heidi Williams made a striking contrast with Ángel's niece. Where María José was dark and definite, Heidi was like a neutral smudge: hazel eyes, caramel-colored hair, and a plain, chubby face. Her expression was open, almost innocent, and she was much too plump, Ángel thought, to be wearing red slacks. He wondered why her mother hadn't told her that.

"Sit down, señorita." Ángel smiled.

Heidi immediately backed, like a child, into the chair. She popped her chewing gum.

Ángel's nerves tensed. "You may be the key to this whole case." He spoke gently.

Rather than act frightened, Heidi perked up. "Me?" she asked in a pleased voice. "How can I be the key?"

"You knew Lisa better than anyone else. You were with her in the bedroom. Maybe something that was said or done—"

"I've already told you everything I remember."

Another interrupter, Ángel thought wearily. "I am going to ask you some of the same questions all over again, Heidi. Maybe they will jog your memory."

With very little prodding, Heidi told him about Lisa's leaving the room on Friday afternoon to go sightseeing with Dr. Fong. "Lisa said that he was a drag." Ángel assumed that "drag" meant a bore. He wondered what Rita Fong would think of Lisa's appraisal. He nodded for Heidi to continue.

She told him again of fighting with Lisa on Friday evening, of making up, of Pepe escorting them both to the banquet, of dancing, and of their midnight walk. She ended her story as she had before: Lisa found a note from an admirer shoved under the door.

"Lisa tore it up and flushed it," she said.

Studying the girl, Ángel wished he could delve into her mind. Was she as naïve and simple as she appeared or was she as devious as a winding road? The room was quiet save for the cracking of her gum and the steady drumming of rain against the window.

"Did you like Lisa?" Ángel asked at last.

Heidi shrugged. "She was okay. We were best friends when we were little and when we were growing up. In our senior year she won a scholarship, and after high school she went away to college."

"What college?" Ángel couldn't remember having asked that question before. It didn't seem relevant, but it would keep her talking.

"A college in the South. Belmont College it's called."

"Did she like it?"

"I guess. We didn't talk much after she started college."

"Did you go to college, Heidi?"

She snapped her gum. "My mom wanted me to go away to college. My dad thought I should stay closer to home for a year or so. I didn't have the grades to go away anyway, so my dad won, and I went to the junior college. Usually my mom wins."

Odd, no mention of what she wanted to do, Ángel thought.

"My mom nearly always wins," Heidi said dreamily. "She wanted me to take Lisa with me on this trip. My dad didn't want me to go at all. I wanted to take my cousin Doreen. But my mom won again. If she hadn't won, Lisa would still be alive, wouldn't she? So did she win?"

"When I get home, my mom will blame it on me. I know that. She'll be real mad at me." Tears flooded the hazel eyes. "But I couldn't help it. I really couldn't."

Ángel fumbled through the manager's desk drawer for a box of tissues. "Why do you think your mother will blame you?" He felt sympathy for the woman-child weeping before him.

"Because she blames me for everything." Heidi sniffed. "She says I screw up everything. But I didn't screw this up," she said, then let out a wail that brought Officer Zaldo running.

Even after she was escorted from the room, Ángel couldn't get Heidi Williams out of his mind. She was surely sick, but how sick? he wondered. Sick enough to kill a childhood friend? Maybe. Maybe not. Mentally he put her above Rita Fong on his suspect list.

"Comisario." Zaldo reentered the room and stood stiffly at attention. Wet half-moons had formed under his arms.

"The two nuns are asking to see you, and I have brought in Señora Bootsie." Straight-backed, he waited for instruction.

"Send in the nuns first, Esteban. Let's see what they want."

◆

After a few perfunctory courtesies, Mary Helen got right to the point. The two top buttons of the *comisario*'s shirt were open, his gray tonsure was mussed, and he was beginning to look wilted at the edges. No sense prolonging his agony with another long conversation, she thought.

"I forgot to mention that on Friday night, the night I thought I saw someone on the cathedral steps, another person was also looking out a hotel window."

Ángel straightened up and leaned forward in his chair. "How do you know, Sister?"

"I heard someone cough. From the sound I knew it came from a window. I remember thinking that someone else was having trouble sleeping and was gazing out into the plaza.

"This afternoon I heard the same cough. And Sister Eileen"—she turned to her friend, who nodded at Ángel—"identified it as Bootsie DeAngelo's cough. Since she is waiting outside for you, we will be on our way."

"Way to where?" Ángel asked warily, but he was too late. Wherever it was, the nuns were already gone.

◆

The *comisario* was shocked by Bootsie DeAngelo's appearance. Blue-black rings circled her eyes like bruises. Her hair was pulled back and tied with a large silk scarf; the tails hung over her bony shoulders. Bootsie looked thinner, if possible, than she had when Ángel first saw her, and it was not becoming.

Chicken bones, picked clean, he thought, watching her

perch on the corner of the chair. "Have you thought of anything you didn't mention the first time we spoke?" Ángel
gave her the opening.

Bootsie's false eyelashes fluttered like two black spiders
against her pale face. Then she fixed him with an icy glare.
"No, Comisario, I have not. And if I had, I surely would have
sought you out and told you. This entire incident is most
upsetting."

"I couldn't agree more, señora," Ángel said with a practiced courtesy calculated to annoy her. "But I have reason to
believe that you were standing by the window of your hotel
room late Friday night. Is that correct?"

Bootsie let out an exaggerated sigh. "No wonder you are
getting nowhere with this investigation if that is the kind of
fact you're going after."

"Perhaps you are correct, señora. Do you remember if
you were at your window that night?"

"I may have been. I've been up late on several occasions
this week. I have not been sleeping well, Comisario. I'm sure
that is not so hard even for you to understand."

Behind the desk Ángel clenched and unclenched his
fists. It is a wonder someone hasn't gone for her little chicken
neck, he thought, watching her drum her red fingernails on
the arm of the chair.

"Do you remember Friday night specifically? The night
you arrived here from San Francisco. Do you remember if you
were by your window that night?"

Bootsie gave his question some thought. "After dinner
Roger and I joined the others in the lounge. We left shortly
after the other couples did. At first I had difficulty falling
asleep because of the strange bed and the rain, but once I did,
I slept well."

"Then you don't remember standing by the open window?"

"When I think about it, I'm sure I did not, Comisario. I have more sense than to stand in front of an open window on a rainy night."

"Are you sure?" Ángel gave her the final bait.

"I'm sure," she said, her smile rigid. "As I said, I'm far too sensible for that."

But not sensible enough to tell the truth, he thought. Why? he wondered, watching her thin back leave the manager's office. Why would the woman choose to lie about something like that?

Officer Zaldo reappeared in the doorway. "Comisario, do you want another American?" he asked briskly. "Or will you wait until after dinner?"

The peal of the bells in the cathedral's lordly tower filled the manager's office. Church bells in the steeples all over Santiago rang out the Angelus.

"It's noon!" Ángel pushed himself up from the padded chair. "We will both think clearer, Esteban, after dinner and a little break!"

"Sí, Comisario," Zaldo snapped, and with a click of his heels he was gone.

Whether it was the hour or Bootsie DeAngelo's emaciated look, Ángel did not know, but suddenly he was ravenous. He gathered up his raincoat and umbrella. Julietta would be busy in the kitchen by now, fussing over bubbling pots, peeking into steaming pans with delicious smells, just waiting for him to taste. He wondered what she was preparing. For once he hoped it wasn't chicken.

◆

Kate Murphy lay in bed with her eyes closed. Her head pounded, and she was burning up. Her stomach itched. In fact, she itched all over, but her head hurt too much to open her eyes to investigate the reason.

Her husband grunted, and the alarm clock went off. Kate waited for a few seconds while Jack made his usual waking-up noises. When he finally sat up on the edge of their bed, she opened her eyes. Her eyeballs felt as if they had been rolled in sand. Jack put his fingers into his thick, curly hair and scratched, and she knew he was awake enough to hear what she said.

"Pal." Her tone was matter-of-fact. She didn't want to alarm him. "I don't think I feel very good."

Jack spun around. "What is it, hon?" His cool hand touched her forehead, and she could tell by his expression that she was on fire. "What hurts?" He scrutinized her face.

"My head is throbbing, and I feel hot and sticky."

"What did you have to eat yesterday?"

Kate groaned and closed her eyes. Had she married her mother? A good meal or a good physic had been her mother's solution to all illnesses.

"Where the hell did we put the thermometer?" He shuffled through the drawer of the nightstand.

"Try the medicine chest in the bathroom."

Jack left the room to do just that. The phone rang. Eyes still closed, Kate fumbled for the receiver and was surprised to hear the voice of Comisario Ángel Serrano.

"I apologize, Inspector Murphy, for disturbing you again," he said, sounding as if he were calling from a cave, "I was wondering if you have any more information on the American tourists."

Kate felt much too sick to get angry. "Comisario," she said, her throat raw, "it's only seven in the morning here in San Francisco. I'm sure my friend has not yet been able to get to Redwood College, let alone to interview the dean or anyone else. As for the others, none of the offices or businesses are open yet."

Kate heard him moan. "Of course, it is seven in the

morning!" He sputtered, "I am so sorry, Inspector Murphy, I don't know what I was thinking of. I should not have been so impatient. I hope I didn't wake you."

"No, no," Kate said, craving a glass of water. "I understand." And she did. Sometimes when you are on a case, you become so absorbed that you lose all track of time, let alone time in another country. "As soon as I hear from my friend, I'll call you."

Jack stood over her. "I can't find the damn thermometer," he said. "Only the baby's, which is . . ." He held it up.

"Don't even think of it." Kate was not that sick.

"I'll call the doctor?"

She tried to think sensibly, but all she wanted to do was sleep. "No," she said. "We don't even know if I have a fever. I'm probably just tired. But what about John?" She tried to struggle up.

Jack's thick hand stopped her. "Don't worry. I'll get him up. Then maybe my mother will watch him."

"Only for the day."

Jack nodded and handed Kate some aspirin and a glass of cold water, which felt heavenly going down.

Later—Kate had no idea of how much later—she heard her mother-in-law's voice in the distance. She felt a cool compress on her head. Waking from a restless sleep, Kate swallowed the warm soup Mama Bassetti spooned into her mouth.

Suddenly she was conscious of the quiet in the house. "Where's my baby?" she asked in alarm.

"He is napping." Mama Bassetti gave Kate some juice. "You should nap, too, Kate," she said. "You'll feel much better when you wake up."

"But little John." Kate felt tears sting her eyes.

"He's just fine." Mama Bassetti's voice was soothing. "After his nap I'll take him for a walk to the park. Then I'll bring him in. He's been in to see you three times already. I think the poor little angel is worried about you. Go back to sleep now, so you can wake up feeling better."

"What's wrong with me?" Kate asked, her eyelids heavy.

"I'm not too sure." Her mother-in-law sounded almost amused. "But I think we should know by tomorrow."

"Tomorrow?" Kate was drowsy. Why tomorrow? she wondered, and was asleep as soon as she formed the question.

♦

Ángel Serrano was embarrassed. How could he have forgotten the time difference? Somehow the days seemed to have run together. Of course, Inspector Murphy's friend had not yet had the opportunity to interrogate anyone else! She must think him a half-wit, although from her voice, she sounded too sleepy to think much at all. Maybe he should have stopped at two glasses of *vino* at dinner.

It was not the *vino*, he thought, making his way back through the narrow arcade of streets to the police station. It was this murder case that was driving him crazy.

He crossed the streets carefully. They were still slick from the rain. It would not do to fall. Ángel avoided the puddles. So far today he had also avoided the mayor, the clergy, and that infernal Héctor Luna from *La Voca de Galicia*. How long would his luck hold?

The newspaper would have a field day with him if he were unable to solve the case before those blasted pilgrims returned to San Francisco. That gave him only two days.

What if he needed to detain them? What would the American Embassy say to that? He didn't know. He'd never had a case like this before. Tourists in Santiago usually lost their belongings, or bumped into things, or thought that they had been cheated. But murdered? Never!

"I do not want to be disturbed," Ángel shouted, and

slammed the door of his small office. He waited until the glass stopped shaking to open it again. "By anyone," he roared. "Is that clear?"

"Yes, Comisario," a small voice answered. It was the telephone operator. She seemed to be the only person left in the building.

Ángel pushed back in his chair, propped his feet on the edge of his desk, closed his eyes, and tried to think. After this morning's interviews, every instinct told him that his suspects narrowed down to Rita Fong, Heidi Williams, or one of the DeAngelos. How could he prove it? None of them had a real alibi, so all of them had had the opportunity.

The key to motive might be with the information Kate Murphy's friend uncovered. For that he must wait until she called him tomorrow.

The weapon! Could he find the weapon? After dinner, he had told María José that tomorrow afternoon she could help Zaldo search the Americans' belongings. When he thought about it, the hair on his neck stood up. Did he need someone's permission to do that? As *comisario* of Santiago he was within his rights. The murder was in his jurisdiction. Or was there some international law governing the situation? He didn't need any more trouble with bureaucrats.

Ángel Serrano spent the rest of the evening searching for a book that would give him the laws for dealing with tourists.

thursday, OCTOBER 14

feast of St. Callistus I, Pope and Martyr

♦

All morning Sister Mary Helen was conscious of a strange foreboding. An unnamed dread hung in the back of her mind like fog over the Golden Gate, waiting for a chance to roll in.

Her three "accidents" were at the root of it, she knew. Three is a charm—she tried to bolster her courage—and if I wasn't harmed in three attempts, surely I'm safe. Perhaps the incidents were coincidences after all.

Yet hard as she tried, she could not rid herself of the ominous feeling. Several times she attempted to read, but she was too distracted. When a tour bus backfired, she jumped.

Her prayers were scattered, and even in ordinary circumstances, she felt little devotion to St. Callistus, an early Pope who was condemned for leniency. That's a twist, she thought, abandoning her office book.

She rearranged the things in her suitcase, tensing when the chambermaid's cart rattled by in the hall. Tomorrow they would fly home, or would they? What would Ángel Serrano do if he had not discovered the murderer? Would he let them return to San Francisco? He couldn't do that. The murder had taken place in Spain in his jurisdiction. They were suspects. Would he detain them all? Wait until Sister Cecilia received that collect call!

"What is it, old dear?" Eileen asked finally. "Have you a case of the fidgets?"

"Sorry," Mary Helen said. And she was. It is very annoying to be cooped up in a small room with someone like Eileen. She stared out of the bedroom window. Soft rain drenched everything. Full dark clouds fought with patches of blue sky, and at the moment the clouds were winning.

"I have cabin fever," she said.

Eileen winked. "That's an improvement. Yesterday it was submarine fever. Your spirits are moving up. By tomorrow you'll be flying high, all the way home."

Mary Helen groaned at the pun. I hope we are on our way home, she thought.

Eileen must have sensed her hesitation. "That nice Comisario Serrano with the name and face of an angel won't detain us, will he?"

"I don't know," Mary Helen said honestly. "But if we can discover the killer, that's no longer a question."

Eileen blinked back any surprise she felt. Only her brogue thickened a bit. "What is it you suggest we do?" she asked.

"Launch out on a new tack. The old ones are getting us nowhere fast."

"What tack is that?"

"Discovering the murder weapon!"

"The comisario said it was about two inches wide in the middle, narrow on the ends, perhaps padded. Have you any idea what we are looking for?"

"That's my point," Mary Helen said. "Let's see if we can find something, anything, that fits the description."

"That sound a little like finding a pimple on an alligator's tail," Eileen muttered.

Mary Helen pretended not to hear. This aging has some advantages, she thought. "In the mystery I'm reading, the victim is strangled with a circular knitting needle that the detective discovers at a yarn store."

Eileen grimaced. "That will teach you to get on Sister Ursula's bad side when she's knitting."

"Let's walk along the Rua del Villar, the street with all those shops. Maybe we can find something that fits the description."

"It is pouring down rain." Eileen's protest was half-hearted at best.

"We'll stay under the arcade. María José always says that it clears up quickly." As a show of her faith in María José's expertise, Mary Helen grabbed up her Aran sweater instead of her raincoat.

♦

Two hours later the two nuns, drenched to the skin, staggered into El Franco Restaurante for a cup of hot coffee.

"One more souvenir shop, and I may begin to wish that *el botafumeiro* had hit me," Mary Helen quipped.

Eileen shivered. "Don't say that even in fun. I don't want to think of the possibility."

Eileen was right. Mary Helen changed the subject before her earlier feelings of dread returned.

"Those shops were so jam-packed with people and things that it was hard to tell what they had," she said, "let alone if it was the right shape or, more important, if someone in our group has one. I'm afraid that our shopping expedition was nothing but a wet waste of time."

Always optimistic, Eileen shook her head. "Not necessarily," she said. "You may have pneumonia tomorrow, but your fidgets are gone!" She dug into her purse and pulled out a dog-eared piece of paper. "And we did pick up a few more souvenirs to take home."

She spread the paper on the table. "Here's our list," she

said. "Let's make sure we have something for everyone. I would hate to leave anyone out."

Sister Eileen ran her finger down their list and, with Mary Helen's prompting, wrote, "key chain, letter opener, medal" by the names that didn't already have "black soap" next to them.

"Are we about done?" Mary Helen asked. She detested this part of traveling.

"All except for Shirley. What are you going to bring Shirley?"

"Can you think of something special?" Mary Helen felt a touch of guilt about leaving her hardworking secretary to wrestle with the last-minute details of the alumnae fashion show.

"There is a nice shop toward the end of the arcade," Eileen suggested, "with brightly colored scarves. One of those might be nice."

It did not take Mary Helen long to decide on a gift. The entire back wall of the shop was filled with colorful scarves emblazoned with flowers and shells and edged with a graceful flowing fringe. Since Shirley was attractive in every color, Mary Helen simply closed her eyes and pointed. Opening them, she discovered that she had picked a large shell-covered one in a beautiful shade of Nile green.

"Perfect," Eileen said, and the salesclerk wrapped it in tissue paper.

"Nine hundred and fifty pesetas."

The old nun rummaged through her purse and found the nine hundred in paper bills. She checked the pockets of her sweater for change. In her left pocket she felt two coins and something else. It was stiff and slick like a piece of shiny cardboard. She pulled out fifty pesetas and with them the Polaroid picture that Rita Fong had taken at the Madrid airport.

While the clerk rang up the sale, Mary Helen stared absently at the picture. It was of Eileen and herself looking weary and disheveled. Rita had caught her with her eyes shut. She'd also snapped three other pilgrims in the background. As she stared at them, Mary Helen's heart quickened. Could that be what they were looking for?

"Eileen!" She pointed to one of the figures in the photo. "Look at this," Mary Helen said, hardly daring to hope. "Can this possibly be the murder weapon?"

The salesclerk, who obviously understood English, gingerly handed Mary Helen her purchase.

Eileen squinted at the photo. "It could be," she said slowly, controlling the excitement in her voice. "It very well could be."

Oblivious of the steady drizzle covering the city, the two nuns flew, like honeybees to the hive, toward the office of Comisario Ángel Serrano.

For one frantic moment Mary Helen thought that someone was following them, but all fear dissolved as they mounted the steps of the police station.

♦

Ángel Serrano's eyes were sore. He yawned so widely that they watered, and that only made them ache more. Inspector Kate Murphy had called from San Francisco at four-thirty A.M. his time with some interesting facts about Professor De-Angelo. Ángel had been awake and mulling them over ever since.

"Sorry to disturb you, Comisario," she began apologetically when he finally answered the phone in a sleepy haze. "I know you are waiting for my friend's report on Professor De-Angelo," Kate explained. In an instant he was wide-awake.

Quickly she told him what Inspector Gallagher had uncovered. Roger DeAngelo had come only recently to Red-

wood College in West Marin. Before that he was a full professor at a small college in Greensboro called Belmont College.
He had a recommendation but not rave notices, and his reason for changing colleges was never very clear. "Health reasons," his application had stated.

Gallagher had remembered that Belmont College in
Greensboro was the same college that Lisa Springer's mother
had said Lisa attended.

Kate told Ángel the years that each had been at Belmont. "For whatever this is worth," she said, sounding as if
she thought it was worth plenty, "Lisa's freshman year coin-
cides with Professor DeAngelo's last year at that college."

"Were you aware of this? That's Gallagher's question,
not mine," Kate had said.

Ángel admitted he was not. "By their own admission,"
he said, "none of the winners of this pilgrimage claims to
have known any of the others before the trip."

"Why lie about it?" Kate asked bluntly.

"That is what I need to discover," Ángel said. Kate gave
him Inspector Gallagher's phone number at Homicide.

"Just in case you need him," she said.

As soon as he reached his office, Ángel phoned Roger
DeAngelo. "Did you ever teach at Belmont College in
Greensboro?"

His question seemed to stun the professor. "Yes," he said
as cautiously as a soldier crossing a minefield. "Why do you
ask?"

"Were you aware that Lisa Springer was a student
there?"

"Of course I was not." The professor's tone was indig-
nant. "When did she attend the school? Perhaps I had already
gone."

"No, Professor, you were there. In fact, her freshman
year and your last year at that college are the same year."

The professor gave a supercilious laugh. "Have you any idea how many freshman students there were at Belmont?"

"It seems to me that a redhead as beautiful as Lisa Springer would stand out even in a crowd."

"Probably," DeAngelo admitted, "which further proves my point. If the girl was at Belmont, our paths must never have crossed."

Ángel had chewed on that conversation ever since. The coincidence was too "coincidental" for him to swallow. It stuck like a popcorn kernel in his throat. It was the only link he was able to find between any of the suspects and the murdered girl.

What was he missing? Mentally he reviewed his interviews with the suspects one by one. Nothing clicked. Frustrated, Angel went through them again. Whoever the murderer was, he was an arrogant bastard, that was for certain. He had undoubtedly shoved the note under Lisa's bedroom door.

If only he could discover who had written the note. "Zaldo!" he shouted.

The office door swung open immediately. "*Sí*, Comisario?" Officer Zaldo stood as stiff as a navy blue board. Even the hairs on his narrow mustache lined up at attention.

Exasperated, Ángel shook his head. "At ease, Esteban," he said, "for the love of God, at ease, before you snap in two."

Hurt clouded Zaldo's eyes, and Ángel felt guilty. "I want you to bring Heidi Williams to me at once," he ordered, like a centurion before his hundred men, and tried not to flinch when Zaldo clicked his heels. Too much American *Mission Impossible* on the television, he thought, watching Zaldo's stiff back exit.

Closing his burning eyes, Ángel pushed back in his chair to think. The sound of quick footsteps echoed down the hallway and seemed to be heading toward his office. A prickle rose on the back of his neck. When his office door burst open with only the briefest knock, he fully expected María José and his sister. He was ready to explode with righteous indignation at their intrusion.

The sight of the two breathless nuns brought him bolt upright. "What is it, Sister?" He tried to keep the anxiety out of his voice. "What has happened?" He swallowed the "now."

"It's this." Mary Helen waved the shiny Polaroid.

Sister Eileen, looking as satisfied as a cat in the cream, stood beside her.

"Look, Comisario." Mary Helen shoved the print across his desk. Ángel skimmed the picture. It was a poorly taken snapshot of the two nuns. Both could be mistaken for fugitives except that fugitives usually didn't look so disheveled. And the photographer had caught Mary Helen with both eyes closed.

"It is certainly not very flattering," Ángel admitted.

"That is not the point, Comisario."

He had never seen Sister Mary Helen like this. Her whole body trembled with energy. She eyed him expectantly as he brought the picture closer to study it. He examined the figures in the background. Whatever is exciting her, he thought, must be in the background because these two are not "it."

Four figures were caught behind the nuns. Two he quickly recognized as the DeAngelos. The third was a piece of Heidi Williams. The fourth person must be Lisa Springer. The amber hair and the crooked-toothed smile gave it away. The beautiful animated face in the photo bore little resemblance to the discolored, swollen lifeless mask that he had seen beside the tomb of St. James.

"Well," Sister Mary Helen asked impatiently, "do you see it?"

Reluctant to admit he hadn't, Ángel continued to study every detail of the snapshot.

Mary Helen groaned aloud when she heard the knock on the *comisario*'s office door.

"*Pase!*" he shouted without looking up from the Polaroid.

The door opened, and stiff-backed Officer Zaldo escorted in a bewildered-looking Heidi Williams. Her red-rimmed eyes shifted between Ángel and the nuns. Obviously she had been crying, and from the nervous way she kept swallowing Mary Helen could tell that her mouth was dry with fear.

"What do you want me for?"

"A few questions, señorita." Ángel was gentle.

"I've told you everything I know." Heidi's eyes began to fill.

"Only one or two more."

"You'd better be careful about your questions," Heidi said. If she meant to sound menacing, she failed. Her words came out in a near whine. "I've just talked to my mom, and she's really mad now."

"Why is that, señorita?"

"My mom says she doesn't want any more questions. She says I don't need to answer questions. She says a cop came to our house and really upset my father. My mom is mad at me, but it is not my fault." Heidi's voice shook.

"Of course not," Ángel said soothingly. "This will be one of the last questions, I am sure." He motioned Heidi to a chair facing him and nodded toward Zaldo.

Mary Helen felt the wind of the officer's quick exit on her back.

"Señorita, have you remembered anything else Lisa said on Friday night when she saw the note that was left under your door?"

Heidi stared at him.

"When she read the note?" he prodded. Mary Helen

figured that Ángel was searching for something, anything, that would produce a lead.

The office air was electric while Heidi thought. "She just said, 'What's this?' when she first saw the paper."

"What's this?" The words triggered something in Mary Helen's memory. "What's this?" Bootsie had asked when she found the small tightly rolled slip of paper on her plane seat. "Belmont," Bootsie had read aloud, and Mary Helen had thought only of the city on the Peninsula.

"Belmont." Her voice almost crackled. "Does Belmont ring a bell?"

Heidi, the *comisario*, Eileen—all three pairs of eyes were on her.

"That's where Lisa went away to school," Heidi said.

"And where Professor DeAngelo taught before he transferred to his present assignment," Ángel said.

Abruptly he rose from his chair. "What is it, Sister?" Now his eyes were on Eileen.

Her face was as white as the wall. "I should have remembered." Eileen's gray eyes were enormous.

"Remembered what?" Mary Helen asked, rubbing her friend's icy hand.

"Don't you?"

"You're the one with the phenomenal memory, Eileen. I've said that all along. What is it that you have remembered?"

Eileen sucked in a deep breath.

"*Agua*," Ángel shouted from the doorway, and Zaldo appeared almost magically carrying a glass.

"I don't know what happened to me," Eileen said after a couple of swallows. "I guess it was such a shock."

"What was a shock?" Ángel hovered over her.

"Remembering that Belmont was the college with the scandal seven or eight years ago. It was the talk of the educational community. A history professor. I can't remember his name, but he was giving good grades to coeds for sexual favors. What made it even more despicable, if I remember correctly, was that he victimized scholarship students, who needed to maintain their grade points, and he picked on only those who were plain. That way, I guess, he figured the authorities would never believe their accusations. He could slough them off as the delusions of frustrated and love-starved young girls.

"It would have worked, too, except that one plain-looking administrator believed the young women. Nothing, however, was ever proved. The professor's wife gave him an iron-clad alibi. No one ever went to jail. The college smoothed it over, and the professor simply went on sabbatical. I have no idea if it was Professor DeAngelo, of course." Eileen took another swallow of water. "It just seems so coincidental."

"Would he murder to cover up an old scandal?" Ángel was thinking aloud. "It doesn't seem necessary."

The giant bells of the cathedral began to peal. Bells chimed from the stately towers all over the city and filled the air with one enormous sound. Mary Helen raised the Polaroid from Ángel's desk. She studied it more closely. All at once her scattered thoughts swung together, like steeple bells, into one long, loud harmonious whole, and she knew she was right.

"I know who did it," she said above the ringing. "I'm not sure why or when, but I'm absolutely sure how."

♦

The smell of fear filled the *comisario*'s office almost before the DeAngelos took their seats.

"What is the meaning of this?" Roger said indignantly, but his dark eyes held no anger, only panic. He plucked at his beard. It was beginning to need a trim. "We are American citizens! What right have you to summon us arbitrarily?" he demanded, trying to sound ominous. Nervousness had raised his voice an octave, and he only sounded silly.

Bootsie's face was mime white, and her long, shoe-polish-black hair was pulled back and sprayed as stiffly as a wig on a mannequin. Her eyes, hard as blue glass, shrieked hatred. She smiled with chilly courtesy at the group.

And an odd group it is, Mary Helen thought. Comisario Ángel Serrano, whom one could easily mistake for an aging and harmless gnome unless you caught the intelligence in his dark eyes; Officer Zaldo, stiff and formal, the parody of a police zealot; red-eyed Heidi Williams, sniffling and chewing her perpetual stick of gum; and two aging nuns.

No wonder Bootsie DeAngelo viewed them with contempt. She had figured them for a knot of fools. Mary Helen's heart began to race. This was going to be fun!

"What is it that you people want anyway?" Bootsie said with the condescending frown of Scarlett O'Hara talking to a Yankee. She touched her husband's forearm as if to restrain his rage. "Perhaps this matter can be simply settled, Roger, and then the *comisario* can get back to his real work of looking for the mugger."

"Do you recognize this picture?" Mary Helen picked up the Polaroid snapshot from Ángel's desk and handed it to Bootsie.

"I have more to do with my time than look at pictures." With a bored sigh, Bootsie glanced at it. "That idiot woman was snapping Polaroids in the Madrid airport if I remember correctly. It is a very bad shot of you nuns," she said, her inflection making "nuns" sound like an insult.

"Pacience is an heigh vertu, certeyn," Chaucer's pilgrim claimed. At that moment Mary Helen found it amazingly true.

"No, dear, behind us," she said innocently. "Do you see who's behind us?"

Feigning annoyance, Bootsie studied the picture again. "Roger and I, part of her"—her eyes flicked to where Heidi was sitting—"and Lisa Springer's face. Was that what I was intended to see?"

"That—and something more," Mary Helen said, feeling strangely like a mongoose toying with a poisonous snake.

"I have more to do than to play your nonsensical games." Bootsie's eyes, sharp as drawn swords, met hers. "What exactly are you getting at?"

"Look at what you are wearing on your head," Mary Helen said calmly.

Bootsie's eyes fastened on the Polaroid, her thick eye-lashes still. What little color she had left drained from her face, leaving deep wrinkles around her mouth and eyes. Her hands shook almost imperceptibly.

The silence in the room lengthened.

"What is it?" Roger grabbed the picture from her stiff fingers. "What in the devil is it that you're wearing?" He squinted at the picture. "It's only that old horseshoe head-band thing you wear to keep your hair off your face." His eyes darted quizzically from Mary Helen to Ángel and back again.

"Unless I'm wrong, that old horseshoe headband thing is the exact size and shape of the mysterious weapon used to strangle Lisa Springer," Mary Helen said. "What I don't know, Bootsie, is why."

"That's ridiculous." The professor's voice echoed in the silent room. "Bootsie would never kill anyone." He turned toward his wife. She was rigid, her ashen face as emotionless as a mask. "Tell them, Bootsie. Tell them you didn't."

Bootsie was silent.

Roger grabbed her shoulders and shook her until her

head bobbed like a puppet's. "Tell them, Bootsie. Do you hear me? Tell them."

"But I did," Bootsie said in a small, satisfied voice. "I did it, Roger. Before that girl brought up Belmont again. We couldn't have that, could we?"

Roger looked baffled. His hands dropped from his wife's shoulders. "What girl? Lisa?"

"She was one of the fat, homely girls you had trouble with at Belmont, you know," Bootsie said in the same flat way she might have said, "One of the girls you taught in Western civ."

Mary Helen's blood ran cold.

"I recognized the hair and the crooked eyetooth," Bootsie said with satisfaction. "She was going to make trouble for us again, Roger. I couldn't allow that."

By now Roger DeAngelo's whole body shook. His already lean body shrank inside his natty tweed jacket. Tears ran unheededly down his cheeks. He stared at his wife as if he were seeing her for the first time.

"Bootsie, why?" he asked, bewildered.

"I told you, Roger. You know as well as I that once she found you, that little bitch was never going to leave you alone. Her note on the plane with that one word." Bootsie's eyes narrowed. "You'd never hear the end of her. I saw you on Friday night, coming down the cathedral steps. I knew whom you had met, silly." Now she sounded like an indulgent parent chiding an errant child. "So when you fell asleep, I slipped a note under her door. From you, of course." She smiled at her own cleverness. "I told her we'd meet in the crypt as soon as the cathedral opened in the morning. Six o'clock is when it opens. What could seem safer? Six in the morning in a church." Her carefree giggle clashed with the stunned silence in the room.

"Once again I saved you, my darling. Once again, Roger,

Bootsie has saved her pussycat." She smiled a cloying smile and put a protective hand on his sleeve.

Roger recoiled as if her fingers were on fire.

Bootsie looked puzzled. "What is it, darling?"

For a long moment Roger DeAngelo stared at his wife. "You're crazy!" he said with sudden contempt. "I've always known you were possessive and suspicious, Bootsie"—his words were rapier sharp—"but I had no idea that you were crazy, too."

Color rushed back into Bootsie's face. It made red splotches on her white cheekbones. "Don't say that to me, darling." For a moment her eyes blazed; then they faded. "I simply could not go through it all over again, Roger. The newspapers, the accusations, the veiled innuendos from the other faculty wives. And worst of all, the pity I saw in their faces. I'd do anything—anything, Roger—to wipe away that superior pity."

Bootsie snatched the Polaroid from Roger's hand and tore it into small pieces. The whole room watched as intently as if they were playing charades.

"Now that's gone!" Bootsie said, and grabbed Mary Helen's pocketbook. With an impersonal glance toward Mary Helen, Bootsie unearthed Anne's travel diary from the purse. "She has been writing things in here all week," Bootsie said, holding the book triumphantly above her head. "I've seen her."

With a smug grin, she ripped out a fistful of pages and shredded them.

"It was you who put those Gypsy women up to snatching my purse," Mary Helen said, feeling a sudden lightness.

Bootsie DeAngelo turned her frosty blue eyes on the old nun. "Who would have imagined that you were so strong?" she said and gave Mary Helen a look of pure hatred.

Then she touched Roger's arm. "All the evidence is

gone, my darling. I've destroyed it." Bootsie was as matter-of-fact as if she'd said, "I just took out that pesky trash."

"Once again I am your alibi. Now you can be mine. We are free to go, aren't we, Comisario?" she asked.

"I am afraid not, señora." Ángel Serrano's voice was gentle.

With a scrape of his boots, Officer Zaldo slipped up beside Bootsie and clicked the handcuffs on her wrists. The manager's small office reverberated with the sound of her shrieking.

friday, october 15

feast of St. Teresa of Ávila, doctor of the church

♦

"Denny is on the phone, hon." Jack Bassetti's voice was soft, and his words barely penetrated Kate's heavy blanket of sleep. "He says it's important." Jack gently shook her shoulder. "Phone, hon," he said again.

Kate smelled his after-shave. She blinked her eyes open. Her husband was dressed. How had she slept through the ringing of the phone? How had she slept through Jack's alarm, his showering and getting dressed for work? What time was it anyway? The clock was fuzzy, but she thought it said seven-thirty. Where was the baby? She propped herself up on one elbow, but her head began to swim. Lowering herself, she closed her eyes. "Why did you let me sleep? I've got to get up," she insisted.

"Just stay put, hon." Jack's voice was soothing. "I've fed and watered the baby, and my mother's on her way. Talk to Denny, now, and we'll talk when you hang up." He placed the cool receiver against her burning ear.

"Hello," she grunted.

"Those damn two nuns have done it again," Gallagher shouted without so much as a "hello." "Even in a foreign country where they can't even speak the language, they can't keep their noses clean. The commissioner from Santiago calls me in the middle of the night. Not that I blame him. He sounds like a nice enough guy and has some sense, considering how anxious he is to get the hell rid of those two."

"What happened, Denny?" Kate's head was throbbing. Even her scalp was on fire.

"I'm not sure of all the details yet, Katie-girl, but from what this commissioner guy tells me, he was afraid that before he found the killer, he was going to end up with a second murder."

"Whose?"

"Sister Mary Helen's, naturally, because you have never been able to tell her to stay out of police business."

"This is not my fault, Denny." Kate felt her temper warm, but she was too tired to argue. "Who is the murderer?" she asked instead.

"Barbara, aka Bootsie, DeAngelo, the professor's wife, Serrano says. He also says that she's probably a certified nutcake as well. Since both she and the murder victim are American, our State Department and the Spanish government did some fancy footwork and decided to let us have her. She'll arrive on the same plane as the rest of the tourist group, accompanied by an officer from our embassy. We need to meet the plane at the airport and take the lady off his hands. Are you still there, Katie-girl? You're awful quiet."

"I'm here." Kate was barely listening. She itched all over. Her neck, her arms, her eyelids, across her midriff, everything itched. What was it? Did she have some sort of rash? An allergy? What had she eaten? Kate opened her pajama top to examine her stomach. What she saw looked oddly familiar.

"I thought if you'd decided to come back to work on Monday anyway, you might want to take a ride to the airport with me this afternoon. See the nuns, pick up the prisoner. You know, get your feet wet again."

"Denny, I'm afraid I won't be back to work on Monday."

Kate was strangely relieved that a decision of sorts had been made for her.

There was an unnaturally long pause before Gallagher spoke. "Then you've decided to quit?" He seemed to be battling his emotions. "Not that I blame you."

"I've decided nothing, Denny." Kate started to giggle. "It's been decided for me."

She reexamined the patch of small red bumps on her stomach. She'd seen those same bumps on two-year-old Stephanie's stomach last week at the pediatrician's. She didn't have to be much of a detective to figure it out.

"I have the measles," she said.

Gallagher guffawed.

"And don't you dare say one word about it to any of the guys!"

"Fat chance, Katie-girl," he roared in her hot ear. "Fat chance!" he said, and hung up.

◆

The plane ride home was long and, by comparison with the week's events, uneventful. Hours dropped away, and a quiet settled over the passengers as the giant jet flew on.

Mary Helen was exhausted. As exhausted, surely, as those medieval *peregrinos* who had walked to Santiago from France or Italy in their thick-soled shoes and floppy hats. Everything ached. She closed her eyes in the hope that the steady hum of the plane's engines would lull her to sleep. No matter how hard she tried, she could not switch off her mind. Lisa's purple, swollen face appeared without warning. Bootsie's manic screams echoed and reechoed in her ears.

Late yesterday afternoon, with a few phone calls, Ángel Serrano had arranged for Pepe's *peregrinos* to bypass Madrid and take a direct flight to San Francisco from Santiago de Compostela.

He and María José were at the airport to see them off. The mayor of Santiago de Compostela sent lovely parchment certificates with Ángel for each of them. Mary Helen examined hers closely and was pleased to see that it declared her officially *una peregrina de San Francisco*.

The ancient city put on its best face for their departure. Low Celtic green hills rolled six deep toward a horizon of steel blue sky. A brilliant October sun made poetry of every flower and leaf it touched. The cathedral towers shimmered in the distance.

María José, her magenta hair aflame in the morning light, clung to the arm of Héctor Luna from *La Voca de Galicia*. "I have really enjoyed meeting you, Sisters," María José said with a broad, white-toothed smile. "This was the most exciting week of my life. I will never forget it."

"And what will you do now?" Eileen asked. "Continue with the tourist business or, perhaps, try for the police force?"

Ángel Serrano's face visibly blanched.

"Oh, no, Sister," María José said, "I think that I may try journalism. Héctor tells me that journalists have lots of interesting adventures and that they must be fiercely independent." Her dark, dancing eyes fastened on Héctor's face, and from the look on it, it was obvious that whatever white magic María José practiced was working on him.

"That may be a very good job for you," Eileen said kindly. "At least it is worth a try."

The *comisario* had grasped Mary Helen's hand with his large, warm one. "Good show, Sister!" he said. His dark eyes twinkled, and a smile lit up his cherubic face. "Thank you so much for everything and, *por favor*, don't come back again."

At first Mary Helen thought she'd misunderstood. But from the jaunty way he hurried her up the steps to the waiting plane, she was sure she hadn't.

Bootsie, clearly as "nutty as a fruitcake," to use Bud

Bowman's appraisal, was taken aboard and settled in the first-class cabin of the plane long before the rest of them arrived. Mary Helen assumed that an officer of the American Embassy was accompanying her. She figured that Roger must be up in front, too, since he was not in their section of the plane.

She wondered what must be going through his mind.

"You can't sleep either, old dear?" Eileen cut into her daydreaming in that statement-questioning way of hers.

"No," Mary Helen said. "I was thinking about everything that's happened. And I can't help feeling sad. I am always confounded by how our actions affect one another. We truly are one body," she mused, more to herself than to Eileen. "In this case one person's sickness caused another's madness and a third person's death. How does that song go that Sister Anne sings?"

> So my pain is pain for you,
> In your joy is my joy, too.
> We are all one Body. . . .

Mary Helen's rather tuneless humming was drowned out by the droning of the engines.

"Right you are, old dear." Eileen was only half listening. "You and St. Paul and John Donne, to mention a few.

"I'm glad the *comisario* arranged a direct flight," Eileen continued. "I dread seeing poor Bootsie again. We would, you know, if we changed planes in Madrid."

"Me, too!" Cora had overheard. "I knew all along there was something different about her."

"Too uptight. She needs to relax, get some exercise," Rita Fong chimed in from her seat, and Cora and she began to discuss the danger signals they both had noticed in the unfortunate Bootsie DeAngelo.

"Hindsight is twenty-twenty." Neil Fong rose from his seat and walked toward the water cooler.

"How are you two doing?" The voice startled Mary Helen. Pepe Nunez, ever the tour guide, hung over the seat. His smile was just as polished as it had been a week ago, his manner just as suave, but somehow there was a small touch of maturity in those flashing dark eyes that Mary Helen hadn't noticed before.

His curly black hair was tousled, and he held tightly to Heidi's hand. Heidi's face radiated so much happiness that she was almost pretty.

"Well, look at you two." The words slipped out of Mary Helen's mouth before she thought.

Heidi's high giggle tinkled through the tourist cabin of the plane. "We've discovered that we have a lot in common," she said, and snapped her chewing gum.

Mary Helen hesitated to ask what. Fortunately Eileen filled up the uncomfortable pause. "Isn't that grand?" she said. "I guess it truly is an ill wind that turns none to good."

Heidi, obviously unable to make the connection between having things in common and ill winds, stared so blankly at her that Eileen focused her attention on Pepe. "After what's happened to you on this trip, you must feel like a seasoned tour guide." She smiled up at the handsome face. "Did Pulmantur offer you a permanent position?"

"Sí, Sister"—Pepe beamed—"but I turned it down. I think I will look into law enforcement."

Mary Helen hoped her face didn't show her shock. She wondered how Uncle Carlos Fraga would react.

"Comisario Serrano did such an excellent job with this case I think it is something I'd like to do. You know, stop crime, arrest the guilty." Pepe smiled at an adoring Heidi.

"Besides, that policeman is traveling first class! I got a stewardess to let me sit up there for a while on the way over, and it was great."

Eleven hours after the plane left Spain, it touched down in San Francisco. Through the magic of time zones it was still early evening.

"The *año santo* tour members are to debark immediately by the front exit," an attendant apparently following orders announced over the intercom.

Mary Helen struggled up into the aisle. Under the suspicious and unconcealed stares of the rest of the passengers the tour group silently filed out, returning as they had begun, gathered like Canterbury's pilgrims "together in a flock."

As they exited the plane, Mary Helen half expected to hear "Godspeed and blessed martyr reward you," instead of "Thank you for flying Iberia."

She scanned the waiting room. Out of the corner of her eye, she caught the rumpled, balding figure of Inspector Gallagher. He was talking to several airport policemen and undoubtedly waiting for the DeAngelos to be led from the plane.

After a moment Gallagher spotted her and gave her a thumbs-up.

"Where's Kate?" Mary Helen mouthed.

"Measles!" Gallagher mouthed back, and scratched at his stomach and face to make sure she understood.

"Here we are!" Sister Therese's high-pitched voice sang out through the terminal. Beside her Sister Anne held a large Welcome Home sign. Sister Cecilia, looking quite "uncollege-presidentish," wore a enormous sombrero.

With everyone talking at once and, to Mary Helen's relief, with no one talking about a murder on their pilgrimage, they drove back to Mount St. Francis College. Amazingly the media had not yet picked up the story.

After much chatter, dessert, gifts, and more chatter, the convent settled into a peace-filled night silence. Exhausted but still unable to sleep, Sister Mary Helen slipped into a back pew in the convent chapel. Only the sanctuary lamp lit the darkness. Its flickering shadows danced across the marble floor. A soothing aroma of incense and candle wax filled the oratory.

In the stillness the events of the last eight days tumbled in upon Mary Helen. It seemed impossible that so much had happened in so short a time. She had made a Holy Year pilgrimage halfway around the world, discovered a murder and a murderer, and nearly been a victim herself. Then suddenly she was back home.

"Lord, how could you have allowed so much to happen to me?" she asked, and with a jolt remembered that today was the feast of the Spanish mystic Teresa of Ávila.

Once after a particularly hectic week St. Teresa was said to have prayed, "Lord, if this is how you treat your friends, no wonder you have so few."

There is, of course, no record of God's answer to Teresa. Nor did Mary Helen get one either. Instead she sat and let the peace and silence wash over her like healing water.

"Let nothing disturb you, /Let nothing affright you," Teresa had written to calm medieval Castilians. Now, centuries later, those same words calmed Mary Helen:

> All things pass,
> God is unchanging.
> Patience obtains all.
> Whoever has God,
> Needs nothing else,
> God alone suffices.

"Tomorrow, Lord," Mary Helen prayed in earnest, "when Cecilia gets the first call from the media, which she most assuredly will, grant me Teresa's serenity.

"And," she said as a much-needed afterthought, "with Teresa's serenity, Lord, send me a touch of deafness. I'm not sure which I'll need more!"